BLACK COMEDY IN ANCIENT SPARTA

"Think of this novel as Koestler or Solzhenitsyn transposed backward in time, and you won't be far wrong."
—*New York Times Book Review*

"Two men tell the tale: Agathon, the Seer, and his disciple Demodokos, the Peeker. They share a rat-ridden prison cell in the ancient Sparta of the tyrant Lykourgos from which Agathon, horny, foul-smelling, lame, mocks the world, its philosophical systems, its political vanities and his own vital history. Their prison cell is as much a metaphor as Sartre's in 'No Exit.' But it is more than that: it is a 'real' place, with corners, four walls, slop on the floor. It is John Gardner's gift to evoke, at once, substance and essence."
—*Newsweek*

Few novels today present as much significance in as many belly-laughs as *The Wreckage of Agathon*, and few books today hold as much hope for tomorrow.

Titles by
John Gardner

GRENDEL

THE SUNLIGHT DIALOGUES

THE WRECKAGE OF AGATHON

Published by Ballantine Books

THE
WRECKAGE
OF AGATHON

John Gardner

BALLANTINE BOOKS • NEW YORK

Library of Congress Catalog Card Number: 71-122888

SBN 345-22472-8-125

This edition published by arrangement with
Harper & Row, Publishers, Inc.

First U.S. Printing: January, 1972
Second U.S. Printing: December, 1973
Third U.S. Printing: February, 1974

First Canadian Printing: January, 1972

Printed in the United States of America

Cover art by Michael Leonard

BALLANTINE BOOKS, INC.
201 East 50th Street, New York, N.Y. 10022

This book is dedicated to Duncan Luke

Therefore with the same necessity with which the stone falls to the earth, the hungry wolf buries its fangs in the flesh of its prey, without the possibility of the knowledge that it is itself the destroyed as well as the destroyer.

—Schopenhauer
The World as Will and Idea

1 Peeker:

"What charge?" cried Agathon, rolling his eyes up, clinging to his crutch, "what charge?" His eyebrows were like tangled hazel and hawthorn and oak moss, a blown-down forest of silver trunks and boughs. His nose was like an avalanche, his eyes were like two caves. "What charge?" he cried, and banged his crutch. "Master, for the love of God," I said, but he gave me a look and roared again, "What charge?" A question obscenely presumptuous, for he was the foulest man alive, by any reasonable standard: a maker of suggestions to ugly fat old cleaning ladies, a midnight prowler in the most disgusting parts of town—the alleys of the poor, the palace gardens—who searched out visions of undressed maidens and coupling lovers, especially old ones, and lived, whenever his onion patch had nothing in it but burdocks and brambles, by foraging in the garbage tubs behind houses. (I have followed him for three years, though I speak of him with understandable detachment, and I know these things I'm telling you for facts.) He was seated on a curb when they came to arrest him, cooling his great horny feet in the gutter, up to the ankles in the indeterminate principle. (His words, not mine.) "I do not overprize sewage," he sometimes defended himself when children teased him. "It's smooth and cool, but also smelly. Neither do I overprize kings." And he would cackle. Occasionally people would laugh and praise him. Usually they threw stones. Either way, he was happy. He was a fool, and I was ashamed of

1

him. He was a troublemaker. When one of the stones they threw hit me and broke my head, he would say, "Tut tut! That's a nasty scratch!" In the beginning I used to resolve sometimes that I would murder him, but he would reason with me and twist my mind and make me believe that I ought to be proud to be seen with him. In any case, I knew that if I murdered him I would have to go back with my mother.

The officers who had come to arrest him stared straight ahead, embarrassed to be seen laying hands on a famous and respected Seer, and annoyed at his stupid question. The old man went on asking it, fanatically, shaking with indignation and wagging his finger at them (he was standing now, lifting one foot gingerly from the cool black sewage to the blistering heat of the cobblestones): "I insist that you tell me the charge!" His tenacious hold on trivial fact, he told me, was the secret of his genius.

They gave him no answer, merely growled, "Come along." The police would have given him a swat if they dared, and I would have agreed with them. But swatting a Seer brings bad luck, and besides, his eyes were red-rimmed and bloodshot, and his tongue was thick: his grasp on lower reality was uncertain. If they swatted him, he'd fall down and splash them with sewage. "Come along," they said.

Agathon obeyed, his rags flying like starlings. He hobbled between the two policemen like a man in pain, but I knew he was ecstatic, the center, once more, of all the gods' and all mankind's attention. The huge stone horse that towers over the temple of Poseidon looked down across the city at him, full of love and awe. Even the dogs looking up at him from their noonday rest admired him, he thought. Magnificent soaring eagle! (It takes no genius to know what Agathon's thinking, except in his trances. To know what he thinks in his trances you have to be crazy.) He hobbled with violent jerks of his crutch and twistings of his face, now and then loosing a horrendous fart, because of his living so long on onions, and so he proceeded with the two policemen down the winding street toward the great stone square of government buildings, the ephors' Hall of Justice. I followed, a little behind them, bringing the jug. I kept by the walls and hurried from one building's shadow to another. He stumbled once or twice and reeled, throwing out his arms like mangy wings. They caught him, wincing with distaste.

"Lykourgos will hear of this!" he squealed. "All Time and Space will hear of this!" And then, forgetting himself, he giggled. (I ducked and hid behind my arm, as I always did in these situations. There was nothing I could do with him.) "Did I ever tell you my theory of Time and Space?"

They ignored him.

Children, seeing the officers pass with Agathon, came running from their yards and houses to follow, joyfully mimicking first his limp, then the officers' official strut (they walked toeing out, so he toed in, for symmetry), and they called out words of encouragement, now to Agathon, now to the police. A young Helot girl came running to mock him, though once he'd saved her when she was chased by a cow. (I was there. I saw it all.) "Bless you, bless you," cried Agathon, beaming like the sun. It was all his doing, this festival spirit, and maybe he was rightly pleased. Ten years ago, those who liked him would have been alarmed at seeing him dragged away to jail, and those he disgusted would perhaps have thrown thorns in the path of those filthy bare feet. They'd had no philosophy, he said. No deep sense of the holiness of things. He'd converted them all. If he'd wanted to, he used to tell me, he could have changed the weather. He had Influence. "Bless you, bless you!" he said to the sullen young officer on his right. Old women in black, with sunken mouths and eyes like open graves, watched him go past. "Remember death!"

he whispered to the guard on his left. The guard stared forward.

(I give you, though I am only an apprentice in matters of this kind, a vision of the world peeled bare: Two officers, shiny and clean as needles, erect and elegant as unicorn horns, march down a sunlit swept-stone street, clumsily slowing their otherwise military pace for the old man between them. Their captive is a smallish, fat old clown with a halo of tangled silver hair ascending from his dome, a beard that shoots from his chin like lilacs, his robe more tattered and filth-bespattered than anarchy, his lips as endlessly in motion as the wind, saying words that play between cracked and crocked. Behind them come children whose laughter unifies Spartan law and those passing absurdities, us.)

Try as he might, he could not learn what charge it was they'd arrested him on. No matter, of course, as he used to say. It would reveal itself, in time, like everything else. "Ah ha!" he said, looking crafty, "I've got it! You suspect me of plotting an earthquake!" He laughed till tears ran down his cheeks and he had to pause, hanging breathless from his crutch. "You overestimate me, friends. Watch this!" He roared, eyes wide and ominous:

"Tremble, mountains! Shatter, air!
Shake Lykourgos from his chair!"

Nothing happened. "You see?" he squealed triumphantly. But he paused again, head cocked, as if afraid he might have started something after all. But old Poseidon the earth-trembler was off somewhere among the sunburnt races, smelling the smoke of thighbones burning, haunches of rams and bulls. The mountains remained as they were, the air did not shatter. It was a holy moment. "Impotent!" he said gleefully. "I'm impotent!" He glanced back at me sheepishly. I've reminded him a thousand times that all he ever talks about is sex.

"Keep walking," they said.

He walked.

I could have told them, if they'd asked, that the old man wasn't as drunk as he appeared, though he was, as usual, deeply, reverently drunk. He stood weaving, hands clasped, in the immense Hall of Justice, struggling to focus the Board of Ephors who gazed down on him. They were the greatest men in Sparta, perhaps the most powerful men in the world, and he knew them all, had served them often in his younger years (if anything at all that he tells me is true). They were greater than Kharilaus and Arkhelaus, the kings; greater even than the Lawgiver, Lykourgos. Though each of them, individually, was merely a man, subject to the usual misgivings of heart and inflammations of liver, as Agathon says, they were, together, more awesome than the oracle at Delphi. They could set aside the oracle as they set aside the whims of common mortals. They were the final masters in all things foreign and domestic, ecclesiastic and secular. But Agathon, being the god's fool, was unimpressed. Though their black robes and square red hats and shaved upper lips were all the same, their persons were various, some fat, some thin, some black-haired, some silvered. He pointed this out in a marveling voice to the guard on his right, and his face squeezed up into wrinkles as though he were closing his mind on the fact like a fist around a stone. I crouched in the doorway, cradling the old white jug in my arms and peering in like a beggar to see what would happen. Nothing did, for a long time. Agathon leaned on his crutch, hands clasped, looking up at the ephors or maybe at the iron trident that ascended almost to the ceiling behind them, and waited with his head cocked. Still nothing. He gave a jerk and I realized he was going to sleep. At last the Chairman stood up, behind the table, and addressed him. I couldn't make out a word he said, and I doubt that Agathon could either. The words were swallowed in echoes that rolled like thunder.

"Blallooom, blallooom, blallooom," the Chairman said.

Agathon considered. "Onions," he said at last, and tipped his head to the other side to see if he was right.

"Blallooom?" the Chairman said nastily.

Agathon considered again. "For several reasons, your honor," he said. He stood for some time sucking his mouth in and blowing it out again thoughtfully and scratching at his seat with his left hand. "Onions are very nourishing, relatively. And they're uplifting: their roundness inclines the mind to unity and completion. Also, onions occur in Nature, which is wonderful. And onions make people cry who wouldn't otherwise." He smiled, rueful, and stretched out his arm. "I like onions. It's nothing personal. I just like them. Also, they're cheap." He began to giggle and couldn't stop himself. I covered my face with my two arms and the jug.

"Blalloooom!" said the Chairman. The ephors conferred, and after a moment the Chairman spoke again. "Blallooom."

One of the guards seized Agathon by the shoulder and turned him around. They led him away. I ducked around the building to see where they were taking him, and when I saw they were heading toward the north end of town, where the prison is, I stopped. It's a horrible place—a sprawling gray-stone mass of buildings filled with sickness and misery, honeycombed with windows like bugs' holes and smoking here and there, day and night, like a garbage dump. I'd be damned if I was going there. He'd earned whatever it was he was getting, and the only bad things I'd ever done in my life were pull him up out of the street a few times so that no one could run over him. I was stupid to follow the old man at all, but I'd be stupider if I followed him to jail. He drew flies. I wouldn't have been surprised if I looked up sometime on a hot day and saw vultures circling over us. Sometimes when he was haranguing a crowd the people standing nearest to him would faint. They really did. I wasn't going. A fat pig's hell on him!

The trouble was, I still had the jug. "I'd be blind without that jug, boy," he used to say. But it was worse than that. Without his jug he'd shrivel up like a prune and all his blood would turn to dust. I clung tighter to the jug's sides and clenched my teeth against the injustice of everything. Was it my fault that he couldn't carry his own damn jug? Nevertheless, I could hardly stand it, watching the poor old bastard jerking and wobbling away in the distance between the two guards, never to be seen again by man, except for maybe the man who swept him up when he dried out. I would have to go live with my mother and sell apples.

Then he yelled, louder than a trumpet. "Peeker!" He jerked away from the guards enough to turn, his whole face twisted like a mop. "Peeker!" His name for me. He calls me that right in front of people. May herds of elephants trample his fucking old bones. He called out again, like the scream of a man going over a cliff for the third time: "Peeker! The *jug!*" I had no choice. I may be an old man myself sometime, though I doubt it. "All right," I screamed, "all right!" So they found out I was his follower, and they put me with him in the cell.

"It's good to have you here with me, my boy," he said, and patted my shoulder. I couldn't think of a suitable answer, except maybe banging my head on the wall or hitting myself with his crutch.

By evening, the jug was empty. He sat, sweating and dejected, at the table in the middle of the cell. The room was full of large flies buzzing a deep dull drone, as if they too felt the heat. "Is it possible that they've brought their Seer to this dismal place to dry him out?" he said. "Have they no more respect than that for Apol-

lo's choosing of his chosen?" He wrung his fingers and
rolled his eyes up, getting into the swing of it. "What
will become of me, here where I can get no wine and,
worse, where I haven't a soul to lecture or rant at or
mock?"

"You have me," I said.

But he ignored it. He was enjoying himself. He
stretched his arms toward the ceiling—they were dirtier
than the horns of a bull that's been goring things.
"What becomes of a Seer when harassment drives him
sane? These are dark times, Peeker! And dangerous
times! The fires of revolution, the daily arrests. Even
the children are sullen and withdrawn as mountain
goats." His eyes grew stern. "These are *wintry* times,
Peeker. The streets are slick with ice. The people move
about silently, mufflered to the eyes."

"It's summer," I said. I understood, of course, that
it was useless to try to persuade him.

"Men are dying out there, you know. Falling asleep
in snowdrifts and never awakening. That's why I bless
them, even when they do me wrong. Also, of course,
why should I curse my enemies and make them hit
me?" He giggled, as I'd expected him to, then sighed,
which caught me off guard. It made me nervous, and I
looked out through the cell-door bars at the pleasant
summer evening stretching away toward the mountains.
When I looked back I saw that, in his vague way, he
had been watching me. He smiled, crafty as usual but
also full of sadness. "How can even a Seer tell the truth
when he's sitting all by himself in a cell, frozen to the
marrow, without so much as the shadow of a drop of
wine, and nobody who loves him that he can write
to?"

"I'm here," I said. "I'm somebody." Then I was embarrassed. "Never complain, never explain," my mother says.

Agathon laughed, *Hyuck, hyuck, hyuck!* Something

between a Helot and a rooster. He asked, "How old are you, Peeker?"

I looked away and blushed. "Twenty," I said. A person ought to have become something by twenty, I admit, but I was sickly as a child. I'm still not as well as I might be. That's why he lets me accompany him. Our two shadows on the cobblestones—his as round as a potato, mine more like an asparagus—remind him that life is fundamentally risible. I ground my fist into my hand and looked at my knees.

"Twenty," he said, and smiled sadly. "Then I see I am many years your senior and can afford to humor you. We'll say it's summer."

"It doesn't matter," I said.

"That's true!" he said, and his eyes brightened for a moment, it seemed to me, then dulled again. "No, it does matter, to a certain extent. Everything matters, to a certain extent, now that our jug's gone dry."

He pushed his chair back, leaned over for the crutch on the floor, and, grunting a little, got up. He jerked over to the cell door as if something I'd said had made him cross. He peered out for a long time, sucking in his mouth so far that his beard and moustache met. Finally he pivoted around to face me squarely, sober as a disreputable judge. His eyebrows went out like two mountain slopes, and his cheeks twitched like an earthquake. "Break the jug!" he said. "A man can be crazy without it!"

I broke the jug.

His eyes widened. "Peeker! It was a metaphor!" He hobbled over to the pieces in a hurry, as if if he got there in time he could stick them together again. He was too late. He looked at me over his shoulder, deeply grieved.

"I'm sorry," I said.

He moved his head slowly from side to side. "Ah well," he said, wiping his hands on his stomach. "Ah well." He leaned on the table and, after deep meditation, sat down. At last he smiled, as if forgiving me; but it wasn't that. He'd forgiven me for it long ago, because he'd known it would happen. He always knows. It had merely slipped his mind.

foreshadowing of Peeker/agathon being same character or projections of a character

summer (peeker)/ winter (seer)

2   Agathon:

I have difficulty maintaining my crafty leer. Last night they had another execution. I couldn't see it—the cell door faces the wrong direction—but I could hear the roars of the crowd. They're something, these people. The roars are deliberate, calculated. As the condemned man's pain drives out his fear, the roars of the crowd grow more intense, less human, ringing like a sound of bees from every pitted, icy wall, to call him back to terror. A man doesn't need to see them marching, every flick of the knee precise, to know this city's been squeezed tight into one man's image—the image of a lunatic: Lykourgos.

Helots passed in the darkness afterward, down by the river, moving quietly over the snow toward the high white hills where they've lived for generations, semi-slaves to Sparta. They passed as quietly as lepers. It must have been some Spartan that died, and his stiff, bullheaded dignity put them to shame. Even a weak, sickly Spartan, a man who's a failure and criminal by his own code, puts other men to shame. I might assert, and prove by double-talk and winks, that the shame is nonsense—a man might as well be ashamed in the presence of a lion's gaze or the logical reflections of a striking snake—but the shame's there just the same. We live by the myths imposed on us, like actors in an endless play. (If you quote me, remember who said it.) In my moments of greater than usual senility I look at myself, befuddled, complex, disloyal to everything I

11

know (my wife abandoned years ago, and my two children, my city, my art, my philosophical rumina- tions), and I look at my jailer, calm, self-righteous, intransigent as a mountain, and though I know him to be no cleverer than a clothespin, I am ashamed. His shaggy eyebrows are thick with ice, his nose is white, as if someone had just pinched it, his coat goes out in the wind like a sail, but his heart's indifferent. He does his Spartan duty.

The boy observes this, of course, and despite all I've taught him, he's greatly drawn to it. He sits in the doorway bent over so far that his vertebrae stick out like the spikes on a dragon, and he peeks up through his hair in wonder at the thickness of our jailer's thighs. I caught him this afternoon flexing the place on his arm where there should be a muscle. "Vanity, vanity!" I cried. I delight, I revel, in his embarrassment. His head goes down, his bony feet and knees come up, his elbows rise as he tries to hide behind his arms. He looks like a bundle of sticks that has come untied. "Ah, Peeker," I say, "poor misbegotten Peeker!" and touch his hand, which he withdraws. At times I torment him, merely to keep my mind alert—and for his good, of course. "At least you could come over here by the fire. You'll freeze, sitting there by the door in all that snow."

"You're crazy! You're truly crazy!" says Peeker. "It's the middle of summer and we've *got* no fire, for which praise God, and you keep babbling about snow!" His eyes roll like a new colt's and his arms go up over his ears, holding onto his head.

I chuckle wickedly. "Ah well," I say, feeling gen- erous. "Time is a matter of the greatest perplexity."

He hides again. "*Com*plexity, you mean."

I nod, benign as Apollo, benign as Athena. "That too."

I will win him over eventually. Not in the matter of the weather, perhaps, but to other valuable opinions. I suppose there's no harm in his obstinate clinging to "facticity," as Thaletes used to say—though it smacks, to me, of niggardliness and concupiscence, even hubris. He couldn't turn into a Spartan if he wished. He hasn't got the chin for it. Helot through and through, my poor disciple, and not even one of the revolutionist crowd: one of those who, instead, endure, blindly imagine that by suffering and piety they will prevail. They too will be bloodied. The word of Apollo's Watchman. And so eventually he'll face the fact that he's ridiculous and become, like me, a Seer. And I'll pity him, of course; that's only decent. These are not predictions but griseous facts.

But ah! A Seer without a book! The first of his kind in the world, probably. I had the best book to be seen, once, or one of the best: a pile of scrolls as tall as a man and as wide as a man could stretch his arms, thick with scratches, column on column, parchment on parchment, all the best pages brought down from the six great ancient books, and all the best pages from the last generation—Solon, Thales, Thaletes, and Gorias the Commentator (his book went into his grave with him). I had, in the oldest section of the book, all the names of the true Akhaians and where they came from in the time of the Great Wanderings, back to the age of the Orchomenians, and which of the heroes were guilty of human sacrifice and which were not, and which of them married their sisters and which took enemies' wives. I had all the names of the tree gods and the animal gods, and the names of the stars, with their characters, and how they became confused with Zeus and Athena and the gods of spirit. I had in that old book the secret of embalming, which not even Homer understood, and the secret of ciphering curves, and the secrets of poisoning. Wherever I traveled in the world—and I traveled plenty for Solon and later Lykourgos—I traded secrets with the wisemen I met, and when I came home I would set it all down carefully, cunningly, hide on hide, adding the new to the old, as did Klinias before me and as Phemios the Doubter did before him; and then I'd lock up the book once more in its secret place. There were men who'd have killed me to get that book, though no one could have read it but myself or a disciple. I wrote in the secret grammata of Klinias, my teacher, and in later years borrowed the alphabets of Prastos and Kalaphos. Nevertheless, I meant it to last forever, safe and sound. (It was hundreds of years old already, I believe, by the time it fell into Klinias's hands. Philombrotos, who kept it in his palace, valued the book more highly than he did the palace itself, though he couldn't read a word in it.) But so much for elegy. The book is gone. Fittingly enough, in this age of universal darkness, and plague, and war. And rightly, perhaps. It could answer none of the final questions: a great, sour garbage heap of facts and figures, tricks, devices. Let Peeker start fresh, as I myself, in my old age, have resolved to start fresh. I will scramble his wits to a fine fury and send him on his way. The gods be with us.

3   Peeker:

The old bastard's crazy as a loon. He's trying to drive
me crazy too, for company. An hour before dawn I
hear this terrible crash and I think the room is tum-
bling down but it's Agathon falling out of bed. "Ye
gods!" he yells, "I've been remiss! Remiss!" I'm thinking he means the gods made him fall as a punishment,
which I happen to believe, but then I see it isn't that.
He comes crawling over on all fours to shake me—it's
too dark for him to see that I'm awake—and as soon
as his breath comes over me like a dead rhinoceros I
shrink back against the wall. "Ah ha!" he yells, "so
you're awake! Good boy! It's time for your education."

"Fat hell!" I say. "It's the middle of the night."

"Count it as yesterday," he says. "We let yesterday
slip by us." He grabs ahold of my hair and I've got no
choice. "Now," he says, "I am going to teach you history."

"History is irrelevant!" I yell. "Education is meaningless. You can't piss in the same mud puddle twice!"
Sometimes you can beat him by an appeal to principle.

But his mind was made up. "Be still, Peeker. History's useful, even when it's false. It strengthens a young
man's character, leads him upward to the knowledge
of Joy and Death. Besides, this is a *personal* history. To
reject it would be inhumane. I'm a *feeling* creature,
Peeker—whatever you may think."

There was a catch in his voice, and, dark as it was,

15

I was aware that he was clutching his heart. Though I know his tricks, I decided to be cautious. "Personal," I echoed, noncommittal.

"Exactly!" he said. "It's the story of my loves and hates, and how they made me a Seer."

He was sounding downright fraught now, and I knew there had to be a catch. At last I saw it. "Loves!" I said. "You mean *women*, master?" It cracked me up.

"I mean women," he said, and his tone was so lugubrious I stopped laughing. I thought of the women. They'd all be dead now, suffocated by his breath. I could see that in a way it was sort of sad.

"OK," I said, though I knew better.

"We'll begin with Lykourgos. A grisly tale of hate."

"OK."

He let go of my hair.

For a long time, once I'd given in, he sat on my bedside not saying a word, just patting my head and thinking, full of woe. The donkeys and chickens started up. It would be morning soon. At last Agathon left my bedside and crawled over to his own bed to find his crutch, then climbed up it and jerked his way over to the cell door to stand looking out, lecturing mostly with his back to me. He pulled thoughtfully at his beard as he talked, except when he paused to scratch himself, and sometimes he'd turn to glance at me, crafty, and would laugh as if in rage.

"Peeker, my boy—"

Zeus only knows why he does these things. Here we are in prison, and the whole world's reeling as if the gods have gone mad—wars on every side—the Spartans moving one by one through the cities of the Perioikoi: Methone has fallen and all its citizens are dead; Pylos, ancient home of Nestor, has been turned to a charred desert; Algonia, Gerenia, Leuktra, and Thalemae are burning. The suicidal Helots are rising in rebellion, terrorizing the outer suburbs; and while the Spartan army pushes out through valleys and plains

like a tidal wave, Kyros the Persian stares across at
Lakonia from the ashes of Sardis. Agathon knows all
this better than I do. The finest Seer in Greece. But he
twiddles his fingers, tells frivolous tales of kings nobody remembers. What am I to do?

"Peeker, my boy, they tell a story of Lykourgos's
great-grandfather Soös. In the dead heat of summer he
attacked the king of the Klitorians in a dry and stony
place, and neither army had water. Near the end of the
day the Klitorians asked for a truce and offered a deal:
King Soös would give up all he had taken in land and
spoils if the two armies, to save themselves, might
drink in peace at the nearest spring. After the usual
oaths and ratifications, the armies moved to a spring
three miles away, and the Klitorians drank while Soös
and his Dorian army stood with folded arms and
waited. When the Klitorians had drunk their fill, King
Soös himself came up to the spring and sprinkled his
face without swallowing a drop, then turned on his heel
and marched his army off through the dust in scorn of
his enemies, relinquishing nothing, since neither he nor
his men had drunk their water.

"No legend, this little Spartan tale! I give you my
word as Apollo's Aid, I see its truth in our jailer's murderous eyes." He leered and winked (it was daylight
now).

He tells about their hero of heroes, Lykourgos.

"Lykourgos, when he was a young man, was king of
Sparta for eight months. While he was king it came to
light that his sister-in-law, the former queen, who'd
been barren heretofore (known to be an insatiable slut,
and feebleminded), was pregnant. With characteristic
self-righteousness, Lykourgos immediately declared that
the kingdom belonged to her issue, provided it were
male, and that he himself had regal jurisdiction only as
the child's guardian. Soon after, an overture was made
to him by the queen, that she would herself in some
way destroy the child, on condition that Lykourgos

would marry her. Lykourgos brooded—grinding his teeth together, if I know him—outraged to blisters and boils by the woman's wickedness.

"I give you the heart of the matter in a vision, Peeker:

> Lykourgos stomps in his fourth-floor chamber, black, oh, black
> Of beard and heart, pacing; and though he's a dwarf, a crack
> Flies through the marble tiles at every step. He turns,
> He kicks the wall. He stomps to the other end and turns
> And kicks again. Dark cracks go up and down the halls
> Like trees, like lightning upside down. The palace falls,
> Lies still in billowing dust! Then, lo! from the towering dump,
> Lykourgos rises, scowling, scattering boulders off his hump!

> > O Lord, let us be fierce and bold
> > Like him, before we grow too old!
> > Oh, let us seize our Destinies
> > As wrestlers seize each other's knees
> > And throw ourselves, head over heels,
> > To where life shocks like mating eels!"

I groaned and hid. He could at least have a little respect for visions. And for dactyls! He was once the most famous poet—or at least second most famous—in Athens. Is nothing sacred to him?

"But that's something else," Agathon said. He cleared his throat and drew himself up, struggling to be more formal.

"Lykourgos played the fox. He pretended to accept the woman's proposal, sending a messenger with thanks and expressions of joy—hah!—but he urged her not to force a miscarriage for fear of impairing her health or endangering her life. He himself, he said, would see to it that when the child was born it should be gotten out of the way. And so the woman came to the time of delivery. As soon as he heard she was in labor, Lykourgos sent people to be on hand and observe all that happened, with orders that if the child was a girl they should give it to the woman, to eat or dandle, whichever she pleased—" He cackled, transported by his imagery, then caught himself and looked angry. "—But if it was a boy, this child of the queen's, they should bring it to Lykourgos, wherever he was and whatever he might be doing. It came about that when Lykourgos was at supper with the principal magistrates of the city, the queen was delivered of a boy, who was soon after that presented to Lykourgos at his table. Lykourgos took the child in his arms and said to those around him, 'Men of Sparta, here is a king born unto us!' So saying, he placed the child in the king's seat and named him Kharilaus, or 'Joy of the People.' All this without a trace of humor or embarrassment, and without a flicker of doubt as to why he behaved as he did or why the queen behaved in the strange way she did. Needless to say (though the story does not report this part), nobody laughed. They were Spartans."

He shook his head, his lips trembling. He found it all very tragic, but also infuriating. He said:

"And later when, inevitably, the lady turned on Lykourgos in rage, threatening to kill both him and the child, and crown her brother Leonidas, it did not so much as occur to Lykourgos to strike out at the queen mother. (She was of royal blood, and wife to his own dead brother.) He packed his trunks and set out to study the legal systems of the world, avoiding Sparta till his nephew should come to marriageable years and, by having a son, secure the succession. Again, nobody laughed. They followed him to the edge of the city, with deep respect for his virtue. He traveled to Krete, to Asia, to Egypt, to Athens. Wherever he went he stood watching, listening, brooding like angry stone. Most of what he saw (as you could guess, my boy) repelled him. When he found things that might be of use to the new Sparta he had in mind, he was repelled by the admixture of good laws with bad."

My master was beginning to shake, now, in his indignation.

"He wrote himself notes: *A species originates, and a type becomes established and strong in the long struggle with essentially unfavorable conditions. On the other hand, it is known by the experience of breeders that species which receive superabundant nourishment are fertile in prodigies and monstrosities (also in monstrous vices). Consider the hearty eating of peasants, the sparse fare of born aristocrats.* His suffering made him a wolf."

He turned from the doorway with these last words and glared at me like a madman, trembling all over. He'd pulled his beard all out of shape in his agitation. He looked like a tree full of seaweed after a hurricane.

"More wolf than *you* are, master?" I said. "He he he!" It was a dangerous thing to say, no doubt, but his anger was infectious. Anyway, I can outrun him. I could put the table between us, and if necessary I could brain him with the lamp.

"Yaargh!" he said, or something like that, and took a step toward me. I jumped out of bed and snatched up the cover and held it out like a bullfighter's cape. His neck swole like an adder's, but he realized his disadvantage and merely shook his finger, sucking his mouth in.

"Look at you," I said. "Supposed to be so wise, supposed to be so full of sophrosyne!* You're like everybody else!"

"Not so!" he roared. "It's because you broke my jug!"

"It was empty," I roared back.

His face moved slowly together like a square knot tightening, and he thought about it. "That's true," he

*From σαόφρων, opposite of σλοόφρων. Ed.

said. His voice cracked. "That's what I like about you, Peeker. Even in this freezing weather, you care about the Truth." He smiled and took a step toward me, but I was no fool. I put the table between us.

Agathon sighed and his face came loose again. I thought he would cry. "Ah well," he said, as usual. The jailer came, just then, with two plates of food. It was overcooked cabbage.

"We only eat onions," I said, to make up with my master.

The jailer said nothing.

We sat down, on opposite sides of the table, and ate.

Agathon was still shaking. "They're all alike, these Spartans," he whispered.

I nodded and went on eating.

He smiled politely at the guard, then whispered again, fiercely, "*I* am not one of these crazy people. I'm Athenian. Fact! A scribe by profession, originally; once chief scribe to the Lawgiver Solon himself. I am educated, civilized to a fault! I conceal it, of course. I've done so so long it's no longer easy to keep in mind. Even with respect to simple things, my mind wanders like a blind man tapping in the grass with his stick. But I manage. Yes! I remind myself by the fact that the rats in my cell—like you, dear Peeker—are not morally offensive to me, though they frighten me, of course—incredibly furry in their brown winter coats." ("Summer," I mumbled.) His eyes burned darker, fuliginous. "They materialize as if by witchcraft at the edge of the glow my lamp sends out or near the embers of my paltry hearth, and they come straight at me, hurrying, their shadows sneaking up on them like cats. Their close-set, coal-black idiot eyes never move, not even to blink. A Spartan would kill them at once, without thought, in righteous loathing. 'For superior men,' Lykourgos says, 'evil is not what is bad by some theoretical system, but that which disgusts him as inferior to himself.' 'He he ho ha,' I asnwer. —But though I

have resided in Lakonia a long time, I have not lost all
capacity for philosophical objectivity and amusement,
especially amusement at my own inferiority. Though I
am larger than the rat, and armed (I have my crutch),
I climb up on my stool and draw my tattered skirts
around my knees and cry, eyes wide, my huge beard
shaking, 'Shoo! Shoo!' —This partly for the jailer, partly for the rat. Only the rat notices, and, being a Spartan rat, he keeps on coming." (I have never seen my
master do any such thing.) "In Athens," he continued
with great feeling, "the rat and I would sit down over
black bean soup, with side dishes of olives and nuts,
white napkins at our necks, and we'd talk of metaphysics. The rat would perhaps not be good at it, but
we Athenians are a cheerful people, infinitely tolerant,
always hopeful. Nevertheless, though I joke, Peeker,
I'm afraid of them. I'm frightened by everything, wor-
shipful toward everything, like any decent Seer."

Our plates were empty. I gave them back to the
jailer and he went away. Agathon watched me, then
belched once, softly for a Seer, and went to sleep. His
snores drowned out the irenic buzzing of the flies.

If ever I have to become a Seer, I mean to be a
gentleman about it.

4 Agathon:

Ah, Peeker, Peeker, poor miserable wretch! He has no understanding of anything! He sits across the table from me, writing and writing—his opinions, I trust, or his youthful memoirs—and he hasn't an inkling that he's falling into their trap. Does he ever inquire of himself or of me why the ephors give us parchment? No! They come, look us over, and leave a great gray stack of it— it's worth a small fortune—and as soon as I hand him his third of the stack (he writes smaller than I) he begins to spill out his opinions like logs down a flume. I should stop him, if I were an ethical person and cared for my fellowman. But alas, I am a sensualist who takes frivolous delight in the way he leans forward and clamps his tongue between his teeth and crosses his eyes, preserving his soul in fustian. When I try to peek at what he's writing, he shades the parchment, blocking my view, with a hand as big as a shovel. Well, I am resigned to it. As I watch each new day's prisoners brought in, lifting their feet unnaturally as they labor through the drifted snow, or when I hear the roars of an execution, I think back fondly to my onion patch and the beautiful women who made me what I am. At times the thought of their gentleness, fitful and dubious as it was, awakens my soul to civilized guilt, and I do what I can to distract him from self-destruction.

"Time for lessons!" I say. "All play no work makes Jackie a jerk!"

His shoulders shrink inward, his head droops like a frond. "For the love of God, master, take pity!"

I fulminate. That too takes up time, after all: delays his pen. When his eyes glaze and I know he's no longer hearing my rant, I descend to pedagogical harassment. "Young man, do you want to be a Seer or a stupid-shit pig?" His choice is predictable and not as amusing as he thinks. "We will speak of Lykourgos," I tell him. He puts down his pen and the blood drains out of his face. I tell him with fulgent rhetoric things of no interest, the nature of his doom.

"Lykourgos was missed, during his time away from Sparta. There had been for a long time an absolute abyss between the rulers and the common people, and each watched the other with hostility. The Spartans, you know, are descendants of old-time mountaineers—tough, rugged, stubborn men, Dorians and various breeds of Northmen, a black- and red-headed mixed rabble of cattle raiders by nature impatient of reasonable law or of complexity in any form." I get up from the table and hobble around on my crutch as I speak, to keep my mind off women. Occasionally I pause behind his chair. He broke my jug.

"To make myself clear," I say, "I must stoop to fact."

He sighs, but I am a tempest. I tell him how it was.

When the Mykenaians were weak from the last of their booty hunts—the invasion of Troy—the Dorians and newer waves of Northmen, who'd been watching all along, perched in the mountains like starlings on a clothesline, swooped down to attack them. By animal courage and stupidity and luck they wiped out the majestic old civilization (only cultural islands survived, refuges for the dispossessed, such as Athens), and they occupied—along with the Helots, who seem to have been there since time began, everybody's slaves—what was left of the ancient cities. They lived as squatters in the burnt-out palaces, like goats nibbling at the cracks in old altars, and they made no effort to rebuild. Record-keeping vanished, the art of writing disappeared, handicrafts decayed, old gods became confused with new ones. Finely wrought weapons of bronze gave way to clumsy iron. Burial in magnificent tombs gave way to quick cremation. "All things were Chaos," Anaxagoras says, "when Mind arose and made Order." He might have added, All things were Mind when the Dorians came down and made Chaos. (But I veer from my matter.)

Even so, a Dorian aristocracy developed, a thing impossible back in the mountains, and it modeled itself, as well as it knew how, on the one it had overthrown. The process took a long time, but old ways hang on, especially among Northmen. The commoners scorned this froufrou new class, bringing the state close to anarchy; and the ruling class scorned the commoners as insolent. Both the commoners and the two kings of the diarchy sent again and again for Lykourgos, but he wouldn't return until Kharilaus had engendered an heir. Lykourgos was in Athens when word came that finally it was done. He started for home the same day, set himself up in the two kings' palace like a statue of its original owner, and began his fierce reforms.

His aim was total reconstruction. He compared himself to the wise physician who brings all the humors to the brink of exhaustion and then, by surgery, diet, and exercise, rebuilds the sick man's constitution from scratch. He went first to the oracle at Delphi to collect his set of laws from the god himself. (This was always a favorite trick of his, a thing not to be inquired into too narrowly.) When he returned to Sparta he broke his plans—or some of them—to his closest friends and then, little by little, to others. He organized a police force on the Egyptian model, one which could operate swiftly, secretly, and without any bothersome scrutiny by the courts. His opposition soon became more flexible of disposition, and the kings, Kharilaus and Ark-

helaus, came to his side. He established a senate of
twenty-eight men—all hard-line old military leaders—
and denied the people any right but ratification or temporary rejection of what they might decide. Then he
began his more daring innovations.

He outlawed wealth. First, he redistributed the land,
splitting all Lakonia into thirty thousand equal shares
and Sparta itself into nine thousand, with a provision
for yearly review and redistribution. Of those who
fought him, some stood trial for treason, some merely
vanished. Nevertheless, men still had money, and
Lykourgos knew from his travels in Asia, especially
Sardis, that treasure hoards, like land, mean inequality.
Finding that it would be dangerous to go about seizing
men's gold openly, Lykourgos took another course and
defeated greed by a stratagem: he commanded that all
gold and silver coin should be called in to be reminted
and standardized. When the money came in—you remember the story—he returned it not in gold or silver
but in iron bars, the coin of the ancients, before the
Asian influence. A great weight and quantity of the
stuff was of very little worth: to lay up, say, three thousand dollars' worth required at least a large shed. Thus
he closed out several vices at once. Who would rob a
man of such coin? Who would even accept as a bribe a
thing by no means easy to hide, a thing not a great
credit to possess or of any worth cut in pieces? Moreover, it was ugly. When it was red hot they quenched
it in vinegar and spoiled it: it couldn't be worked.

The trick had further implications. It ended trade.
Foreign nations—"inferior breeds," Lykourgos called
them—scorned the coin of the Spartans and would not
sell to Lakonia. No more fat merchants came with ship-
loads of trinkets or finely carved furniture or spices. No
more rhetoric masters, fortune-tellers, whores, engrav-
ers, or jewelers cast their wide, comfortable shadows
on Spartan soil. As for local arts, all but the useful were
outlawed. Spartans made bedsteads, chairs, tables, gold-

en cups. In time, for reasons I could never make clear
to Lykourgos, they made nothing but cups—neurotic-
ally elegant—and left all other work to the Helots—in
effect, though not technically, their slaves. An incredible thing, when you muse on it. The Spartans stood over
the land like gods, grandly posing with their round
shields and swords, while a more populous race which
they judged inferior—a civilization as separate from
theirs as the woodbine is from the elm tree—provided
the bulk of Lakonia's blacksmiths, shipwrights, masons,
bakers, cooks, woodcutters, messengers, longshoremen,
saddlers, shepherds, dry cleaners, doctors, foresters,
carpenters, bowmakers, weavers, unguent boilers, ditch
diggers, even wine inspectors! Any fool should have
guessed what trouble it would lead to! But the Spartans were clever, intuitively. They developed an almost
unconscious theory that the one thing Helots were incapable of was fighting, even to prevent, say, the rape
of their wives or the murder of their children. And the
Helots, who'd been losing for centuries, believed it. I
don't credit Lykourgos himself with inventing this in-
genious weapon, but no doubt he knew how to wield it.

Then came the masterstroke that almost killed him.
He destroyed the last refuge of gentility—fine manners.
He ordered, backed by a Rhetra from the god, that all
Spartan men should eat in common, of the same bread
and meat, and of kinds officially specified, and should
not spend their lives at home, lying on costly couches at
splendid tables, delivering themselves into the hands of
their tradesmen and cooks, fattening themselves in corners like hogs, destroying both their bodies and their
minds. No man henceforth could indulge in the Sardinian luxury of daintiness or effeminacy. The prince-
ling who could not stand the chomping and slobbering
of honest warriors must sicken on it and die.

When the law was announced, all who opposed
Lykourgos gathered in the central square of the city to
wait for him. (The sun beat straight down. The three-

story stone buildings of the government, with those wide
sterile columns and tier on tier of marble steps, trapped
the heat inside the square like oven walls. Hawks cir-
cled in the sky overhead as if riding the crests of the
heat waves. At the crowd's edges, Helots watched,
loaded like animals, and hobbled donkeys waited with
their eyes shut.) When Lykourgos appeared, dark and
morose as a volcano, as always, they met him with no
overt sign of hostility, drawing him into their snare.
He came toward them, and when he had approached
too near for retreat they rushed him, hurling the stones
and sticks they'd hidden until then behind their backs.
It was holy, and I was there, I witnessed it! He stood
his ground for a moment, like a man undecided as to
whether saving his life was worth the trouble, and
splashes of blood appeared on his forehead, his bare
shoulders, his legs. Then he laughed, a single irate
snort, as if he had glimpsed for an instant the full
senselessness of life, and he turned, stretching his arms
out before him, and ran. His mouth gaped, his black
hair flew out behind him, his feet slapped down on the
pavement as if he were clowning. But he outran them
—or outran all but one, a young man named Alkander.
He was right on Lykourgos's heels, and when Lykourgos turned to see who was so close, the boy swung his
stick and popped Lykourgos's left eye like a grape.
Lykourgos stumbled. When he got up he was holding
both hands over the eye, and blackish blood came bub-
bling like oil through the cracks between his fingers.
Alkander stood still, terrified, no doubt, and the crowd
behind him stopped too. With the one eye he had left,
Lykourgos looked at the boy. Then he said, "Come
with me."

Alkander hung back, glanced at the crowd. They
looked like they'd just remembered they'd missed their
lunch.

Lykourgos said again, "Come with me."

The boy obeyed, looking at the ground, and Lykourgos led him to his house. He made Alkander his personal servant and bodyguard, and in a few weeks Alkander worshiped Lykourgos as he would a god.

Nobody laughed.

I pause for questions and comments. Peeker is asleep

Ah well, ah well. It's for my sake I lecture him, not his. When he sits asleep, skinny legs aspraddle, feet sticking out under the far side of the table, beneath where his hands hang (his head is balanced on his square chin like a dancer on the wedge of four square toes), my mind, left to its own devices, falls back, like a boulder returning to earth, to thoughts of my beautiful Tuka, my beautiful Iona. I am a man in the clutch of goddesses. You too would wink and leer, break wind, speak poetry. I have been blinded, deafened by holiness; they have severed the frenum of my tongue as boys slit a crow's.

But I hardly show it. No trifling comfort. I showed it less in the insouciant days of my onion patch, my peeking through windows, my jug. Yet even now I manufacture distractions: my wonderful weather, my pedagogy, my fond recollections of lunatic converse with kings.

I must wake up Peeker and explain to him that THE WORLD IS A SHRIVELED PUMPKIN.

I'll tell him tomorrow. Let him rest.

5   Agathon:

By daylight I have a splendid view. It has, like all
views, its drawbacks—chiefly the fact that I view it
through a squat Kretan door which, most of the time,
is wide open to the elements, or open except for nineteen crude iron bars on an iron frame, so that the north
wind strikes me not as Zeus sent it, but sliced. Snow
drifts to the legs of my table, then melts, turning my
floor to mud. It's a cell that hasn't been used in years—
hence the absence of the outer door—but the prison's
bursting its seams just now, thanks to the revolutionists'
plots, the Messenian saboteurs, the sickness in the sea-
ports, the general worldwide climate of rapine and destruction. No doubt they thought I'd be indifferent to
cold, being a philosopher and a messenger from Apollo.
I endure, however. I can sleep, wrapped in my horrible
blankets, curled up to the right of the door, my feet
near the hearth, where the wind gets me on the re-
bound, reduced to an irritable turbulence full of damp-
ness and unwholesome smells—my own. Sometimes,
though not always, they cover the door for me at night,
thanks not so much to their kindness as to my craft.
When I came here, two weeks and three days ago, I
used to sit by the door every night making marks on the
dirt floor or in the drifted snow with my crutch, pretending to plot the positions of the stars. When my
jailer glared at me, as if to ask what the devil I was up
to, I would merely roll my eyes up, open my hands in
wise-old-Athenian despair, and murmur, "It's going to

be soon, my good man, very soon! Look! Ares in the
ascendant!" But I wouldn't tell him what it was that
was coming soon, would merely cackle as if with no
hope for Sparta. It made him nervous. They don't believe in knowledge, and their councilors scorn the
opinion of the Helots (which I used to promote when
I was loose—partly from meanness, partly from conviction) that earthquakes will soon destroy this wicked
land. But it made him nervous just the same. Whenever
he's sure no inspectors will come, he puts wide planks
in front of my door to block my spying on the stars. I
accept it philosophically. I say, "Jailer, dear friend, a
man of my years has no time left for grudges. Apollo
bless you! I'm his Seer, you know. He does what I tell
him. I snap my fingers and he jumps."

But despite drawbacks, my view is impressive. I look
down from my low hill to the beautiful Eurotas River,
gray blue and glassy, virtually abandoned at this time
of year (a few young idiots swim there at times, proving themselves, as usual, or possibly washing). The
snow-covered summits of Mount Taygetos rise to the
west of the river, a few Helot huts against their base,
sending up threads of smoke to the home of the eagles.
On the east side of the valley there are the glittering
bluffs where the shrine of Menelaos is, and beyond the
bluffs the pale-blue ridges of Mount Parnon. Only a
Spartan would leave such a view to mere prisoners and
plant his best houses where a civilized man would dig
sewage ditches. It's not, I suspect, that Spartans have
no eye for scenery, and not that they're so stupid as not
to know that a fine landscape can pick up a doomed
man's spirits. It's their stony superiority: they disdain
their own inclination toward beauty ("even pigs make
aesthetic choices," Lykourgos claims), and they disdain
such paltry sadism as giving a prisoner nothing of interest to look at. As usual, I can think of no revenge.
"Such splendor!" I say, wringing my hands and clutching my chest with my inner arms like a man about to

faint. I faint. He leans on the bars and frowns (I watch through one eye), then goes away.

I begin to think he is, all things considered, a harmless dog, no more to be feared than, say, Peeker. He's fierce, dangerous, not to be toyed with, he lets me know by the twist of his eyebrows and mouth; but he's one of the older ones. Though his face looks only middle-aged, his hair is the color of milkweed pod. I would not play games with Lykourgos's new generation. Or would I? I would. I've done it a hundred times with my antics as wobbly old arrow of the far-shooter Apollo. Clearly, the urge toward self-destruction in a civilized man is irrepressible. I've played my games with Lykourgos himself—never doubting the outcome, which now is upon me. —Or us. I must not forget my faithful Peeker, my footnote, my apistill. Civilization, mother of the arts, implies a failure of healthy imagination. So Lykourgos. Hence his insistence that girls go bare, and that burials, not to mention tortures and executions, take place in the heart of the city, for all to see. Babies look over their mothers' breasts to watch small boys beat a smaller, weaker companion with iron bars—the coins of the Spartans. Gangs of young thugs, in their war games, knife Helots in the streets, and passersby, wrinkling their noses against the Helot smell, give thoughtful criticism.

My jailer, I suspect, would find knifing me distasteful, though he would do it. Though he never talks to me, naturally, I believe he occasionally listens to me when I teach him things of interest. I never teach him anything true. What little I know of reality I'm saving, in hopes of bribing him with it, when my case gets even more desperate. I told him this morning that in the old days (the days of Theseus and the rest) goats were male, sheep female. This is seditious, actually. It cuts to the heart of Lykourgos's theory about women, namely, that women are merely a variant sort of men. "In the process of time," I said, leaning heavily on my crutch and looking skyward thoughtfully, but smiling and smiling to keep his attention, "sheep and goats became separate species." (Peeker hid his head.) "No one fully understands it, but the evidence is irrefragable. It has to do with our erroneous notions of time and space. We define objects in terms of the shape of space they displace, and we forget that old men are what they are because they're old. You follow me?" He looked at me, very cross, and I had an inkling that he did not fully understand. "Time is a thing," I said, and, leaning closer to him: "It bites."

Peeker and Tailer as aspects of
Agathon

6   Peeker:

We still don't know what the charge is, and the old
man's still done nothing about defending himself. It's all
insane. What's the matter with him? The ephors aren't
fools. They know his value to the state. Why don't they
talk to us then, come hear our side? Lykourgos is a just
man—even righteous, in fact; Agathon says so himself.
I keep asking myself, *What's happening? What's happening?* and I kick the walls and pound on my head
with my fists, but I know the answer: *Nothing's happening.* There's an execution almost every night, but
Agathon just babbles on. The crazy old bastard will let
us both be executed and he won't even lift a damn
finger! Who can I get to come listen, give us justice?
We're needed, now more than ever—the endless wars
in the north and west, the rumble of revolution all
around us. . . .

I don't know why it is—the muggy heat after yesterday's rain, or the queasy feeling I always get when I
eat too much cabbage, or the way my poor master's
flibbertigibbeting mashes my brains—but I feel more
confused, more unreal, more hopeless every day. Again
and again it strikes me: *This is serious! They're going to
kill us!* It's as clear as a vision, clear as a white duck in
a dark-green pool. I turn to Agathon, scared shitless,
and he does something crazy—some moron joke, or a
bump and a grind—and I'm disoriented, like a man
cast out of Time. Have we all been fooled? I wonder.
Is he merely insane? He teases the guard unmercifully,

like some impudent, fat nine-year-old, and he teases me,
teases himself. My mother would be laying plans. Is he
doing that, behind a facade of clowning? When someone is driving a cart for my mother, she does everything the driver does, a little ahead of him. Her shoulders go "whoa," though her hands are folded in her
lap; she pulls the team to the left or right with reins
invisibly rising from between her locked thumbs. "Zeus
helps those that helps theirselves," my mother says.
Who helps those that help Zeus?

Nothing I do can make him admit the seriousness of
things. I was sitting at the table, trying to write—Agathon writing across from me—and I said, "Master,
what is Lykourgos planning?"

He said, "My boy, let me ask a more significant
question. Why are we sitting here writing when we
could be gathering beautiful icicles to save up for summer?"

"In Apollo's name—"

"No no, my boy, I'm in deadly earnest. Why are we
writing?"

"Because they give us parchment," I said.

"And why do they give us parchment? The stuff's
expensive."

"God only knows."

The old man deliberated, then shook his head. "No,
we must think this out more soberly. Do they read what
we write?" I had no answer, so he answered himself.
"It seems unlikely, yet every three or four days they
come and take what we've written. —But do they read
it?" he asked himself again, and answered, "Probably
not." The dialogue amused him and he began to throw
himself into it, turning his head one way for one voice,
the other way for the other, like a rhapsode.

"They will preserve it, for the record?

"Doubtful. Their poetry is oral. They have lost the
art of writing music down. Their communism dispenses
with the need for public records, so they say. They do

not even write down their laws, on Lykourgos's theory that when laws are written, men abandon the sense for the letter.

"Then why do they give you parchment?

"God only knows. Because I used to be a scribe?

"You must do better than that."

"Master," I said. But he was engaged. He began wagging his finger at himself, lecturing himself pedantically.

"Perhaps they do it for their scornful amusement, using you as they occasionally use the Helots. They seize some Helot in the marketplace and take him to a house and give him wine, and they force him to drink it, like it or not, until he can barely stand. Then they lead him lurching and staggering to the eating hall where all the young Spartans and their older advisers are seated at their tables, brotherhood by brotherhood, and they make the drunken Helot dance and sing and struggle to play the flute. He kicks up his heels and clumsily lifts his filth-smudged, wine-bespattered skirt, showing his crooked, hairy legs, and he blunders into tables where the young men throw pieces of food at him or cover his head with a messy iron pot or reach out to trip him or slyly, as if lovingly, seize hold of his private particulars. They applaud his antics and give him more wine until he vomits and passes out, and then, roaring with scornful laughter like a wolf pack's growl, they strip him of his clothes and hurl him like a grain sack through the window into the street. The dogs there snarl and bark at him, but the Helot lies still, philosophical as stone. According to Lykourgos, the example of the drunken Helot teaches temperance to Sparta's young." He laughed.

"So with you, then. Yes. They take what you write to the eating halls, where they read it aloud to the boys and advisers, who laugh in outrage at your laborious intortions, and answer them in the laconic way Lykourgos has made popular: 'Wisdom acts. Stupidity labors to explain itself.' And thus they purge the State of sickly reasoning.

"That's it, no doubt. Yes. Praised be Apollo!"

His expression became glum.

"The trouble is, you can never know if you're right or wrong, and until you do you must pull your nose and scratch your ear and ask the question some other way, in a predictably futile but inescapable search for certainty."

Agathon strongly disagreed. "False! Sir, what is certainty to me? I'm a Seer. Truths move through my mind like fish. I watch them, follow them into the gloom, turn indifferently to nearer fish, tapping my fingertips, marveling at the grace of their fins, and brooding, alarmed, on the emptiness of their eyes."

He considered this point and became conciliatory.

"Perhaps they give you parchment, Agathon, in hopes that you'll set down something they can condemn you for—some crime or indiscretion. They read, still as tigers in their dusky rooms, and watch through the dark, rustling ambiage, for some dire phrase to pounce on. A sudden summons then, a hasty trial . . .

"No! Ridiculous! In Sparta, justice is for Spartans. Especially so in this age of universal war. They'll waste no trial on me, much less on Peeker. Sooner or later, when he's sick of making a fool of me, old man Lykourgos will nod his head and noble Agathon will hobble from his cell, joking and leering and impishly aiming the tip of his crutch at the nearest guard's toes—or will be dragged from his cell, if we tell the truth, screaming and pleading, wringing his fingers, offering bribes, threats, promises, and that will be the end of poor old Agathon's adventures and ideas."

I tried to break in, but the other Agathon was quicker.

"Is it possible that they send what you write to Lykourgos?

"What would *he* care?

"And yet I wonder. He was interested once in all you said. He searched for years for the hiding place of your book."

He nodded thoughtfully.

"An amusing theory. Old one-eyed Lykourgos sitting black-bearded and heavy as a sack of murdered men's bones, shriveled small as a lizard's corpse, waiting, waiting in the temple at Delphi for the god to make up his windy mind, waiting, passing his time with the writings of his half-cracked lifelong critic. Is it possible that even Lykourgos has moments of doubt, so that he can't resist spying on the meditations of his enemies? Or is there even in him some flicker of the old Akhaian delight in ancient secrets, grand ideas?"

As if only now aware of my presence, Agathon looked at me, lachrymose. "Peeker, my boy, I've wasted half the afternoon sitting here with my crutch across my knees and my chin on my fists, brooding for your sake on why they bring us this parchment and take it away as they do our chamber pot when we fill it." His tone grew more poetic. "The sun is low. Only the icy crests of the bluffs to the east of the river still gleam with Helios's fire, and in the darkened valley Helot workers are driving goats and cows up from the river through the snowflakes to their barns. I can reach no decision on the parchment business, but I think we can solve the problem. We'll assume that all the answers are true—that our writings are for the eating halls, that what we write will either condemn us or save us in court, and that the letters all go to Lykourgos. I call this method Calculus."

I sighed, leaned on my hands.

"A wise solution," he said. "What matters in the world, my dear young friend, is not so much what is true as what is entertaining, at least so long as the truth itself is unknowable. So Homer understood. The question is, will it still entertain us tomorrow? Will we change our minds and hoard these writings in some secret place and offer the ephors only, say, obscene drawings of women? —Why not?"

And so I gave up. It's plain that my master has no respect for my opinions and no concern about my safety. The hell with him. I begin to suspect that a Seer is not someone who sees more clearly than other people, but merely a man who is forever looking in the wrong direction. I am going to figure out a plan of escape. If I think of one, see if I tell him!

7 Agathon:

Strange developments! "Magic is afoot in these woods," in the words of Alkman. I must begin at the beginning.

It was dusk. The first stars were beginning to appear above Mount Parnon and the wind was turning bitter cold when, pausing in the little song with which I was warming the cockles of my heart and entertaining my fellow prisoners for a mile or so on either side, I heard my jailer coming down the row of cells to the right of mine, feet crunching in the crusted snow, dragging a plank. He appeared at my door and glared at me, his bearded lips pursed to a kind of pout, steam blowing from his nostrils. I put aside my melody, rubbed my freezing hands together, and tried to look apologetic—for I do understand his problem. My very existence, for him, is criticism. My paunch condemns his asceticism; my timid, wholly irrelevant grins deny the iron-chained order of his soul. He went on glaring.

"Dear jailer," I cried, snatching at my crutch and rising from my table to welcome him. "Bless you! Always alert," I cried, "like a rabbit!"

His black eyes grew violent, and I corrected myself: "Like a bear."

I was too late. He spit, only vaguely in my direction, and set up the plank and turned away to get another. I spoke to him again when he returned with the second plank—"Any news of the wars?"—but he ignored me. When he came with the last plank he paused and looked at me a moment, not yet dropping it into place, and I believed he was struggling against a temptation to speak. For a man of stone, he was in agony—a brute straining toward thought. I said nothing, of course. There are times when even humor is out of place. His mouth worked, his underjaw twitched, and for an instant I had hopes that his eyes would cross the way Peeker's do when he's intense—but he looked away, instead, and I was disappointed. What was it he wanted to say to me? Some word of animalistic rage? Some news of how horribly I'm to die? Strange to say, I think not. His iracund, muscle-bound face was like a child's —it made me remember my own poor son Kleon, back in Athens. Without thinking, I stretched out my hand to him, and suddenly, with animal fury, he slammed the plank into position, shutting me in. He left then. I caught only a glimpse of his legs cutting the dusk like huge, slow stones, a statue walking.

So much for the evening's beginning. It was an omen, clear as an eagle carrying flowers above your left shoulder.

Darkness settled. I fed my rats the portion of our supper Peeker and I had saved for them, and after that, feeling in no mood for art or talk with Peeker, I took my constitutional, walking around and around my table, deepening the trench my crutch end has cut in the hard-packed earth of my floor. Every few rounds I would pause at the cell door to look out, watching for revolutionists' fires, listening for the outbreak of a riot or the noise of an execution. There was nothing. It did not calm me. Quiet nights are the worst. You keep waiting, wondering which direction the trouble is going to strike from. (I can seldom foresee any troubles that involve me directly. That's how it always is, people say. Tieresias. Kassandra.)

Somewhere near midnight, as near as I can tell, I was startled by a hint of movement outside the bars but inside the lean-to of planks. I stopped, trembling like a leaf, clutching my heart. (Even as a younger man, I was never up to this kind of thing.) Peeker's eyes were open, bright as an owl's. Nothing stirred. For a long time I waited, trying to see past the glow of the lamp on the table between me and the door. It was no illusion; that I knew. A wolf, some young Spartan here to murder me —I could not guess. Then there was another movement and something fluttered to the floor inside the bars. A minute later a dark, bony hand came through the bars and the index finger pointed at the scrap of thin parchment. Some trick by my jailer! I thought. Is it possible? Sucking my cheeks in, slow and wary, I moved closer to the scrap and, four feet from where it lay, I reached out with my crutch to drag it toward me. The rats in the corner watched, torn between snatching the note for dessert and keeping clear of the creature behind the bars. I stooped then, keeping my eyes on the dark doorway, picked up the parchment and glanced at it in haste. My glance caught and stuck. All the unreasonable pleasure in life I thought I had abandoned years ago churned up in my chest as if to drown me, and I reached out to steady myself on the table. The messenger behind the bars stirred, and I whispered, "Wait!" He stayed.

The message was from a woman—a girl—what should I say of a sixty-year-old child? The note was from my beloved Iona. I was in no condition to read it just then, but I would know that furious, childish scrawl if I found it carved on the moon. I taught her how to write, I'm ashamed to admit. I am ordinarily an excellent teacher, and Iona was a brilliant student; but Iona learns what she chooses to learn, especially from me. I stared at the writing without reading it as I used to sometimes stare at her mouth, not listening to her words. It came to me then that the light from my lamp made the messenger vulnerable: the jailer, if he were to look from the side, would see the shape crouched under the planks and would sooner or later realize it

was somewhat too large for a frog. I turned and blew
out the lamp, then went to the door and peered out.

"Hah," I said, stroking my beard. It was a boy I
had seen before—no more than nineteen, I would
guess. It's hard to tell a Helot's age, especially of late.
The war's been hardest on the Helots. Malnutrition
stunts them in their youth, labor and flight make them
old before their time. He had slanted eyes, like Iona's,
and a face too much like a skull. His eyes flicked continually from side to side, the eyes of a boy who's spent
most of his life on dark unpeopled streets or sprinting
up lightless alleys in the city of his enemies.

"Iona's all right, young fellow?" I asked.

He nodded. It meant nothing. They always nod, eyes
flickering away.

"She's not sick? She hasn't got the piles? Her stools
are normal?"

"No, not sick." I had to read his lips.

"Not in prison, either?"

"No."

"Good. I take it she'll get out of Sparta, then, as
I've always so wisely advised her?"

"No." This time he spoke aloud. I raised my hands
to hush him.

"Tell her she must," I said. "Tell her if she doesn't,
the consequences will be dire."

He smiled and, seeing his smile, I knew him. Her
grandson. So she'd brought him into it too. She was
crazy.

"Young man," I said, "your grandmother is crazy." I
began pacing hastily back and forth in front of him.
"We must try to help her, poor thing. I know how you
must suffer, seeing her wander about like a lamb some
horse has kicked, hearing her babble her curious language—but we must be patient and kindly and do what
little we can to give her comfort. Could you tie her up
in the cellar, perhaps wall her up someplace, with a hole
to pass in food through?"

He smiled again. "She learned it from you."

I straightened up, indignant. "Nonsense! All I offer is mild and harmless confusion." Then: "You must force her to do as I say, get clear of Sparta." I spoke earnestly now, on the chance that he was an innocent. "Do it for my sake."

"No," he said very simply, stubborn as a mule. "The revolution is on."

I sighed. "You've caught it, then—her craziness. Why couldn't she have had mere measles, say, or the seaport plague?"

He ignored me. (Everybody ignores me.) "I'll be back," he said, "if I can."

I nodded. "No doubt. The cell next door is empty. They killed the fellow."

But he was gone. He went across the snow and into the trees without a sound.

After his visit I couldn't sleep, or anyway I thought I couldn't, grieving for them—or for her, or for myself. But in the morning rats had nibbled my fingers as usual, so I'd slept after all. There's a lesson in that. All human feeling is a slight exaggeration.

8   Agathon:

When he got up this morning, Peeker wouldn't speak to me. He resents his lack of divine omniscience. A healthy condition in young people. He pointedly ignored Iona's note, which I'd left on the table, and when the jailer came and I greeted him like an old friend, Peeker turned away and folded his arms and stared with intense unconcern at the back wall. I ate. He stubbornly eschewed the table. I understood his point of view, and in my youth I might have sympathized. But now that I am old and cachexic, I need my nourishment. When I'd finished my food I ate his. He remained intractable.

Toward noon I said, "Peeker, it is my duty to tell you a story."

He laughed, full of violence and grief. That too was excellent, from my point of view. I am determined to make him a Seer.

"Sit down," I said kindly, persuasively.

He sat. I dragged my chair from the table to the cell door, where I could sit with my back to the glare of the snow, and when I had made myself comfortable, I spoke to him as follows.

"Peeker, my boy, as you've observed yourself, I am much, much too old to be in love. It's undignified. Also, it's against my philosophy, I think. Nevertheless, you see before you a lover. Dignity and philosophy are for mountains."

Peeker laughed more violently than before. I waited

45

for him to finish (gasping, clutching his head between his knees, and stomping up and down), then resumed.

"I met her many years ago, when my wife was still here with me in Sparta and I was still on excellent terms with Lykourgos. He had less power in those days: I was satisfied with snarling obscenities at him, or laughing till I wept at his high-toned pronouncements.

"I was, I must explain, an attractive and witty young man. This furfuraceous, fucoid mop that now shatters from my brow and spatters obscenely at the world from my chin was an august brown; my eye was aurora-borealic; my every speech was delicately perfumed. I had not yet succumbed to the fluxion of the world."

He was groaning, trying to crawl under the bed. I decided to alter my style.

"What I meant to speak of, Peeker, was Iona—the lady who sent the epistle last night. I mean to lay bare my sufferings and sorrows."

His feet stopped struggling, and after a moment he backed out from under the bed. He studied me, to see if it was a trick, and then, with a hopeless sigh, sat down on the bedside as before.

"Fat hell," he said without spirit. Even his hair, hanging almost to his elbows, looked despondent. His eyes were two red holes.

I nodded and told him the tale.

She was a Helot—that is, a captive. Originally the word meant, I suspect, a captive from Helos. Such matters are always obscure in Sparta. Spartans are not, as they express it, hoarders of knowledge. In the beginning, people say, the Helots were slaves to particular masters; but Sparta's communism did away with that. Now they are simply the property of Sparta, not exactly slaves but not Spartans either, more like the cows and goats they herd or the fields they till. They do all the work. (Spartans are warriors, Lykourgos says, not drones.) The Spartans have nothing to do with the

Helots except, now and then, to hunt one down and cut him to pieces, or hang him for smiling at a Spartan girl, or put him on display and laugh at his dancing or the foolish way he talks. —They do, in fact, speak oddly: softly and slowly, with grammatical forms I believe to be older than those of the Spartan dialect. Once you have stupidly fallen in love with a Helot woman, their language becomes as beautiful as the music they play— not the clean harsh flutes of the Spartans (nor the rich, sophisticated music that comes from the Athenian harp) but gentle, Phrygian lyres that, crude as they are, move even a sensible man to tears. The Spartans scorn such music, of course. I may say in its defense that it conjures a world, an impossible world, admittedly— the innocence of Athenian childhood, the summer calm of a just state at peace. It's healthy for a man to be re- minded of such things, however they may mock him. (More healthy for a free man, of course, than for a Helot.) I stood with Lykourgos once at an execution in the square, and as I watched, full of rage at Lykourgos's foul laws and howling in secret at the needless brutality of the legal murder, I heard, above the thwunk of the executioners' bars, some Helot's lyre behind me, far down the street. The sound was so distant I was only half sure it was not my imagination. In any case, I heard it, and suddenly all my anger gave way to grief and despair and searing love for some unreachable ideal. Tears filled my eyes and I nudged Lykourgos with my elbow. "Listen to the lyre, old horse," I said. He watched the execution. "The music of weaklings," he said.

They never go near the Helot huts, except for more labor at harvesttime or else for theft or murder. (You seldom see it happen. You come upon a bright-red stain on a stone path, or an early-morning cluster of workers bending over something in a hayfield.) But my wife and I walked where we pleased in Sparta, and, be- cause I was of use to him, or because he coveted my book, Lykourgos let it pass. We had far more in common with the Helots, we found, or anyway I did, than we had with our Spartan hosts. This was while I was still a guest, an "adviser," honored though despised. We began to visit certain huts fairly often, usually for some festival—a funeral, a wedding, one of the innumerable game days or days of sacrifice Lakonia honors. The talk was a relief after all Lykourgos's damned aphorisms. The Helots have no more education than the Spartans, but the Helots at least aren't ignorant by choice. They have among them men who can recite nearly all of Homer, and not just for the supposed morality. They have excellent, uninhibited singers. They have women among them—Iona was one—who can cook as well as an Athenian. They have dancers and lyrists and, best of all (or so I thought as a callow youth), people more eager to play with ideas than to eat. Among these last, the best of the lot was Dorkis, Iona's husband.

We met him at his house. Iona had heard of our visits to some of her Helot friends—or so I imagine, knowing her—and, being a lady who would not be outdone, she sent a messenger to invite us to join her family and a few close friends for some pious festival—I've forgotten which. I was, at least from a Helot point of view, a person of importance: an Athenian, heir to the old Mykenaian and Ionian civilizations, no Spartan savage come down from the Dorian mountains. I was, moreover, the personal guest of Lykourgos, living in his palace, at times his unofficial diplomatic envoy to Thuria or Antheia, even Messene. What power she must have thought she had within her grasp! She had even then the fires of revolution in her, though she wasn't yet aware of it. She would show me what culture the Helots maintained in semisecret, would ravish me with food and flowers and music and her clever husband's talk. I would become her ally, her ornament, and she would become the greatest lady in the underground civilization of the Helots. How the Spartans would have

laughed! Goats might sooner pretend to civilized manners! And I, too, laughed, to tell the truth. I was a
cocky fool.

We went. It was one of the better huts. One might in
fact call it a fine house. It was large, anyway, by Helot
standards, and newly limed, which made it a fair
parody of Lykourgos's place. We passed through the
courtyard and stood in the doorway, my wife and I,
looking in at the round room with its hearth in the
center, and we were simultaneously dazzled and
amused. There were huge wall paintings, all on arcane
religious subjects and done in the most ungodly Oriental style. Bright drapes and beads hung everywhere,
charging the room like a harvest of biffins and snow
apples; the furniture—leviathan painted tables and
carved chairs like behemoths at rest—burlesqued Athenian elegance; and wherever there was space there were
fresh fruit and flower arrangements with figurines set
in their leaves, and small clay lamps. The decorations,
I learned later, were Iona's work. She had a kind of
genius along that line. It was all, that night, like some
magical cave from the dream of a savage—light, shadow, color, incessant movement. But the crowning
achievements were Dorkis and Iona herself. He was
dressed like some apterous mythological bird, in azure
and gold and burnished black and scarlet, with barbaric golden earrings like those of Sardis, and though it
should all have been lewd, bumptious, he brought it
off: his smile and eyes were brighter than his garb. He
was no man of Helos, one knew at once by the slant
of his eyes, but an Easterner. (He claimed mixed Ionian
and Asian descent; his father had been an omen
watcher on the island of Hydrea.) His wife, still axis of
all that aureate churning and flash, wore a white chiton,
unembroidered, pinned at the hip and shoulder by
black two-headed serpents made of iron. Her breasts
were like cream, like snow-capped mountains, as perfect as sacrificial doves, and exposed to the very halo

of the nipple. No naked Spartan girl could have dreamed of competing. I gave her a hasty, embarrassed salutation—I was no voyeur, a dedicated amorist—and turned my attention to Dorkis. With a smile like sheet lightning, at once ironic and benevolent, she took my wife's arm, and I watched them go, my wife (dressed in black) like Pallas Athena and Iona like—well, a bacchante who'd bear watching.

"Ah, Agathon!" her husband said, and we embraced in the Helot style. (He was several drinks ahead of me —as were they all. But he wouldn't hold his advantage long. He was used to Helot wine; I wasn't.)

"I've heard of you," I said. "I'm glad we've finally met. You have a wonderful house." I had, in fact, heard of him. Among the Helots he served as physician and sometime fortune-teller. Whether or not he told fortunes truly, he was not, from everything I'd heard, one of those crackpots who are forever pushing men back into the swamps—urging them to barbaric sacrifices in times of war, or stirring up the crowd to unusual cruelty, like that of the old days, in the whipping ceremony at the festival of Orthia. You have seen such men—wizards, witches, demagogues, not honest prophets: demon minds that feed on disaster. Dorkis was not one of those. To the Spartans, who knew nothing of his standing within his own culture, he was one of the most useful and responsible of servants (technically, he had been elevated to the hollow status of "New Citizen," something between a horse and a Spartan Inferior); he was the man in charge of selecting and preparing the food for the communal eating halls. It was said that he'd been, before the redistribution, a personal servant to the palace. His power was enormous, at least in potential. He could have poisoned every man in the city, if he chose to—though one knew the instant one met his eyes that whatever the Spartans might do to the Helots, Dorkis would not turn poisoner. But he had other powers too, as history would show. He had

the Spartans' trust. They could hardly believe any evil
of him, even after it was proved. This not only because
he was obviously brave and noble (despite his curiously
Oriental stance), but also because they gave him little
advantages. Like masters everywhere, even Athens,
they knew the art of corrupting the elite among the
people they dominated, and letting the elite take care
of the rest. They forgot two things, in his case: his odd
religiosity, which made him in fact incorruptible, and
his wife. Dorkis had one further hook into power. As
master of the communal eating halls, he knew all the
important Helots—vineyard keepers, olive growers,
goatherds, potters, wagon masters, the lot. Most of them
owed him favors.

So, as I was saying, I'd heard of him—and had
speculated about him. When I praised his house,
sweeping my arms toward the painted walls, he laughed
and shrugged, boyishly modest. He'd been an athlete
once, a javelinist barred from the Olympics only by his
station, and when he shrugged you saw that he still had
the chest and shoulders for it. He said, "Oh, it's nothing, nothing." And then, quickly, extending a hand to
one side and pivoting, he invited me to meet his guests.

The house was crowded and noisy as the sea with
party cachinnation, but I no longer remember clearly
who was there. A man named Kebes, a vineyard keeper
whom I'd met before, the largest young man I have ever
seen, close to seven feet tall and still as stone; a woolly-
bearded goatherd who'd done well enough that nowadays he seldom sniffed a goat but who somehow nevertheless maintained a perpetual dudgeon; a small, ironic,
testy man whom I later met often but whose name I
never learned (he had a son who was insane; he became a famous arsonist and roof crawler in the later
days of the revolution); two or three Helot priests.
There were always priests at Dorkis's house. Religion,
as I've said, was one of his fascinations. Sex and wine,
sad proofs of life's caducity, were the others. There

were various other people there, well-off Helots and
their wives, an Athenian ex-patriot or two, a pet liberal
Spartan, all milling, lounging, battening each other on
wine and fanny patting. I talked through nearly the
whole evening with Dorkis. Tuka, my wife, talked with
everyone, as usual. She was radiant, casually elegant as
a mountain temple, so conscious of her easy superiority
of taste and class that she could lay them aside like a
shawl. "These Spartan markets!" she said, and stag-
gered, face and body, as if she'd been hit on the side
of the head by a timber. "You take an armload of iron"
—she struggled with an invisible load—"and all it buys
you is three eggs and a cauliflower. But OK, at least
it's better going into the market than trying to get out.
On the way in you've got protection, but on the way
out all these people have these armloads of iron they
can't see over, and every time you turn around you get
zonked." She reeled, carrying the invisible cauliflower
and eggs, being zonked. "It's so absurd, really. Why
use money at all—as my husband tells Lykourgos." (I
never did.) "Why not let people just buy things with
lies and promises? It would keep everybody on his
toes." Everyone laughed. Iona said scornfully, laughing
with the rest, "Clearly unfair! Tuka would own the
whole world in a week, and we'd all have to move to
Africa." They laughed again, and Tuka launched a
story. I turned back to the men.

Dorkis was pouring wine now, the thick, resonated
honey distillation the Helots drink straight and the rest
of the world mixes one-to-six with water. "To Lykourgos!" he said, and grinned. He liked me, it was manifest; and—who knows why?—I was delighted. I knew
from the first that I was doomed to show off for Dorkis
as I would for some girl.

"To psychotic coherence!" I said. He and the priest
beside him laughed. We drank. But Dorkis was thinking, impish. His eyes brightened and snapped into focus
on distances, like an eagle's.

"That's the trouble," he said. "Coherence."

I smiled. He liked me. Ah!

His eyes snapped over to me, then away again, and he tipped his head back, thinking out his phrases. It hit me that he too was showing off. I was honored. "There's a sense in which everything has to balance," he said. His right hand peeled away like a seagull, illustrating balance. "The world's a great big clutter of truths, some of them conflicting but all of them true. Each truth is a kind of stern god. Turn your back on one—" His hands danced out, turned their backs.

The priest beside him shook his head sadly, a little drunk. "We must not presume," he said. He had a weak chin.

Dorkis ignored him by nodding agreement, a favorite trick of his, I learned. He opened his arms with loving-kindness for the whole world. "Pursue one single truth, never glancing to left or right, and *pow!*" Light sparkled from his eyes with the word, the boxer's pow of his fist. He was glorious, bright as a thousand garnets. He could have said "Circles are square" and I would have been hurled to the highest reaches of philosophy. I drank and filled my cup. "There's a sense in which nothing is true," he said. "Triangles, for instance. All the laws of geometry fail when you try to draw a triangle on a round pot. The sum of the angles changes, or else the lines aren't straight." He hunched his shoulders, more like a wrestler than like a potter, laughing with delight at the difficulty of life and pretending to struggle over lines on the side of his cup.

"It's simple," I said. "You smash the pot and draw in the rubble."

He laughed. "To Lykourgos!" We drank.

"That's the way it is," he said. "Life. Experience. It's like something alive, forever changing its shape. There's a sense in which as soon as you learn its laws it's become something else. It wreaks havoc on ethical theories."

I laughed, merely from good humor. If I wanted to be hypercritical, I might have observed that Dorkis was inclined to be sententious.

"Everything's air," he said. "The breath of God." With this phrase he again opened his arms wide, like a man just home from the city calling his animals; and I laughed.

The priest smiled and nodded to show he was awake. He looked puzzled, however.

Dorkis said, "You have to ride it, like a bird."

"That's so," I said. I realized with pleasure that I was drunk on two cups, and the whole evening lay before me like a meadow. "Ethics," I said, "is some theory a man imposes on the world. A man makes up a set of rules, or some fool priest makes up the rules—" I wagged my finger at the priest. "And you try to make the rules inside you fit what's outside. If the world outside is nothing like what your rules say, or if it fits your rules on Tuesday but then on Wednesday it changes . . ." (This was not my usual view, but I was pleased by it, and I've held it ever since, for sentimental reasons.)

The priest shook his head and waved his cup. "I'm sorry, but you're both quite mistaken."

"Priests would be beggars if people weren't always mistaken," Dorkis said.

The cheerful talk went on through dinner, some splendid thoroughly unspartan meal I no longer remember except in isolated images: my wife, Tuka, gleaming, talking with fine wicked wit about Korinth; some fat, dark lady who looked like a grackle bending her head to hear what the testy man said through the side of his mouth; Iona holding up a wide clay black-figured dish as if doing a dance with the cluster of shadows on the white stone wall behind her. Dorkis and I shouted, telling stories with obscure points. His teeth and slanted eyes glinted, the muscles of his cheeks bunched up like fists, his hands flew wildly, now like a boxer's, now like

some delicate artisan's. The drunker he got, the keener
his mind became, it seemed to me. I grew duller, but I
made up for it in noise. At some point I slept.

Later he sat on the soft couch with his arm around
Tuka, his hand on her breast. She talked lightly, clever-
ly about silversmiths, and Dorkis laughed till tears
came, ravished by her brilliance—the quick, dingy wit,
the lightning-fast plasticity of face, the clowning body.
He clung to her tightly, head against her shoulder. I
was a little surprised by all this, but it seemed not unnatural. I went outside. The trees went round and
round like big black chariots.

I stood for some minutes sucking in the air, trying to
get my mind clear, and then I walked out into the
garden, momentarily convinced that I was interested in
vegetables and flowers. I picked a leaf and held it up
against the moon. Awe went through me like a pain,
and then, for some reason, I lost interest. I urinated.
When I returned to the back steps of the house Iona
was leaning against a pillar as if with native and accidental grace.

"You have lovely breasts," I said. "I couldn't help
but notice."

She smiled. I was full of woe.

"Come roll with me in the garden," I said. I put my
hand on the pillar she leaned on, and she smiled again,
studying my face.

"If I followed my inclinations—" she said. She remembered the cup in her hand and took a sip.

I put my hand on hers and she looked down. For an
instant my mind cleared. She was confused, less certain
of the game than I had imagined—or was she acting?
She filled my mind with jungles. Birds and tigers. I was
tempted to press her and perhaps I would have, but
Tuka was standing in the low, square doorway, her skin
white against the black of her hair and dress. She was
smiling the slightly crooked smile she gets when she's
had too much to drink, and she was looking at us up-

from-under like a bull. It struck me with terrific force that Tuka looked like Lykourgos.

"Let's go home," she said.

We went.

9 Peeker:

Stories, stupidities—he never lets up! The ephors came this morning, three of them, to collect our writing. I gave them nothing, though I wanted to. The old man's talk about why they collect the stuff got to me. Agathon gave them a big messy pile of things—stupid damn drawings of dogs.

I was afraid when they came—all those guards and people with banners and all those swords—but when they'd stood there at the cell door a little while, talking with the jailer, asking whether we were eating and how we were sleeping nights, I began to feel less afraid. Agathon sat at the table serene as a mountain, smiling at them the way he'd have smiled at a delegation of children, and when they spoke to him he would answer as if they'd asked some other question, like a deaf man. Their spokesman—I didn't hear any of their names—was a tall man with pale-blue eyes, young for a man with so much power. His legs were hairless, like a young boy's, and pale from his spending all his time indoors. He stood with his head thrown forward a little, like an important man being taken on a tour of a city's defenses. He had a sharp mind, you could see at a glance, but what he might be thinking was as obscure as old astrologers' charts. He glanced through Agathon's drawings and didn't smile.

When I saw they were about to turn away I said, "Sir!" The spokesman turned back with his eyebrow lifted, impersonal and polite. "Son?" he said. I was moved—all choked up—at his calling me son. A feeling went through me, like the shock from an eel, that I could trust him. Why would he be here visiting us if he didn't care that we got justice? And the way he stood, perfectly erect, not slouching the way some tall men do, or erect except for the thoughtful and considerate bend of the head and shoulders, not a slouch but an invitation to us to think of him as a friend—it made me think of a ship's captain or an iren guiding his troops. His mild eyes fixed me like pins.

I said, "Sir, we've been falsely accused." My eyes filled with tears. It was like a plea, but I wasn't ashamed. He put me at ease.

"Oh?" he said.

He was waiting, and I said, "My master's the loyalest man in all Sparta. He's too proud to say so himself, sir, but it's true. He's a man of the deepest integrity, sir. That's why people hate him. And he's a good man, absolutely law-abiding, only there's certain people that spread rumors about him—people I could name: old Bottje, for instance, the rich old goof that peddles horse manure in the vineyards. I mean, they resent the way he dresses and things. Also, he puts them to shame. It's the truth. They're mediocre, you know, and my master's a genius. People can't stand that—they say things in public and then there's Agathon showing that all they say is wrong. That bothers people."

The ephor merely listened, far away as the mountains, the eagles that fly beyond the rims of the farthest mountains, but I could see he was taking it all in. He'd weigh it, maybe begin an investigation. I glanced over at Agathon. He was looking at me with quizzical interest, as if I was talking about somebody he didn't know.

The ephor was still waiting, looking me up and down with cool but not unfriendly detachment, the kind of thing you expect from a good administrator. The others stood a step behind him, one of them fat and kindly, soft-looking, rubbing his little hands together, eager to be my friend, the other ephor short and square, stony-faced, the kind that might be your friend and then again might not.

"Lykourgos knows about him, sir," I said. "Agathon worked for Lykourgos for a long time. He was one of his top advisers."

"But Lykourgos is at Delphi," the ephor said. He was honestly concerned. He sucked in the corner of his lower lip, thinking about how he could get through to Lykourgos.

"Well," I said, "the kings know about Agathon too."

His eyebrows lowered a little. He was still looking at me hard, judging me carefully. "Do you think they'd care?"

He was right, I knew. What was justice to them? But I was excited. The ephor was a man who leveled with you. I'd been right to trust him. Now I wished the shit I'd written something to give them, some kind of point-by-point defense. That reminded me, and I said, "Sir, what's the charge against us?"

His eyes were still coming at me firm as nails and his look was still mild, but his mind was a thousand miles away, reconsidering our whole case. Then he looked past me, over my head, remembering something. He worked it out, made some decision, then turned to the jailer. "See that they get everything they need," he said. Without another word, he left, striding across the sloping field with the other two ephors hurrying behind him and the soldiers and men with banners running to catch up.

Agathon smiled. "You played it brilliantly," he said.

I could have hit him with a chair, but I kept my temper. We had hope now. "You're crazy," I said. "I mean *literally.*" And it came to me that it was true. He was a great Seer, yes, and he was a good old man, but he was out of his mind, insane. I'd been cowed by him before. I hadn't realized that a genius can be as stupid as anybody else at one or two points; but I knew now. I wasn't playing, I was pleading with that ephor with all my heart. And if Agathon couldn't see that, it had to be because he'd spent so much time seeing through men's lies he'd forgotten what plain truth sounded like. I glanced at him to see if my guess about him was true. He was still smiling, and he'd rolled the pupils of his eyes up out of sight. It scared me, that sudden realization of how crazy he really was. I was going to have to fight for us both—with no idea what it was I was fighting or who it was that was against us. There he sat, filthy and fat, lewd, with those horrible eye whites staring at me and cracks of dirt around his neck and sweat beads on his forehead and the tip of his nose. He was helpless, I could see it now, which meant not only that I had to do it all, I had to outmaneuver his craziness to do it. I wanted to cry. But there was still that tall, cool ephor. There was hope.

I decided to work the whole thing out in writing. That was what they'd given us the parchment for—I could see that now.

What are the most likely charges against Agathon?

1. Corrupting the youth, mainly because of his singing.
2. Friendship with Helots; hence, possible complicity in the revolution. (Nonsense.)
3. Talking too much about the kings, etc.
4. Public nuisance (smelling of onions, breaking wind, etc.).
5. Bad personal appearance.
6. Molesting old women.

I kept staring at the list. I couldn't believe it. Surely there had to be more to it than that! Surely they could see that all these were mere foibles or jokes!

When I glanced over at Agathon, he was looking at me as coolly, as rationally, as the ephor had, his interlaced fingers resting on his beard. The complete trans-

formation unsettled me. He was solemner than a funeral pyre. He said, "I'll tell you another thing about
Lykourgos, my boy. He gets headaches."

I waited.

"He's had them all his life," Agathon said. "He's
asked me about them once or twice, since I pretend to
a smattering of medical knowledge. I suggested that he
have himself poisoned: then all our headaches would
end at once." Agathon laughed wildly, then sobered.
"He rarely smiles at my jokes. He merely stares at me,
mournful, and sometimes shakes his head. I have a
theory about his headaches, though. He gets them from
clenching his teeth. I told him once: 'Lykourgos, that
which is unnatural, Nature destroys. You're a doomed
man.' 'All life is doomed, *finally*,' he said."

You see what I have to contend with.

10 Agathon:

Peeker labors on. God bless him. As the soldiers labor on, dying for freedom (both sides) at Stanyclarus Plain and along the coast. I can gather no news, either by normal or by extraordinary channels, on the plague.

Last night, unluckily, my jailer did not put the planks up over my door, so that Iona's boy couldn't visit me, if he meant to, for lack of cover. I sat wrapped in blankets beside the door squinting out into the ghostly snowlight, hoping to catch some sign of life, some sign that he was at least there, waiting for his chance. The sticks on the hearth crackled pleasantly, but my mind was full of Iona, Tuka, my poor unlucky children, my childhood friend, poor Konon. I watched the stars, unnaturally bright and distinct, riddlesome, imperceptibly turning above me, counting my hours, and they mixed themselves up, somehow, with my thoughts of people. I scoff at astrologers and tease my jailer with the antics of those Great Pretenders, but I know I too am a kind of pretender in matters of Destiny. I clown, pretending to experience what in fact I do experience: I mime and burlesque my own nature in an abaxial attempt to get it clear; but I understand nothing, for all my fine reputation. I strut or rant or giggle or taunt reality with obscene little gestures, like some actor imploring tier on tier of silent observers to show some reaction—laugh, throw stones—but the stars remain aloof, expressionless, creating—perhaps even purposefully (as an audience voluntarily gives the actor time)—the span of my existence. At times, squinting up, furtive, humbly amenable, I am filled with a superstitious fear that they know the plot, and possibly control it. Or that, in any case, someone, Something, knows the plot. How else can I explain these "impressions" that occasionally come to me—clear knowledge of distant things, things still in the future, almost always things of no interest to me whatever? No; precision: I have an unreasonable intuition of deadly inevitability, both in myself and in the world. The skull behind Zeus's mask.

I used to feel it at times with my son Kleon. I would observe him at play, transforming the pebbles on a path into houses, ingeniously constructing and peopling cities, or talking to imaginary friends under a roof of low-hanging branches behind the goat pen. In all he did there was a gentleness, an insistent faith in the goodness of things, that, turned on harsh actuality, would make him, inescapably, what he would be. When he was overtired, as a small boy, and things went wrong for him—some game interrupted by a command to go to bed, or his will frustrated by the recalcitrance of matter (a stubborn pony, a pebble that obstinately refused to stay put on the wall he was building)—the gentleness would give way to an alarming rage, a childish yet terrible nihilism that filled me with fear. The change I would see in Kleon at such moments made his future seem to hang on blind chance: given the right set of accidents, he would grow up to be the best of men; given the wrong accidents, he might become the worst. I fully credited this doctrine, the fortuity of time, but for all the certainty of my intellect, I would find myself struggling to penetrate his future; anticipate and control it. The point is, I caught glimpses which seemed to deny —no, overwhelm—my doctrine: I felt moments of emotional certainty, however illogical or nonsensical, that I was *onto* something, that I was suddenly face to face with some potential more real than all the others—

moments of heightened awareness, as it seemed, that cried out with all the fixed authority of a parent or a king or an oracle—sudden and final as an earth-splitting, river-building stamp of star-rimmed Pegasos' hoof: *This is it.*

So, too, with Iona. Throughout my long affair with her, I again and again experienced periods in which it seemed that whatever strange hold she had on me had relaxed a little; I might eventually free myself of her cacodemonic influence. I would meet her with pleasure at some Helot party or walking on the street, the same pleasure I'd have felt on meeting Solon unexpectedly, or my father, or some fellow poet-sage. We'd talk casually, brightly, Iona and I, and I would think, *At last we can be friends*. And then one day, at the height of my confidence, I would turn and catch her out of the corner of my eye, and she would smile and I would know I was trapped forever. She was my Great Bitch, my ambsace, my doom. If she had said, before Lykourgos and all the ephors, "Kiss me, Agathon," I would have done it. And it's a matter of fact that whenever she sent me out into the hills for thorns and stones and wild flowers for some room decoration, I dropped all my labors, poor miserable wretch, and went. (I'd sit baffled, marveling, as she wove bits and pieces of the world together into charming, riotous wholes of blooming confusion, substance triumphant. "Are you going to use *that?*" I would say as she toyed with some black, shriveled olive leaf. She took it as a challenge. She'd have used the Kolossos of Rhodes if I could have lugged it to her house.) It would all have been simple if Tuka hadn't had equal, if not greater, power. Between them, I was as helpless as a ship in a hurricane. I was never short on will—I am capable even of violent opposition to what I disfavor. But there were forces, both inside me and outside, that turned my will to jelly. It was sexual partly, of course. If I feel the itch of it even now, a sensibly impotent old Seer, no wonder if in my middle thirties I walked crouched over or hopped on one foot. They were the two most beautiful women I'd ever encountered, and when I touched either one of them I was fiercely aroused, driven madder, in fact, than I've ever been since by Apollo. (An accident of time and situation, perhaps. Old, I look at ladies fifty years my junior and wonder that any man alive is moderately sane.) But it was more than that. They were, both of them, goddesses in the only sense of the word I understand. They were embodiments of heavenly ideals—conflicting ideals—that my soul could not shake free of. Tuka, even on those awful occasions when her mind came unhinged, had the precision of intellect, the awesome narrowness of purpose, of a mathematician or a general. She knew, beyond any shadow of a doubt, what she wanted from life and why she wanted it, and she would stalk her desire with the single-mindedness of a carpenter driving a nail. Iona wanted not some one thing but everything; she had a mind as wide, as devious and turbulent, as a poet's, and she went for what she desired like a swarm of blind bees in a windstorm. I danced with Tuka once, at one of the Helot festivals, and when the dance shifted and I turned to Iona she whispered with a fixed smile and eyes like a Lystragonian's, "Get out! Don't speak to me! Get out!" She was enraged, jealous of my dancing with my own wife, and when I begged her to be reasonable she snatched her veil from the back of a chair and quit the place. Dorkis, though he grinned, looked baffled and meek. She had always been too much for him, though they both pretended it was merely his respect for her independence. (Perhaps it was. Perhaps I'm too hasty.) "You should go after her," I told him. "It's not safe, out on the streets at night. Suppose some young Spartan fools should come across her, out there alone." He left at last, reluctantly, more afraid of perturbing Iona, I think—invading her privacy, he would have said—than of what any Spartan thug might do. I

wanted to go after her myself. I couldn't stand Iona's
rage, and she knew it. But Tuka's eyes held me, nailed
me where I was like bat's wings on a barn door. I
understood again, that instant, the two women's power
over me, and I wondered, riding the current of their
bedazzling rage, what I was riding toward. I would not
think about it. The future was blind chance, and I
would wait it out. But whatever is deepest in a man told
me I was lying. *This was it.* A glimpse of Destiny. I was
sure of it. But this was *what?*

Many years later, after Dorkis's execution, her power
over me changed its form, though not its intensity. She
accepted, rightly, her blame for his death, and accepted
something else more strange, her mysterious identity,
through me, with Tuka—alter ego, mirror image, in-
cubus. And so Iona committed a kind of suicide:
curbed her will and physical desire with the same
whimsical violence she'd once used to execute them.
There was for her no question, now, of our being
lovers—though now, curiously, since Tuka had gone
home to Athens, there was nothing material to prevent
it, or nothing but the fact that Iona's heart had turned
to iron and stone and cleansing sulfur fire. Iona's hair-
line had begun to recede, there were shiny wrinkles
crossing her forehead and fanning out at the corners of
her eyes, and her flesh was no longer as firm as it had
once been. Nevertheless, even now when I met her it
was like meeting a dryad in the woods. Her shape
sealed off reality: beyond it, nothing of the same intensity existed. She controlled me absolutely, and though
I clowned, exaggerating the foolishness and invertebrate
absurdity of my sad condition, neither of us misunderstood. I waited for her to assert her will, as I wait for
the stars, and she did nothing. I learned the meaninglessness of space: the two women, one in Athens, one
beside me, were equally remote. "Iona, my lovely
Iona!" I said, and wrung my fingers in theatrical despair. She smiled, girlish, pretending to be flattered, but

her eyes were as cold, as aleatory, as the Kyklops eye of Lykourgos.

And so I believed, again—and thought I would go on believing—that everything was chance. But one day around twilight, when I was sitting on a hillside where horses grazed, the strange conviction came over me that there was no longer a city of Methone. I set out, that same night, walking. Three weeks later, when I arrived at Messene, I encountered the first of the refugees laboring—emaciated, half crazed, silent—toward the sandstone ridges of Stanyclarus. The war would come there too, I could have told them. The wheat-yellow plain would burn to white ash, the villages would belch up smoke. I went on to Methone. Snow was falling. There was no sign of the Spartiate army. No one had buried the city's dead. This time there could be no mistake. I had foreseen it, I'd *known*. But I'd known what? The sea stretching out from Methone was lead gray, dark as spoiled wine, mute. There were no birds. I saw what I took to be a corpse huddled on the stone stoop of a doorway. The arm moved, like a black leaf stirred by wind. "Go away," the old man whispered. "Plague!" I fled.

on becoming a seer

11 Agathon:

But this is clear: I loved my wife—loved her second
only to adventures and ideas. We were children together. My father was an oil merchant, well off but by
no means nobly born. A kindly, gentle, reflective man.
His chief hope of rising in the world, after the death of
my beaming, extrovert younger brother, was my clever-
ness. (No one could have guessed in those days that
within a generation Solon's middle class would be gov-
erning Athens.) I was sent to a teacher by the name of
Klinias, attached to the house of Philombrotos, Tuka's
father. He was an arkhon, her father; a member of the
all-powerful landed aristocracy, and one of the most
powerful men in the ruling oligarchy. I did well. Klinias
was no fool (he had studied with Thales in Miletus),
and I was, in my lugubrious, angry way, ambitious. I
lived, along with another boy, Konon, in Klinias's stone
hut at the edge of Philombrotos's grounds, and when I
wasn't studying or rabbit-hunting or trying to ride some
horse to death (punishing all horses for my brother's
demise), I did chores, sometimes for Klinias, sometimes
for Philombrotos. I first saw Tuka when I was working
in the vineyard behind Philombrotos's house—a small,
private vineyard that served his kitchen. She was standing with her slave in a window high above me, looking
down at me with a bold, steady gaze that unnerved me.
I couldn't guess how long she'd been watching or what
stupid thing I might have done in front of her. I was—
what? Nine or ten? In any case, I was observed, like

something in a cage, like something owned, and I could do nothing about it. I was very conscious, of course, of my social class—and hers. My father was a democrat who liked to talk about the grand contribution of the merchant class, but I wasn't fooled. I didn't miss the exaggerated politeness with which he greeted the rich, and I didn't miss the eagerness with which he encouraged my study. The girl went on staring, and I worked faster, fuming. Someday I was going to be avenged.

She was there again the following day. It must have been more than an hour she stood there (her slave two steps behind her) watching, smiling now and then, pretty much as you'd smile at a turtle in a jug. I decided to ignore her, and I did, for perhaps three minutes. When I looked up again, she was gone. That was worse. I stood with my fists clenched, baffled, furious, staring into my half-filled basket. Then suddenly, as if dropped like apples from a limb or like gods shot down in the lightning from Olympos, she was there—she and her two friends, girls, their slaves not far off, behind them. The three girls stood ten feet from me, their hands folded, their clothes clean and elegant, startling next to the homespun of ordinary workers.

She said, "What's your name?"

"Agathon," I said.

They laughed, and I knew I was blushing.

"I'm Tuka," she said. Her voice was softer, gentler than wind in leaves. It filled me with alarm.

I laughed scornfully, and she looked puzzled. I mumbled, "I have to work."

"We'll help," she said.

I shook my head. "You can't. It has to be done right. A person like you—"

She tipped her head far over to one side and looked at me. "How silly!" she said. The half whisper resounded through me like a judgment. They laughed again, like birds, and fluttered away.

She came alone the next time, or alone except for her slave, and said, "I want you for my friend."

I said I couldn't be. I had to study.

She thought about it. "I bet there are things I know that you don't, Agathon."

I laughed. I knew where I was strong. Who but Konon and I could read Klinias's book? I said, "Like what?"

She thought again, then came to me and took my hand. A sensation stranger than touching a fledgling in its nest. After a moment she kissed my cheek.

I was doomed.

We played together throughout our childhood. She was a tomboy, a good head taller than I was. I liked her looks because she was my friend, but I knew in gloomy secret that, except for her dimples, her soft voice, she was ugly. Her head was enormous, and her nose, though handsomely shaped, was a size too large. She couldn't compete with prettier girls in looks, so she did it by wit. She had the slyest tongue in Athens—a mind like lightning and that soft, near-whisper of a voice that kept her victim from knowing what had happened to him until he came to, days later, in his bath. Her father, who was elderly, in fact decrepit, neither approved nor disapproved, exactly, of our friendship. He was the busiest man in Greece: he knew only instants of his daughter's life, and even those instants, when he gazed fondly out to where she played on the lawn, or when he watched her at her harp, were befogged by his official concerns. Or by his dearer love, to be exact. He had no time, no room in his heart, for any love but Athens—beautiful, albescent as an aging virgin, irrational, tyrannical, deep-dreamed as a wife inexplicably wronged. The city was his goddess. When he spoke to the assembly he pleaded like a lover or a supplicant, scolded like a husband or a priest divinely shunned. The clouds above the Acropolis, the pillared,

honeycombed white buildings, chamber rising out of
chamber, the rolling-gaited crumple-horned cows of the
valleys below were in every syllable he spoke. For all
the studied, peculiarly statuesque dignity of his bearing,
he seemed, like any lover, a man perpetually at his
wit's end. It was the time of the war with the Megarians,
and Athenian politics were in chaos. As I grew older
I became involved in all that, as Klinias's student.
Tuka's father knew me as a record keeper before he
recognized me as Tuka's beloved old playmate.

I have no idea what games we played, through all
those childhood years. I know that we sometimes
had long talks, the slave girl observing in silence from
her place, and sometimes I tried to dazzle Tuka with a
grim, disturbing theory I had about the *prima materia*.
She was a master of pretending to listen, and sometimes
she made me think of what I thought were brilliant
things. They were wasted on her. She was un- if not
anti-philosophical; a musician.

Sometimes I would listen for hours while she played
the harp. It was a big concert instrument, studded with
jewels, imported walnut braced with gold, a gift from
her father on her twelfth birthday. He meant to make
her the finest musician in Greece, and he nearly did it.
When she performed for me (or for anyone else) she
treated her playing lightly, casually, as though it had
come with ease and had no great importance for her. If
the fingers moving too fast for sight made some slight
mistake, she would cavalierly repeat the mistake when
the phrase returned and would build it into her varia-
tions, cunningly flaunting her pretended indifference to
precision. But I knew—better than her teacher, perhaps—how far she was from indifferent. Early in the
morning, when the birds first began singing in earnest
and all the herbs in Klinias's garden and all the grass
and shrubbery rising toward Philombrotos's house were
newgreen and bathed in dew, I would hear Tuka at
her practice. It was a lovely sound, those rich low notes

like far-off herders' bells, the tinkling high notes like leaves rustled by a breeze on a tree made of silver, but it did not seem for beauty's sake she played. She would work one phrase again and again, doggedly, her mind calcinating by patient violence the stubbornness of fingers and wires. Hunched in the coolness of the morning, concentrating on Tuka from my patch of sunlight on the swept-stone steps of Klinias's hut, I could feel her whole spirit contracting to that phrase, excluding all reality except for the ten or fifteen notes that refused to submit to her will. The phrase would come more and more quickly and lightly, and as her will gained ground she would begin to lead up to the troublesome phrase from farther back and from farther back still until suddenly —and I too could feel it—the recalcitrant phrase could no longer resist her but would fly by under her fingers as if by choice, like a storm in the wind god's hand. Then suddenly, as if without a trace of pleasure in her mastery of the problem, she would move directly to her next problem—not even playing up to it, simply turning to it, single-minded as a spider—and the battle of music against wires and stubborn flesh would begin again. I would sit fascinated by Tuka's mind—her compulsive need to appear casual and offhand in public, and the cold-bloodedness of her assault on beauty— until the first excitement of the songbirds waned, the dogs, roosters, and donkeys of Athens lost interest in announcing morning, and the brume on the Akropolis had lifted. Klinias would nudge me with his foot, and I would look up as if surprised, though I'd been waiting for him to come drive me like a goose to my morning chores. I'd jump up, clowning obsequiously, to go for water at the well beside the vineyard.

But the best, and worst, was when Tuka played at night, alone. Sometimes it would be long after dark, and Konon and I would be in bed, half asleep, when the sound of her harp would float down to us. She would play, then, as if feeling were all there were in the

world, and nature had no resistance. I would open my
eyes and lie motionless, listening with every nerve to
the music moving through the night's deep quiet like a
god out taking a walk. Konon, beside me, went on
breathing slowly and heavily, untouched by it, and Klinias slept on in his tangled mass of covers, his horny
feet protruding from the bottom, his crow's nest of hair
from the top. I looked from one object to another in
the room, and everything that detached itself from the
general dimness stood transmuted. The large clay water
jugs by the door had a new roundness—a volume and
canescence that had nothing to do any more with space
or time; they existed in a new dimension, brimmed
with amrita, like the music. The big wooden astrolabe
in the window, suspended against the stars beyond like
some enormous flying machine from the farthest of the
planets, had now some emotion in it, as if it had been
transformed from a thing to a portent. Konon, whom I
aternately loved and fought, one moment scorning him
for his stupid ideas, his arrogant selfishness, his cunning, the next moment admiring him for an instant's unexpected kindness, some leap of thought I could not
have made, some comic sally I wished I'd thought of—
Konon, still as a sleeping child beside me, his tanned
arm resting close to my shoulder as though in his sleep
he had reached toward me, became now clearly what
he was, independent of moment-by-moment dissilience:
my friend, mutable, infinitely valuable because the vision of eternality which the music gave implied that all
of us would pass.

The harp soughed on, sorrowful even when the
phrases joked, and the whole night seemed to listen,
brooding on itself. Sometimes I would slip out of my
bed, not waking Konon or Klinias, and would cross
naked to the door and through it and up to Philombrotos's big house. I would scale the wall, clinging to
the ledges of the polished stone by my fingertips and
toes, and when I reached her window I would hang

there watching her play. Her slave lay on her pallet, pretending to sleep. Tuka sat in her chiton, facing away from me, and her movements, as she played, were not like those I saw when she played for an audience: it was as if, now, she was inside the music, moving only as the music moved, swaying for an instant, hovering, sometimes touching the dark wood beam of the harp with her face as though the harp, too, knew the secret. I was torn by contradictory emotions, like the music, and, like the music, I turned them over and over, as if by feeling them intensely, not with my mind but with my body, I might grasp them. I felt outside time, as if all things merely temporal, coldly dianoetic, were of no importance, and I felt at the same time a strong urge to go to her, show her my nakedness and plunge her obscenely, painfully into the world. But I hung undecided, the music moving in my chest like wind, like annulate waves, the cold night air moving softly across my skin, until my fingertips and toes ached from clinging, and I climbed back down. When I saw her by daylight it was as if what had happened in the night were unreal. The girl I had seen at her harp might easily have been anyone or no one, a spirit, but this daylit girl was Tuka, my friend, almost sister.

There was, it is necessary to mention, a third Tuka, besides the musician and the tomboy-friend, and this third was Tuka-not-quite-sane. I would stare in disbelief, shrinking back, wincing, struggling to make her fit with anything I knew of mundane reality. I could connect it with nothing I'd ever felt—or, anyway, could remember feeling—and with almost nothing I'd seen. At times it wore the mask of rage. For some reason no one ever caught at the time or could manage to reconstruct later, an argument with her younger brother would suddenly turn to a conflict in which the clear and unquestionable goal was her brother's death. She would say things, at such times, from which no human being could defend himself. For instance: "You're stu-

pid, *stupid!* Your *eyes* are close together!" Foolish, in-
significant. Nevertheless, I would see him suddenly
made helpless, limp-kneed as a man who's been
stabbed, and I would see the cold, hard shine of her
face—oh, brighter, neater than a Spartan knife—and
I would wait in horror for her to say it was only a joke,
to tell him she didn't really hate him. But she would
say more, as if the instant were final, there were no
future mornings to get through with him: "You don't
know what people say about you, do you. Your *ears*
stick out. Every time you turn your back, your friends
all *laugh!*" He would cry, howl with grief, and could
no more understand her dismissal of his humanness
than I could, watching. If adults were nearby—even her
slave—they would stop her. Her father would cry out
sharply, "Tuka, go to your room!" and she would go.
The slave would whisper, "Tuka! Tuka!" I—we who
watched—would be left numb, like people who have
witnessed, on a clear spring day, a death fall from a
horse. She went beyond all turning back, exactly like a
wolf or a striking snake that has no idea of continua-
tions. And yet, unbelievably, Tuka would make up,
later. She would explain, as if kindly, apologetically—
but cunningly laying the blame on her brother—"You
made me mad." He would distrust her, at first, as I was
distrustful in later years when she did the same with
me, but Tuka had dimples and a clever tongue, and the
gods had given her winsome ways; in time he would
become confused about what had happened, and he
would believe again that Tuka loved him. Partly this:
she made the attack seem reasonable—made it seem
that some fault in her brother, or in me, later, explained
her rage. And he—and I, later—would shift his attention to his innocence or guilt, and would forget the
other-worldly reality, the murder. So once her father
said to me with the same mad shine of the skin, "Get
out of this house!"—said it with such out-and-out avul-
sion that I would have done it except that I was not, or

anyway not in the same way, crazy. I said, though I was a young man then, and arrogant, "I can't do that. I can't just walk out and take your daughter away forever." Thinking: *You shit-eating son of a bitch.* The old man trembled and got hold of himself, scratched his way back to civility.

Then again sometimes Tuka's madness wore the mask of sadism. At times she turned it on her slave; once she turned it on children. Her father's house stood, as I've said, on a hill. The lawn on the west side sloped down gently to a flagstone terrace where there were tables and benches of stone and, behind them, lilacs and high stone walls. Once, not long after I'd first moved to Klinias's hut, I stood watching timidly from the edge of the lawn, in the shadow of the roundhouse, near the palisade, while Tuka, three of her older cousins, and a number of younger children played near the house. The older cousins were boys, two of them very dark, the other light, with eyes as pale as well water. The younger children were playing with a wagon, a toy version of a four-wheeled mulecart.

Tuka and the older cousins sat on the grass pulling up shoots and biting off the tips and talking loudly, teasing each other. The oldest of the cousins, one of the dark ones, offered to have his slave pull the smaller children in their wagon, then changed his mind and pulled them himself. They let them, and he careened around with them, two at a time, scaring them and making them shriek with joy. He would cut the lawn's slope, almost spilling them out, turning downward into the grade at the last moment, and sometimes he would pretend he was going to run them into the stone benches. The children in the wagon screamed with happiness. The ones who weren't riding yelled, "Me! Pull me!" Then—I don't know whose idea it was— the game changed. Tuka and the older cousins lashed the tongue of the wagon to the wagon's front panel so that the front wheels wouldn't turn, and they set one of

the children in and sent him, with cheerful cries of
"Hang on!" and "You're not scared, are you?" clatter-
ing and bumping down the hill. They aimed the wagon
away from the tables and benches, at first. But I watched
the path changing, sweeping, ride by ride, toward the
tables. I crept closer and hid behind the bushes at the
edge of the lawn. My heart was pounding. Tuka said
softly, lighter than a swallow, "He's so stupid he won't
even jump!" And she laughed, a beautiful lilt, unreal
as ghosts. I watched her line up the cart, talking and
laughing with the child, and I watched her eyes as she
started it down the hill. I watched the child's face, ten
feet away from me, when he realized he was going to
hit. He screamed, but the cart made almost no sound
as it struck. They came running down the hill. "Are
you hurt? Are you hurt?" There was a splash of bright
blood on the child's forehead. *They're insane!* I
thought. I meant rich people—all of them. But I was
watching old Philombrotos's daughter. If there are dead
men who walk, or if there are satyrs, and a man can
meet them on a mountain path or beside some lake,
they can be no more strange, no more removed from
ordinary human feeling, than Tuka was at that instant.

Klinias, passing my bed that night, paused and bent
his head toward me nearsightedly. He cleared his
throat, making the sharp Adam's apple bob below his
frail beard. "You comfortable, Agathon?"

I nodded, my covers pulled up to my nose.

Though Klinias was rarely demonstrative, he leaned
down, as if thinking it out as he did it, and tousled my
hair. He said, "Homesick?"

I shook my head.

He studied me, awkwardly tipping his starved-wood-
chuck head and frowning, lips pursed. The ceiling timbers were pitch black, sooty, above him. Then at last:
"All right, youngster, come out with it." He clumsily
touched my shoulder. The fist was bony, and the punch
hurt. In love as in almost everything, he was inept.

But I told him. He looked over my head as I talked. I was crying at the end, as I hadn't been able to cry at the time. My fellow student Konon watched me with a look that teetered between pity and scorn. I said, "Why did they do it, Klinias? *Why?*"

He cleared his throat. "Don't think about it. You just get to sleep, my boy." He patted my shoulder and grinned, showing the holes where he'd lost teeth.

I whispered, "I think they're crazy."

"No no," he said. He stood up and cleared his throat again and tugged at his loincloth, and scratched one hairy, bare leg. "We all do strange things sometimes," he said. But he stood there thinking for a long time, fiercely scratching his head, making the dandruff fall like snow. "You boys get to sleep," he said at last, and went over and sat on his bed. His lips were pursed. Then he straightened up a little and pulled in his chin, like a man about to burp, and said, "We'll talk this over in the morning." But we didn't.

It had one other mask. Once I was playing with Tuka and her younger brother, and one of us, I don't remember which, broke a large clay amphora that stood just inside the door. Her father was passing, abstracted as usual, but the crash of shattering pottery brought him to himself. He said, "Tuka!" Tuka and her brother ran out of the room, quick as snakes. It astonished me, but it didn't occur to me to follow. Her father walked past me, almost running, as though I were invisible in the dappled light, and called to her again from the doorway. She didn't answer, and he went after her. When I reached the doorway he was standing on the lawn, red-faced, sharp-nosed, the shadows of maple leaves splotching his cloak, and they were running from him, laughing. He came back at last and walked past me again without seeing me, his gray mouth working in spasms.

I said to her later, "Won't he get you, when you go in to eat supper?"

She smiled, showing her dimples. "He'll forget by then."

"Still—" I said.

"Oh, Agathon, *A*gathon!" she said.

I tried again. "If *I* were your father—"

She clasped her hands as if in prayer and tipped her face, grinning. "You'd get a huge net, and you'd make these elephant traps all over the lawn, and you'd get a sling full of sharp stones and nails and things, and you'd get some slaves with bows and arrows that shoot flaming torches, and you'd have these trained wolves and some puff adders and moray eels, and if some little child ran away from you—"

Her brother laughed, wildly gleeful, and I too smiled. But all the same, it left me uneasy. I couldn't answer her—I never could, because her way of thinking ruled out sober discourse—but just the same it was *wrong,* I thought, full of righteousness, to make a fool of a grown-up. Not because of what he could do to you. It was wrong to know that he would forget, even if he would; wrong to know that he would chase you only so far and then stop. Do you love your father? I should have asked. But I was too young to think of it, and she wouldn't have understood.

Klinias said, "Ethics gives us generalizations, rules. Er-hem. But the first rule of ethics is: Never judge par*tic*ular cases by general laws." He nodded, pleased that he'd thought of it, then strode on.

I ran to catch up. We were climbing the old stone path toward where the shrine of Menelaos scrapes the clouds. He was teaching on the hoof, as he called it. I said, "Then ethics is nonsense. What good are rules if the first rule is: Don't believe rules?"

"Fiddlesticks," he said. "You take too narrow a view. Ethics is like medicine, to be taken only when needed. A man can enjoy good health in any number of ways. People who understand one another are beyond mere ethics. They can do things quite innocently to one another that it would be vicious to do to a stranger."

"Maybe," I said. (I was, as I've told you, a morose and rigid young man.) "But how will she know not to do those things to strangers?"

Klinias stopped climbing, leaned on his stick, and turned back to face me. He smiled. His hair shot out like red sunbeams. "My dear young Agathon," he said, "you take this world too seriously. Look there!" He pointed upward to where the big, rough boulders hung on the side of the bluff, the homes of eagles. "You know what those rocks are thinking?"

Konon looked too, eyes narrowed. He said, "They're thinking of rockhood."

Klinias laughed. "Exactly! They're thinking, *I am a rock, I am a rock. Not a tree, not a goose, not a goat's blood pudding, but a rock.* That's what holds them together! And what is our quester for truth, here, thinking?" He laughed again and bobbed his head, delighted with himself. "He's thinking: *I am a human. Is Tuka human? What is a human?* If he isn't careful, we'll be carrying him home in loose atoms."

Konon jerked one shoulder and gave a sort of sneering grin. "Poor ol' Agathon's in love," he said. He ducked as if I were going to hit him and picked up a pebble to toss up and down.

"In love!" Klinias said, and looked at me in amazement. Then he laughed again. "Of course!"

"The shit I am!" I said, forgetting myself in my wrath.

"Here now," Klinias said. "*Here* now!"

Konon went into a laughing fit, maybe at Klinias's startled, stern face, or maybe at me. I went for him with my fists. Klinias was yelling, "*Here here here!*" and banging the stones with his stick. The mountain walls screeched it back at him like crows.

We were hardly aware, for all Konon's teasing, that what we felt for each other was love. She was my closest friend, closer even than Konon. When we were in our teens I would sometimes walk with Tuka, holding her hand, her slave behind us, sullenly observing, but even then I misunderstood. I knew, I suppose, how I felt about her, but she was to me some higher form of life, as distant from me as a goddess would be from a cow. She knew other boys, lean and elegant, boys of her own class, whose fathers had mansions in the country, and though I knew I was smarter than they were, I understood my lot. I chased and tumbled humbler girls, kitchen slaves mostly, and Tuka and I would sit on a hillside talking about them, refulgent as the sunswept hills, and we would laugh and laugh. Her eyes sometimes flashed. I stubbornly misunderstood. As was proper and right, of course. Her father was an arkhon: his land, his wealth, his power sprawled for miles.

Then, when I was fifteen, I met Solon, who brought about a change, a whole new world.

We were in Philombrotos's high, timbered central chamber—five or six of the chief rulers of the city, my teacher Klinias (dressed in the fine cloak Philombrotos had given him), Konon, and myself. I was often in on important deliberations at this time. I had no part in them—Konon and I took notes, carried unimportant messages, filled the wine bowls. As for Klinias, he was a sort of adviser to Philombrotos. He would sit with a great frown, pink eyes gazing at his toes, and would never speak until Philombrotos would say, "Well?" Klinias, who was extremely nearsighted, would look up, vaguely in Philombrotos's direction, pulling his fingers through his hair like a comb, and with great shrugs and greater pauses and throat-clearings that made his Adam's apple bob, would deliver his delicately reasoned-out opinion. There were those who said in mockery that he was king of Athens. He wasn't, but he had a kind of sixth sense about what the commoners would accept and what they wouldn't, and what they'd do. It was Klinias who brought Solon to the attention of the oligarchy. "A profoundly philosophical person," Klinias called him. Meaning: very tricky.

It was a heady summer day, late afternoon: light splashed through the room like something alive, making every painted and polished surface gleam as if newly oiled. All the city leaders were gathered, including the older Pysistratos, all sitting in their usual genteel poses, Philombrotos at his glinting marble table, Konon and I at our wooden desks, the slaves unobtrusively waiting in their places like furniture; but the meeting didn't begin. I looked out at the hills and wished I was there. Then at last a slave came to announce a guest. Philombrotos stood up and bowed. Except for Pysistratos, who merely looked frosty, as usual, the others stood up too, as if the guest were someone like the King of Sardis. The slave reappeared, drew back the drape, and in walked the fattest, silliest-looking man I have ever met. (Only Kroesos himself is said to have been fatter, who weighed seven hundred pounds.) Solon was in his middle thirties, but nearly bald already. His nose was pink. No one needed to be told he was a wine merchant, without a drop of noble blood in his lineage—despite what people say now. His flesh jiggled like a mile-wide field of flowers in a breeze. He spread his legs and stretched his milk-white arms like a man meeting his concubines after long separation, and said, "Gentlemen, God bless you one and all!"

Klinias winced and focused his pink eyes harder on his toes. The slave closed the big door, bolted it, and stood waiting, holding the door hook. Pysistratos looked dour.

Philombrotos said, "My friends, meet Citizen Solon."

They approached him gravely and tentatively and, one by one, shook his hand. "I'm honored!" Solon said. "Deeply flattered!"

Philombrotos said, "Not only is Solon one of our city's most brilliant merchants and a widely admired philosopher, he is, they tell me, one of the favorite poets of our commoners."

"A terrible condemnation," Solon said. "Such taste!" He kissed his fingers in despair.

Philombrotos himself led Solon to his seat. They made a ludicrous couple—Philombrotos tall and lean and frail, keen-eyed, masculine, sensitive to the point of palsy, Solon fat as a monstrous baby, with a face as impish and androgynous (he had pretty lips) as Pan's. Solon eased himself down, though the seat was marble, saying, "Thank you, God bless you!" his flesh all aquiver, and he let out his breath in puffs.

Philombrotos talked of Solon's virtues. His father had been a wealthy man named Euphorion, a commoner who'd proved that arithmetic could be worth as much as vast holdings, but who, in middle age, had decided to give away all he had to the poor. They'd erected a statue in his honor. He'd died when Solon was under twenty, and Solon, having what he called a modest taste for luxury, had in four years (with a bare minimum of double-dealing, he often said) made a fortune as large as his father's. He had sympathies—and some influence—with both the rich and the poor, and he was famous with both for his extraordinary good sense. In these times of political chaos, no man was better qualified to bring the two parties together.

The city leaders knew all this already, as Solon was no doubt aware, but he accepted the flattery of the recitation, even relished it, tapping his fingertips and beaming like a child. They came at last to the point. The war with the Megarians had come to a kind of stalemate, not so much because of the difficulties of war as because the commoners believed they were being taken advantage of, which they were. It was always the commoners and slaves who were killed, the aristocrats —a handful of powerful families—who collected the spoils; and whenever troubles came up at home, the war was blamed for their having to go unsolved. The problem was simple: how to trick the commoners back into battle and beat the Megarians once and for all so that problems at home could, where necessary, be dealt with.

Solon was radiant, gorging himself on the power the leaders were lending him, but though he could not hide his happiness, he pretended the thing was difficult. "Awesome!" he said, and rolled his head from side to side obscenely. He giggled, a laugh like a girl's. "Simply awesome! Gentlemen, we stand at the rim of a new and startling age—a whole new spectrum of human emotions! It's a thrilling and terrifying moment! History will remember us either as monsters or as midwives to gods! Let us struggle to prove ourselves midwives, the Mothers of Humanism!"

"Humanism?" Pysistratos said, looking skeptical.

"It's a new word I've made up," Solon said. "You don't like it?"

They were offended, repelled by everything about him, not just his word—though no one in the room had any inkling yet that this pig would steal their power. But no one, on the other hand, could miss his confidence, and it was catching. You'd have sworn by his manner that he had in mind some hero, completely unknown to them, who could stand with the heroes of the First Age, like Theseus, or at least the Second, like Akhilles. Though Solon was grotesque, a sort of hog in the bath, he could solve their problems, they all knew, with a snap of his dough-white fingers.

"Let me think on it," he said. He sat forward and rubbed his knees. "Let me *pray* on it—for a week."

"In a week's time—" one of the leaders began.

"Come come!" Solon said. He threw up his hands in alarm. "Against the vast span of futurity—"

They gave him a week.

Solon had, as he said himself, a great advantage over them: he had no dignity.

Within two days we heard the report that Solon had

gone mad. He played the lyre half the night (he had no ear, could hardly tell note from note), he danced stark nude, he approached wealthy ladies with obscene propositions. His family confined him to his house and went about in mourning. His physician let it out that he was "possessed." On the fourth day he escaped and ran straight to the center of the city, with a tin cup and some leaves on his head and, pushing aside the more familiar nuts, prophets, soapbox orators, he climbed up onto the herald's stand. When people gathered around him, some in amusement, some in dismay, he began singing, thwanging out horrible noises on his lyre and rolling his eyes:

"I come as a messenger from Salamis the fair!
 The news he sends this town my verses shall declare!"

And then, in mad, mock-elegant dactyls, he called the commoners to one last valiant attempt against the Megarians, an attempt all their own, to be led by himself, indefatigable, mad Solon. The victory, he hinted, would bring on a whole new age for common men. He swore solemn oaths that Apollo was inside him. It was a long poem, and brilliant in its way—the best entertainment seen in Athens for years. If it was full of joking, it was earnest too. For all his reading, for all his self-mockery, he had a childlike, merchant-class patriotism that couldn't be scoffed away. When he talked of "a man's debt to his country" it didn't sound hackneyed: it made you think, coming from Solon, of merchants' iron cash boxes and the famous scrupulous honesty of the old-guard Athenian tradesman. It was a brand-new metaphor, in Solon's mouth: more telling, at least for that audience, than all the silvery Homeric talk of Philombrotos. Some agreed to join him on the joyous impulse of holiday spirit, others because they believed the god—or anyway truth—was in him. (That might seem strange to some people, but in Athens we were not of the opinion that gods are necessarily morose. Whatever strikes true, strikes deep and honest, whatever fills the furthest mountains with beauty and hope, we attribute to the gods.) He got a fair party of men behind him, and Pysistratos, along with other civic leaders, got him more by sober reasoning and bribery.

At the end of the week he'd asked for, the leaders met with Solon again at Philombrotos's house. He arrived late again, and this time he was carried in on a litter by four of his slaves. He hadn't slept all week; I doubt that he'd eaten. He looked terrible. The leaders said nothing, but you could see they were distressed. This sick, decrepit thing that could barely wave its arms was to lead the Greeks to victory! But they waited to hear what he would say. He told them his plan, and it was that afternoon that I myself joined his army. I watched Philombrotos as Solon, with much ambiage, unfolded the scheme. The old man squinted in acute embarrassment. He could see that it would work, but I knew he would rather be dead than have beautiful Athens so deflowered. When the vote came, he abstained, and when he left, afterward, he did not speak to the others.

I saw Tuka in the entry hall. "Praise me," I said at the top of the steps. "I'm going to be a soldier."

"You're crazy," she said. She stared at me hard, then laughed. "Are you going to talk them to death with metaphysics?"

"I may not be much with a dagger," I said, "but I'm sneaky."

She laughed again, but now she knew I meant it. I was looking up with new eyes at where the Akropolis scraped the clouds.

After a moment she took my hand. She said, "You can't. I forbid it."

"It's out of your hands," I said. "I'm a citizen of Athens."

She went on looking at me, then glanced back at her

slave as if for help. None came. Tuka shook her head. "You haven't a chance. How you do overestimate yourself!"

I was angry. "I'll pick on someone little," I said. "I'll see who's wounded and sneak up and get them from behind."

She turned away. The slave went on watching with eyes full of darkness.

I started out and Tuka called to me. I kept going.

Two weeks later I fought the only battle of my life. (We trained like fools, that two weeks. Most of the men, though all of us were young, were veterans. All I learned was to be scared to death of good soldiers.) Word went, by a supposed renegade, to Salamis, to tell the Megarians that, according to our ancient custom, the chief women of Athens were at Kolias, giving sacrifice to Keres, unattended except for their slaves. The Megarians could capture them with ease, for pleasure or ransom. The Megarians bit. We moved the women and children out and, clean-shaven, dressed like girls, we danced and played by the shore until the Megarians arrived. They came pouring out of the ship like unleashed hounds, and we danced and smiled and tightened our fists on our daggers. We got them all and hardly lost a man, but it was horrible, a matter for shame. The one that came for me was a big, handsomish man that thought he would have me right there on the sand. I opened up his kidneys with both hands on the dagger, and the look on his face was like a child's, shocked, betrayed. He pushed me away—there were people fighting all around us, bumping against us, stepping on us—and he lay twisting and kicking in a circle and I couldn't get the dagger out. Blood spattered all over and soaked up in the sand and people slipped in it. I tried to strangle him, but even dying he was ten times stronger than I was. He pushed me away as if I were unimportant, an annoyance, like a swarm of gnats, in the way of his dying. I was crying so hard I could hardly see—a dead Megarian lay across my left leg—but I got a rock and lifted it over him. When he saw what was happening he lay still a moment and gave up. I killed him. He look of indifference shook me to the heart. Then I lay in the sand and sobbed and yelled obscenities at Tuka. I believed I saw her, shining like a mountain, naked, smiling at me, her slave in the distance. A strange experience. When the battle was over we sailed for Salamis, still in our women's clothes, all bloodied now, and took it. I didn't fight in that one. I was unfortunate, which no doubt saved my life. When I jumped to the rocks from the ship I broke my leg.

I was in bed for two months. Tuka came to see me and talked to me very soberly, softly, about how a girl shouldn't let the boy she loved go to war without her blessing and promise. I wasn't impressed, she was still old Philombrotos's daughter. But the rustle of her skirt as she crossed the room, the small shy weight of her hand on my arm, frail as light, made me feel I was bleeding to death inside, hopeless, wicked, unpardonable. I was painfully, totally aware of her, as though her barely perceptible scent had replaced the air I breathed. I hated myself passionately, and, in my despair, blamed it all on her as I would on the gods if they were nearer. (I had lied to her about the broken leg— she thought I was a hero.) She said, looking away from my eyes and smiling, sly, that when I was well she had a gift for me. I got better at last, despite my wish, and agreed to meet her near a huge old olive tree behind the vineyard where we used to play, to collect the gift. I bathed and dressed myself elegantly, swearing and growling at myself all the time (the mind is a tricky instrument), and, clenching my teeth and exaggerating my heroic limp, I went out to meet her by the tree. She was lying a pool of sunlight, naked as a goddess. Her slave sat at a distance, with her back turned. Sudden, searing shame overwhelmed me and, beating on the ground with my fists, I told her of my lie. I was unworthy. She calmed me, drew down my face to her breast. I collected.

12   Peeker:

O gods, gods, gods! Was ever anything alive so cruelly mistreated? I'm being driven insane, and there's no one I can turn to. I thought it was more damn flibbertigibbet when I read what he wrote, his plan for me. But he means it! He's going to unhinge me!

Yesterday we saw a murder, right before our very eyes—some fellow sneaking across the field, trying to stay out of sight in the tall grass, coming toward the prison—toward one of the cells farther down—and all at once there's these two men on horseback galloping straight at the man out of nowhere, Spartan soldiers, and I heard the grass whizzing and the noise of the hoofs and I saw the man on the nearest horse twist— that's all I saw—and when they'd gone by there was a javelin standing like a leaning signpost, and nothing, not even the javelin, was moving. It was as if I'd been staring at the thing for hours, but that was a trick my mind played, because the riders reined up and turned back and I watched them get down and lift up the body and sling it across one of the horses, and then they remounted and rode off.

"Agathon!" I said. I sort of choked it out. But he was standing right behind me, he'd seen it all. It was as if he'd been expecting it.

He shook his head and went back to the table. "It's going to be a long, hard winter, Peeker."

I went ferocious for a minute. I sort of jumped at him and grabbed his crutch and I was going to club him with it. "Winter, winter, winter," I screamed. "That's all you can say. It's crazy! Even if it's a fucking metaphor it's crazy."

He was waiting to be hit.

I felt angrier than ever. The room went blood red. "People die right in front of your eyes and you just fart around, tell stupid shit-ass stories about girls and old dead politicians, and people are actually *dying!* There's some things a human being doesn't have to stand!"

He rolled his eyes up at me. I had the crutch up to brain him. He said, "Nonsense."

I swung down. I don't know what happened because I just flipped out, zero, a tingle across my brain and then nothing, as if it was me that was hit—Apollo maybe. I don't know. I never saw anything like it. When I came to he was sitting on the bed, holding my head in his lap and patting me as if his mind was a million miles away. I shook my head. It hurt like hell, but I couldn't find a lump when I felt around for one. I remembered I was going to kill him and I felt awful. He was a good old man, though he stunk to heaven, especially up close. I started crying, and he started patting me again. I said, "Master, I'm going crazy."

"I know," he said. His voice was thick, like a person's at a funeral. The end of his beard touched my neck and tickled, and I thought how vicious it was that a person could be annoyed by a fucking tickle at a time like this. I cried harder.

"I really am going crazy," I said.

"I know," he said again. He could hardly bring it out, and I cried for him.

After a long time he said, "Peeker, I'll tell you something." Suddenly, absurdly, his voice was cheerful. "Our jailer's going to speak to me yet. I have no doubt of it. This noon when he brought us our plates of smashed worms—or whatever it is—he stood outside my cell door with his arms folded for half an hour, watching me eat. I ate, first my plate then yours, very slowly and delicately—partly because it's the only way I can trick my stomach into willingness, partly to teach him fine manners by my example. When I finished I wiped my lips very nicely with the piece of my robe I reserve for the purpose, and I said to him, 'Jailer, I'll tell you an interesting fact. Everything we study, we modify by our study of it. Hence truth eternally eludes us.'

"He did not look convinced, just held out his hand for the plates.

" 'Take crabs, for example,' I said. 'We poke them with a stick to find out how they behave, and they behave as if poked by a stick.'

"He folded his arms, the plates dangling from his fingertips.

" 'This is of course a very simple example,' I said. 'Take a subtler example, such as atoms of light. Light, as you know, is one of the four great elements—in common parlance, fire. We study it by bouncing it off polished stones, or bending it in water, or squeezing it through holes. And how does it behave? It behaves as if bounced or squeezed or bent. We learn nothing. We merely cause *events*.' I bent closer to him, waving my finger to keep his attention. 'Has it occurred to you that sundials do not measure time but *create* it?' It had not, I saw. 'Time,' I said, 'is actually a thing, like porridge.' I folded my arms and beamed at him, triumphant. The left side of his mouth twitched very slightly. He withdrew."

"Master, you're insane," I said.

He smiled. "That's more like it! Before you were saying *you* were. If there's one thing I hate it's youthful arrogance." We laughed.

When I woke up again it was dark. He was patting my head. When it came back to me I said, "Who was it, master?—the one they killed."

"Some Helot, I expect."

"Was it someone you knew?"

He didn't answer for so long I thought he'd forgotten the question, but then he said, "No doubt."

"And you didn't think anything about it?" I realized I was lying with my head in his lap and I felt silly. He was saying:

"Oh, a thought or two may have passed through my mind. I may have thought how brave and virtuous the man must have felt, sneaking across to the prison. And I may have thought how brave and virtuous the soldiers must have felt, nailing him down like a rabbit. I may have had a passing thought about rabbits, or field mice, or stones."

I sat up, pushed the hair out of my eyes. I was still seeing it—the horses, the javelin sticking up like a signpost. "You don't believe in anything, do you?"

"I believe in the gods," he said.

I said, "Hah!"

"That too," he said. "Magic is afoot when a doomed young man says 'Hah!' "

Doomed. I began to shake all over. He launched some idiotic story.

13 Agathon:

Lykourgos, in his time, was a great general, though one very different from Solon. He comes, after all, of Dorian stock, and he once wore all the dignity of a king. Philombrotos greatly admired him, during his stay in Athens, and he would have admired Lykourgos still more if he'd lived to see him lead his crack troops into battle. You would hardly find them in girls' dresses, with coy smiles, and flowers in their hair. They train naked, hour on hour in the summer heat or the winter wind, until their hides are like leather and their muscles are like pliant wood. They learn to fight, as they learn to march, with precision, every movement clean as the closing of a trap. The iren gives his signal and they draw their swords as if with one single muscle. He calls out again and they advance a step like the spikes of a single harrow. I cannot tell whether to laugh or shake in terror. When a man moves his hand by an inch too much, the iren signals him out of formation and bites his thumb. The man does not scream. Not a muscle of his face stirs.

When they fight they wear breastplates and groinplates of metal, and feathers in their hair like the Philistines. (The Dorians were neighbors to the Philistines once, generations ago. The two people are very much alike, but the Philistines have had no Lykourgos.) As they march to the attack, the Spartans play their flutes, a piercing, deadly singsong thing in the Lydian mode, with no trace of joy, no faintest intimation of mercy.

They destroy a city, kill everything alive in it down to
the humblest dog, and send their ultimatum to the next.
All this is Lykourgos's work. Only a fool would deny
that it's effective.

I had been working under Solon for six months—
and had been married a year—when Lykourgos arrived in Athens. I was twenty. Solon had as yet no
official position (it was that year that Philombrotos died
and Solon replaced him as arkhon), but he was in fact
already what Klinias had been called in jest, king of
Athens. Philombrotos and his fellow arkhons, and even
Pysistratos himself, did nothing without Solon's consent,
yet they hated all Solon stood for. Philombrotos knew,
as everyone did, that when and if Lykourgos returned
to Sparta it would be as Lawgiver, exactly the position
Solon was worming, or rather pigging, his way into in
Athens. When he found the two men in the same town,
Philombrotos couldn't help himself: he had to bring
them together. He made Lykourgos a guest at his palace,
assigning him three of his best slaves, and invited Solon
to dinner. I too, along with Tuka (and many others),
was invited. Though I lived in the house, I did not see
Lykourgos until the night of the dinner. He kept to his
room like a sick man or a misanthrope—both of which,
I soon discovered, he was. Philombrotos went to visit
him, and they would talk, with the slaves outside the
door, for hours. I can imagine how it was. For old
Philombrotos, the world was falling apart. A fat wine
merchant was the city's only hope, and if he saved the
city it would be at the expense of what made the city
fine. It would be like saving a beloved wife from enemy
spears by whoring her. He was beginning already to
talk in a politely disparaging way of Draco's laws,
"written in blood," he said. He would giggle as he said
it. You couldn't be sure how to take him.

So no doubt on those visits to Lykourgos's room,
Philombrotos sat in troubled silence, trembling faintly,
as he always did the last few years, and Lykourgos

delivered sentencia in his quiet, angry way, like talking stone. The old man couldn't help but agree with all Lykourgos said, but he could see no way to get from where Athens was to Lykourgos's iron vision. In his own house common blood had seized a place. Tuka, pregnant (or so we thought), had threatened suicide if she couldn't marry me. She meant it, at least at the moment. Or if she didn't, Philombrotos couldn't be sure. There'd been a wave of suicides among the old families in recent months. ("Changing times," Solon said mournfully, rolling his eyes up, looking pious.) Philombrotos wept. He was too weak from his civic troubles to fight. When we met in the halls, now, we bowed as we had in the old days, as if we were no more than fellow citizens. I forgave the old arkhon, and I did not mind my victory. I was Solon's aide, and Solon was the future.

But Solon was a better man than I. When he learned of the invitation he was distraught. It was dusk, and we were sitting in the room in his house where he did all his reading and writing. (He read as he ate, gluttonously, and he kept a book like Klinias's, as if he fancied himself a sage.) The room, that evening, was full of shadows. He was always strangely reluctant to light his lamps before nightfall. I could never tell whether it was miserliness or one of his superstitions.) He said, "This is awful! Horrendous! It can't be done!" He pulled at his cheeks with his fingertips and made nervous clicking noises.

"Why not?" I said. I took great delight in undoing his grandiose posturing. That was, I think now, my chief use to Solon. In his old age he was a relatively dignified man, considering.

"It's unthinkable!" he said. He had a habit of filling the air with exclamations while his mind raced ahead, figuring. "It's one thing to borrow a poor old man's nuptial bed as if by drunken mistake. It's another to make him bow and humbly abandon it to you."

I shook my head, smiling. A new kind of Midas. Everything he touched turned obscene.

He fiddled with the stick on his desk that he kept for luck, still tsking and clicking like a carter. "You know what he's after. He wants to set us side by side and see whose way is best. But he has no choice! Why can't old men be reasonable?"

"I imagine he knows he has no choice," I said. I was thinking of myself and Tuka.

"Then he's one of those people"—he lowered his voice—"who make their slavegirls whip them." He wrung his hands, then giggled.

It came to me that he was chiefly embarrassed for himself, the figure he'd cut. "You'll come off all right," I said. "You're an Athenian."

"No I won't," he said. He pouted. But he thought a moment and his face grew foxy. "Yes I will!" He sent me home.

The night of the dinner, Solon was, to no one's surprise, late. The wide room was filled with dignitaries. We were just beginning to eat without him when a slave announced his arrival. Philombrotos got up, with difficulty, and took a step or two toward the door. Solon came in, spread his legs apart and threw out his arms, exactly as he had the first time I'd seen him. "Gentlemen, God bless you!" he said. And then, to Philombrotos: "Forgive me. I've taken a liberty." He waved at the door, where his house slave waited, and a moment later the old man—a Korinthian, I think—came in wheeling a cart of Spartan wine. Where Solon had gotten it, God only knew. No Athenian would normally drink the stuff, though the Spartans vow by it. Exiguous food and drink is their national emblem. Solon snatched up a bottle from the cart and held it aloft as if it were captured treasure. "To the grandeur of Sparta!" he said. For an instant everyone was stunned. Who'd ever heard of a thing so unpatriotic? And yet it wasn't, of course. His words pierced some ludicrous old error. Then, first one or two, then more, we all cheered and laughed and even clapped. Lykourgos's features worked as if in agony. At last he too laughed, seizing his pleasure as if to strangle it. "Bless my soul!" he said. It was like a voice from the heart of a cave. Solon sat down in his place of honor by Lykourgos and talked all that night about wines. He happened to have brought along a poem of his on the white wines of Sparta. Philombrotos watched him, baffled and weary, like a man brought against his will from beyond the grave.

Two days later, at Solon's house, Lykourgos said:

"The trouble with a genius is that he dies. The state falls to ordinary men, and they destroy it." They were talking of Solon's wild improvising.

Solon smiled. "I'd rather be destroyed by ordinary men than by System."

"In my system," Lykourgos said, "there will be no ordinary men."

Solon thought about it and nodded. "True, perhaps," he said. "And when you die, there will be no room for genius in all Lakonia except your grave."

That night, Solon gave me a sheaf of writings. "Read these," he said. "Tell me what you think."

I glanced at them and knew whose they were by the handwriting, though it was one I'd never seen. It was as dark and spare and severe as Lykourgos himself, and even harder to decipher. I said, "Shall I take them with me?"

He nodded, thinking about something else. "If you lose them, God help us both."

They were aphorisms, fragments, God knows what. I took them with me and, compulsive scrivener that I am, copied some of them down. I included them later in the book, when I got it from Klinias.

Our vanity would like what we do best to pass for what is hardest for us. Slaves make a difficult virtue of acting like slaves.

The will to overcome an emotion is only the will of a stronger emotion. Opinion is desire.

Strong character, virtue, means shutting the ear to even the best counterarguments.

Madness in individuals is rare; in groups it is the rule. Good government is predictable, and irreversible, psychosis.

That which each age considers evil is the atavism of an old ideal.

Every system of morals is a sort of tyranny against Nature and Reason. That is, however, no objection, unless one should decree, by some system of morals, that tyranny and unreasonableness are bad.

Religion, politics, and art all give us herding-animal morality (Thou shalt not shove). By what secret rules do the great priest, the great king, and the master artist live?

The great State is the mechanical image of some great man. It has no faults he did not have, though it cannot have his virtues. Good. Private virtues make empty talk at parties.

Imprisonment and execution are not great evils, merely mirrors, too clear for cowardly eyes, of reality as it is.

Greatness is impossible without religion. A man must know himself God.

I returned the parchments to Solon. He said, "Well?"
"Stark raving mad," I said.
"Terrible, but not insane." He tapped the desktop

with his stick. "I admire his courage. It's going to be a great experiment—a great adventure. I wish I could see it." He giggled.

I shrugged. "So when he gets it going, go see it."

His eyebrows went up in alarm. "Good heavens no! I'll send some friend." He smiled.

"Don't look at me," I said.

"Don't worry." He laughed. "When the time comes, you'll beg me to let you go. You see, you're a tyrant. His mirror image."

"That's not true," I said. He really seemed to mean it. "What makes you say that?"

"Sheer whimsy, my love." He laughed again, glancing over at his slave. Solon's mind, I could see, was far away.

I told Tuka later what he'd said. She said, more soft, more sweet than morning bells, "It's really true, you know. You're a tyrant." She had a marvelous capacity for defending the wrong if it seemed to give her power over me. This time, for some reason, I was persistent. It was this, partly: she had an irritating way of forever comparing me with her father. Either her father was good at something, like taking care of the tedious details of daily life, busy as he was, and for me it was simply impossible, or else her father was bad at something, like listening to things his family said, and I was exactly like him. It was her father she wanted to be married to, not me.

"Tell me one single thing that I ever did that was tyrannical," I said.

She sighed as if there were thousands and took my hand. "Agathon, look at your fingernails. That's disgusting!"

But Solon's prediction was right, in a sense. It was at my request that, two years later, after travels for Solon had inclined my spirit to wandering, I went with Tuka to Sparta. Lykourgos had just pulled his money trick. In Athens it would have meant civil war. (Solon was skirting war hour by hour, straddling the chasm between the commoners and Pysistratos.) Lykourgos's nightmarish vision of men was becoming actuality. I had to see it. It may be I thought I could stop it.

One last word on all that. The truth is, I was much impressed by Lykourgos's Sparta when I arrived. Though I came full of scorn, even humanistic outrage—though also full of admiration for any man who could bring it off—I was impressed by the studied simplicity of the world Lykourgos had recreated. I saw his whole scheme, now that I was here, in the simplest and most lucid terms, and I was amazed at my former narrowness of vision. A matter of simple geography. Sparta was agricultural, required a huge labor force—not slaves but something almost slave, because that many slaves would be a threat to the master race—and required, above all, the reactionary temper which keeps a farmer regular of habit and stable. Athens lived by trade, a thing requiring liberalism, tolerance, flexiblity. Neither was right or wrong, then: the Just Life was a mythological beast. I would study the world for its images of aspects of myself. I wrote poems about it.

For example:

Is it utter fancy that once one's mind
was clear, one's heart pure?
fancy that once one's will inclined
to what one loved for sure?

On a stone road where donkeys grazed
high slopes above our heads,
and rocks like giant wolf skulls gazed
at the vast march of clouds,

we found a small, improbable
stone shrine—a barren place
where none would watch but a carved wood doll
with a staring, Dorian face.

Carnations bloomed inside the shrine
and coins lay on its stone;
someone had swept to the road's rim
where the cliff wall rushed down.

A mile beyond that, high in the hills
past ruined silver mines,
juts that once spanned waterfalls,
old houses choked in vines,

we reached a huge gray-granite church
some god had pushed akilter.
Children played at its black mouth;
goats watched from the altar.

On the road, donkey path, two young workmen,
blackened as if by fire,
smiled, holy, then moved on,
patient as old desire.

Well, good. Who past the age of two has not experienced a hunger for simplicity? I wrote many poems of this kind when I first came to Sparta. But enough of that. I have been, like Lykourgos, a desperate man all my life.

14 Peeker:

"You'll never make a Seer," Agathon tells me in a voice of scorn, trying to nag me into it. But I'm no longer fooled. It's true. I won't. I don't even want to be anymore. I watch him sitting at the table, breathing with his mouth open—the August heat's deadly for a man as old and fat as him—writing, writing, hour after hour, not all the wisdom he's collected from sages but the squalid details of his onion-stinking life: I see him wake up in the morning and sit up suddenly, with a startled look, remembering his project (he's writing it all for my sake, he says), and I see him stand up at the side of his bed, trembling all over, tasting his sunken mouth, dusting his lips with his dry tongue—then he splashes water from the corner bowl over his moustache and beard and forehead (like King Soös, I think, and laugh), then wipes it off with the back of his hand—all this absentmindedly, thinking only of his crackpot project; and I think, *Where's your spooky gift gotten you, old man?* "Mus' get busy," he mumbles, and glances out through the cell door, worried, checking what time it is by the slant of the sun.

It was different, in the beginning. I had personal problems, you might say, and Agathon was some kind of hope. I don't know. I'd be peddling apples with Mother, and she'd keep saying things to me, trying to make me mind my business: "Mind them baskets, Demodokos. Money don't grow on trees, you know." And sometimes, to herself, "Spare the rod and spoil the

103

child." And then she'd holler, "Biffins! Snow apples!
Fresh as a day in spri-ing!" I would hurry along behind
her, trying to catch up to where she went striding like
a war-horse, eyes like a rooster's, her back loaded like
a mule's. She could carry four times what I could carry,
and she liked to remind me of it. "It's not my fault," I
would say. "When I was little you didn't feed me right."
"Hah! Accusing his poor mother!" she would say. (But
she liked it when I stood up to her. I'd hear her telling
people, "He's not much to look at, good Zeus knows.
But he's got spirit! He'll be my death!") I would run
along behind her, trying to catch up, and then a bunch
of those girls would go past, Spartan girls naked as
jellyfish, and I'd look down as long as they were coming toward me but as soon as they passed I'd peek
back at them, those beautiful beautiful swinging asses,
sleek and powerful and arrogant as the hams of deer,
and all the muscle and bone would go out of my knees
and the apples would go rolling. "Mind them baskets,
Demodokos," Mother would say. Sometimes as they
passed they would swipe a couple of apples from the
basket and would smile at me, and that was worse
than anything. I wanted to talk to them, ask them what
their names were and where they lived. But I was
afraid. As I got older—fifteen and sixteen and seventeen—I thought I'd go out of my mind. My mother
kept watching me, watching, watching, watching.
"Stick to your own kind," she'd say when she'd see
me sort of peeking sideways at a troop of Spartan girls.
A laugh. I felt the same thing with Helot girls. I would
strip them with my eyes, imagine the blush around the
nipples, the softness of bush between their legs, and
then when I looked back at their faces I would practically faint from the beauty of their mouths and eyes,
wanting to say "Hi!"—wanting to tell them I cared
about them, tell them I'd listen to whatever they might
wish to express, listen for ninety-nine years. I wanted
to know if they were happy, what they dreamed at

night, what they liked best to eat. I would watch them talking with good-looking boys or the boys that could always think of something funny, or the moody ones with knowing smiles, and then I'd look at how skinny my arms and legs are and I'd want to kill myself.

Sometimes when we were peddling we'd see Agathon. My mother would give him a wide berth, merely working the crowds that gathered when he talked. Sometimes she stuffed beeswax in her ears to defend her soul. —Not that he always had crowds. Sometimes he'd be sitting all alone, sprawled out over some steps with his thumb hooked in the jug handle, and he'd be singing, louder, more raucous than thunder. Or sometimes he'd just be standing on a corner, like a blind man waiting for help across the street. Sometimes he'd be playing with children. They liked him— they always liked crazy people. He'd try to skip rope with them, clinging with both hands to his jug and gasping for air like a weight lifter as he bounced, kicking out one foot, then the other. He drew large crowds when he wanted to, though, because of the crazy way he talked and because of the way he could mimic people: you'd swear the man he was mimicking was inside him. But naturally what the crowds liked best was his prophecies. He wouldn't do that often. He had to wait for the mood to come over him, and sometimes, no matter how he strained, it wouldn't, even if he was leaning on a horse. (Horses make impressions come, he says. He used to make me lean on horses sometimes when he was trying to teach me to get holy impressions. I hate horses. The smell makes me sick, and if I shut my eyes, feeling woozy, they turn around and bite.) Anyway, when we'd see him prophesying I'd go watch from way in back, jumping up and down to see. "Come away from there," my mother would say. "A man's known by the company he keeps." And sometimes he'd preach. "Your bodies are naked, pretty ladies, but your minds are tucked away like things obscene!" Once he said, exactly in the voice of an old woman we knew "Husband, talk to me! You haven't spoken a word in sixteen years." The old man Agathon was pointing at was a garrulous fool, but what Agathon said was like an icy wind, and it made the old man cry.

And then one day as I was working my way around the edge of the crowd selling apples with Mother, the old man pointed his horrible shaking finger at me and yelled, "You, you miserable misbegotten wretch! Why such sorrow on this day of joyous festival?" I could feel the whole crowd's eyes on me, and my heart was like a hot coal at the root of my throat. I tried to be smart-aleck: "Because of girls," I said. "Oh, master, all because of girls! He he he!" The whole crowd laughed, but the Seer's eyes were solemn as the plague. He said nothing. The crowd grew still. Then he said, "The gods are in that boy!" Everyone was scared. The old man said, "Come with me!" Everyone was looking at me. My feet started moving toward him: I couldn't do a thing about it, even when my mother started screaming. I sank down on my knees when I got to him, because my legs had gone weak. He got down on his knees too, so he could look me in the eye. He was breathing hard, excited. "I'm going to make you a Seer," he said, and smiled. The holes in his teeth were like craters.

You've got no choice, when a Seer says a thing like that to you—even if you know for a fact he's a crazy old drunk. Which I didn't, for that matter. You never know anything about a Seer, unless you happen to have such bad luck as to become a disciple. I mean, they're special, mysterious. A little like the ephors used to seem to me, or the revolutionists when someone would whisper, pointing them out in a crowd. I remember the first time I saw one. Someone said, "Look! That's Wolf." That was what people called him, not his name. I followed the furtive, pointing finger and couldn't tell which man they meant. "The one with the gray sash," someone said. He turned, just that instant, and I saw his face. He looked like anyone, mouse-colored curly hair, quiet, friendly eyes. You couldn't believe he had killed people, gutted buildings with midnight fire. He nodded, seeing me staring at him. Maybe he thought I was someone he ought to know. I nodded back. —But all that's not the point. I might have passed him a hundred times and never given him a second thought; but now, now that I knew he was a famous revolutionist, he was a riddle, unfathomable, no longer Helot, no longer even human, some baffling and terrible alien. I saw one die once, an execution. Snake, they called him. He'd been blinded and beaten horribly, but he was awesome. He died like a god, almost laughing at us, holding back only from gentleness and pity. Even the Spartans felt it.

And that's how it was with Agathon. He might stink like a man, he might share certain features with ordinary men—two eyes, a nose, a beard, a paunch—but he was special, set apart. His mind was different from a merely human mind. Augurers, now—the people who pretend to read the future from bones or goats' intestines or the flight of birds—they're not special; they know it themselves. Either there really are things in bones or guts or patterns of flight that have readable meaning, and they know how to read it, or there aren't, and the augurers are fakes. Either way, it's no stranger than reading from a parchment, or pretending to read when you can't. But Agathon, he can run his hands over a cane and say, "The man who owns this cane once murdered a chicken farmer." Or he can become very still, standing in a field as if listening to the wind, and it will come to him that war has broken out in Amyklai. He *knows*.

He's crazy, of course, to think he can teach me that. It's a gift, for better or worse. And because it's natural, easy for him, he thinks if I learn to relax or something, zonk! I'll get a vision. I used to try. I'd practically pass

out, trying. He'd stare and stare, trying to figure out
what the hell I was doing wrong. His face, his whole
body would become a mirror of mine, trying to feel
out in himself where my mistake was. He'd say, "You
haven't suffered enough, boy. *That's* the trouble!" His
eyes would be glittering like sunlit pits of ice, and I
knew as sure as day what he was thinking. He was
going to get me beat up, or kicked by a mule or something. I'd keep clear of him. It was for my sake, he said,
that he started us prowling the streets at night, getting
us pounded on as peeping toms. It was a lie. He'd been
doing it for years and the only difference now was that
he didn't have to drag his own jug. I should have left
him as soon as I knew for sure I would never be a Seer.
I thought of it. Time after time. But then I'd find him
in the road, knocked down by a cart or something, and
I'd see that his moustache was all gucky with blood,
and I'd be scared. He'd do it on purpose, I think, to
keep me with him. Or else one day he'd pause, looking puzzled, in front of some house, and after a while
he'd go in and we'd find some woman crying, and tears
would be streaming from his eyes too, and there'd be
a young man sitting in the corner, dead. And so I
stayed on—a victim of Destiny. It was sickening, but
I was trapped. The same way Alkander is trapped with
Lykourgos, I guess.

I saw him once. I was close enough that I could
have reached out and touched him. Lykourgos had
been walking in the square in front of the Hall of
Justice, and Agathon had caught sight of him and had
run up to him, wringing his hands and making faces
and God knows what—and Lykourgos stopped, looking
sad, tragic even.

"Agathon, for the love of God," Lykourgos said,
very low, so no one would hear. He stood with his
arms slightly bent, his hands hanging limp, as though
Agathon were a terrible torment to him.

"Have I offended thee? Have I *offended* thee?" Agathon squealed.

"Agathon," he said. It was like a plea but also like the warning growl of a dog.

I watchèd Alkander. He stood two feet behind Lykourgos, towering over him, naked except for his sandals, the sword and dagger harness, the wide iron bracelets on his wrists—they too were weapons. He looked casual, limp, but I saw that he was balanced on the balls of his feet, and his eyes were closed to slits. His mind closed out everything in the world but Agathon. Should the old man so much as spit in the direction of Lykourgos's feet, he'd be dead before the spittle hit the pavement.

I tried to say "Let's go home," but my throat was dried up with fear.

"The revolution's upon you, Lykourgos," Agathon said. "I warned you! I warned you! As long as time lasts, you'll be known as the murderer of a thousand thousand men. And all for blind ego!" He cringed, leering and winking, but I saw that he made no move to touch Lykourgos. "I haven't offended thee, I hope? You see how it is, sir. The god says 'Speak!' and I speak."

"The god indeed!" Lykourgos said. He tried to turn away, but Agathon was around him, quick as a rabbit. Lykourgos gave up, simply stood, one hand closed over his beard, his one eye patiently staring at the pavement. "*You* tell *me* of pride," he said. "Shame, Agathon. Shame!"

Agathon grabbed hold of his belly and laughed. "Brilliant!" he yelled. "O philosopher!" He laughed and laughed, but he was furious. Alkander watched him. "I've given up Athens, my wife, my children, even poetry, to cry out a warning in the savage Spartan wilderness, and you say it's from pride!" He was drooling in his rage, but still faking laughter. I too, like Alkander, watched him. He was wrong: the anger proved it. But Lykourgos was incapable of answering his scorn. The old Lawgiver's mind and heart were as simple and rural as a barn: I could see in his patient, mulish stance all the country generations that led up to him—fierce men plowing straight furrows behind oxen; farm owners rising to bless the food in a big spare dining room of thrashers; country politicians, red-faced and laconic, campaigning not with clever appeals but with facts drawn up like wagons.

"We're old men, you and I," Lykourgos said. "Let's come to truce."

"O deathless gods, hear what he asks of me!" Agathon said. "O motionless mild Apollo, behold this indignity done my old age!"

He was wrong. Any fool could see it. Even if Lykourgos was all he said, an enemy to the laws of earth and heaven, still Lykourgos was a man, had rights. He could burn cities with one word, but he couldn't get justice from Agathon, yet was too just a man to destroy him. Alkander saw it too. I don't know how I knew that, but I knew. The crease beside his mouth moved like a tingle in the back of your mind, but he did nothing. I wanted to talk to him, let him know I understood how it was between him and his master. People think Alkander's a machine, a sort of walking weapon to protect the old man, but I knew better. I would have let him tell me whatever he wanted, and I would have kept all his secrets safe.

"Hate is bad for digestion," Lykourgos said.

"Like murder," Agathon said, and laughed a little wildly. "Like war. Like plague."

Sudden as August heat lightning, Lykourgos lost his temper. "Go home, you sick, fat old fool. Go home before Alkander breaks his leash!"

Agathon laughed, but immediately backed away. "Rage on, old one-eyed maniac," he said. "Your world is crashing down around your ears!"

Lykourgos raised his head a little and his one eye

bored into Agathon. "My laws will survive," he said. "Among my enemies, you alone know the future, and you alone rave. A sign of your despair."

Agathon spit, not just in Lykourgos's general direction but at him. Alkander's hand gave a jerk, but the rest of him kept still, almost relaxed.

I sidled away, following my master. "I'm sorry," I whispered. Alkander slid his eyes over and looked at me, angry at first, then thoughtful. A week later when I saw Alkander it seemed to me—though I couldn't be sure—he nodded.

So anyway, this: I will never learn to be a Seer, but I'm learning things, with Agathon. It occurs to me that I have learned to be patient with everyone but Agathon himself. And with my own self, of course . . . For Agathon, and for myself, I have no forgiveness. Why is that?

But the walls of our cell are close, remember, close as the air we gasp to breathe, and Agathon makes no effort to hold back his farts. He snores and moans and grumbles in his sleep, and he talks talks talks incessantly, about nothing but himself, the most self-centered, self-pitying bastard I've ever seen. "Well, he's seventy," I tell myself. "An old man must have some privileges." But when he wakes up he smacks his lips, and when he eats I hear his teeth cracking. And when he isn't talking or cracking his teeth or sucking at his dry, loose, black-cracked mouth, he's writing his endless, revolting life story, mile on mile of self-congratulation.

"Peeker, my good man, sharpen my pen."

"You sharpen your own fucking pen," I say.

"Ah, manners, dear boy! There is no pulchritude in swinish manners!" Pursing his lips as he says it. Squinting like a pig.

Why should I work up forgiveness for an ugly, sick-minded old man who scorns everything on earth but himself? Or maybe especially himself. And why should I resign myself to what I am—lackey for a madman, hungry maggot in a hole full of maggots, dreaming every night of soft-bosomed girls with light coming out of their pink pink skin like leaves in springtime, with eyes as lonely as graves?

15 Agathon:

I sat with Dorkis on a hillside, looking down on the lake
where Iona, Tuka, and the children—our two and their
three—were swimming. It was a fine, warm day, and
we'd been drinking Helot wine all afternoon. The little
stone aerie he'd borrowed for what he called his flight
to meditation stood above and behind us on the hill. I
kept watching Tuka and Iona, my chest full of pain.
Dorkis talked. He was thinking of leaving Lakonia. It
was against the law, but Helots managed it every day.
The Spartans didn't waste much time policing Helots
in those days; they kept busy enough policing themselves and making incursions into the holdings of their
neighbors—the ephors' idea, not Lykourgos's. Goats
grazed to the right of the lake and beyond it. The boy
who was watching them sat, just visible to us, on an
outcropping of greenish rocks near the top of the hill
to our right.

Dorkis talked of the hopelessness of the Helot situation. There had always been atrocities. The ephors for-
mally declare war on the Helots every year, so that a
Spartiate won't be guilty of religious impurity if he
kills a Helot out of hand. But it's always worse in time
of war. Because of the troubles in Messenia—in town
after town, Spartan governors had been assassinated
and public buildings burned—and also because of the
increasing number of Helots openly talking rebellion—
Lykourgos had recently revived the old institution of
the Krypteia, whereby young Spartan warriors were sent

out into the courntryside with an iron ration and a dagger, to hide among the rocks by day and kill Helots by night. It gave the young fighters combat practice—but that was only part of it. Helots far outnumbered Spartiates throughout Lakonia, and Lykourgos was convinced that in unsettled times the Helots needed terrorizing to be kept in place.

At all events, a young man Dorkis knew had been murdered two days ago by Spartan boys, and Dorkis, as a physician, had assisted the old women in preparing the body for burial. It had shaken him. His voice had a new thinness, like that of a man recuperating from a loss of blood. There was a sense in which it was criminal, he said, for a Helot to bring up children in Sparta. It robbed them of self-respect, which was to say, freedom. On the other hand, he was a leader of a sort. Now, if ever, the Helots needed leaders. I acknowledged it with a nod. It was not a decision I cared to help him with. I myself would leave, probably. I'm easily scared off. I could have said that running away might also rob his children of self-respect, but I couldn't advise him to do what I might not have the courage to do myself.

His sharp, black-eyed stare was fixed on something beyond the farthest of the hills, and his lower lip was pushed forward, making his cheek muscles taut, the slanted eyes little chinks, like slits for bowmen. "Agathon, have you any power left with him?"

I shook my head. "Not a drop."

He grinned. "How'd you blow it?"

"I never had it to start with," I said. "He keeps me around to tell him Solon's theories, which I do—I have them all down in my book—and he listens like a stone."

"Does he really?"

"No. He sort of half listens. But the contrast is somehow obscurely useful to him."

He swung his gaze back to the hills. "Could he be

killed, do you think?" He asked it as one would ask for predictions on the Olympic games—except that his voice was feeble.

I kept quiet. He had his elbows on his knees; his hands hung perfectly relaxed.

At last he said, "You haven't answered. I take it he could, then."

"Anything alive can be killed, one way or another."

He said no more, merely smiled, abstracted, like a bullfighter watching the parade before a fight he's unsure of.

After supper, when the last of the children were in bed and Dorkis and Tuka were cleaning up the mess and sipping wine and talking, he patting her fanny from time to time, sometimes laughing till he wept— Tuka was in top form—I sat at the edge of the lake with Iona. Except for the stars and the flickering light from the hut behind us, the world seemed empty, abandoned, as if plague-struck. There might have been no Sparta, no Lykourgos, even no Athens, only the immense, studded sky, the hills, the water, the curve of Iona's arm. The lake was perfectly still, as smooth as black marble. I felt safe, as if time had stopped forever. Also, I felt hungry for Iona, or for something more, a new life, peace.

She said, "Did Dorkis tell you what he's considering?" Her voice was so quiet it might have come from inside me.

"Which?"

"You know." Then: "The assassination."

"It's a bad idea." My voice, in my own ears, was donkeyish. It had a quaver and my body felt callow.

"He told you, then?"

I nodded.

"Why is it a bad idea?"

"It just is." Because I'm a coward, I should have said. "Some ideas are just bad. There's no explanation, they just are."

"Ridiculous!" She laughed, her amusement breaking over the frown, not quite ending the frown but transforming it, deepening the dimple.

"Maybe so," I said.

She went on smiling, thinking, then lay back in the grass, put her hands behind her head, and pursed her lips. "I know why you say it's a bad idea." Her flat voice again, businesslike. "The truth is, you don't want him dead. He interests you."

"That's irrelevant. Of course he does." It was a lie, in fact. Nothing was of interest but her mouth and the line of her hip, the shattering sweetness of her voice. I listened to the crickets, my heart tripping rapidly and lightly, as if I were standing looking down from the roof of a tower. The water lapped at the shore, very quietly.

"You'd give up anything, anybody, for an interesting idea, even a monstrous one like his." Her voice was half serious, half mocking. Coming straight at you (except with questions) was Iona's last resort.

"An idea or an adventure," I said.

She lay still, looking at the stars. I could feel her baffled annoyance, and it pleased me. At last, with a brief, ironic smile, she said, "All right, smart one, explain."

"It's nothing," I said, still mysteriously uneasy but also tingling with some more than sexual pleasure. "It's a cliché I have. Ghost of my youthful metaphysics. What is the ultimate reality? Adventures and ideas. An adventure is when someone pokes you in the mouth. An idea is when you think pokedness."

"You can't believe that's what life's like!" She was indignant, smiling and scoffing at once, and probably aware that her indignation was sexy.

"I do believe it. So does Dorkis. That's what he means when he talks about riding reality like a bird."

She turned her head to look at me. "Only part of him believes that." Her eyes were dead serious now, though the look was still gentle. "What's best in him makes adventures *out* of ideas. Such as killing Lykourgos."

That was sharp, I thought. Foolishly, I hadn't expected it. I should have guessed that her half jokes, her dimple-flashing ironies weren't all she had, were the ambiance, say, around something she knew for sure. I felt a little flicker of excitement, sexual, and wished I'd brought the wine. "So people can *change* reality," I said

"Of course they can," she snapped, then knew she'd been made fun of. She turned her face away. After a while she said, like a sigh, "You really are serious, somewhere behind all those masks. It would be interesting to know sometime what you really think."

"So I'll tell you," I said, and smiled, boyishly world-weary, wondering what I'd make up.

She slid her eyes at me. She was thinking about it too. The new beginning. Peace like the night around us.

I looked at the stars. "All talk between men and women is a prelude to sex," I said. "You're aware of that?"

"That's really dumb," she said. Smile with dimple.

"Right." But I said, "Because adventures don't begin in ideas, they begin in emotional impulses. For instance, Dorkis and Tuka don't think of making love, they merely think as far as clearing the table, separating themselves from you and me, setting up the potential for a new reality—a new adventure. When it's happened they'll realize what's happened, that is, they'll crystallize the event to an idea, which will signal that it's over. An idea is the conceptualization of a reality which no longer exists."

"Boy," she said. But smiled.

After a long time, which I foolishly imagined she'd been using to brood on my theory, she asked, "Do you think they're making love?" It was one of those straight-at-you questions that made a lie, a joke, impossible, made all my normally devious ways seem shameful.

"Would it bother you?"

"I'm not sure." The tone was so straight, so nakedly trusting, it unnerved me like the whisper of a god. Also, it filled me with lust.

"Strange how I love you," I said. It wasn't what I'd meant to say. I leaned on my arm beside her and, after I'd thought about it, closed my hand on her breast. The effect shook me to my roots, hurled me back into the innocence of childhood. The softness of her flesh was like a sudden bursting of wells in a desert, like sympathy, kindness, and understanding I'd forgotten I deserved. It was as if all I'd been when I was good, when I was young, had lain in moldering disuse until that instant. All the tension I'd hardly known I felt came unwound. I was clean. She searched my face, knew everything in it.

"Don't," she said gently.

I kissed her and she put her arm around me, kissing me back. It was all overpowering—her very breathing slaughtered my ears—yet with a piece of my mind I didn't believe it, quite; no more than I really believed in the gods, or believed there were Helots being murdered somewhere in these hills. She was a good lover, a woman who knew how to play to men. The suspicion made the night terrible.

"I love you," I said. It sounded to me more convincing, and far more dangerous, than most of the things I said in those days. Other girls I'd made love to I hadn't lied to. Then what made me say it? Panic seized me. Did I not love Tuka, then? I couldn't remember. I drew away from her abruptly to look at the water and think. I ached. My groin was as charged as the bottom of the sea and my chest was like wind in a cave. I knew, beyond any shadow of a doubt, I could abandon everything I had in one moment, without remorse, for the taste of Iona's mouth, for her walk, her voice, her breast in my cupped band. Presumably in six months I could drop Iona for somebody else's mouth, or perhaps for a camel trip. I was outraged. —Did she love me at all? I wondered then, in fresh panic. The whole world was dead and putrefact.

Seeing that I remained still as a rock, Iona sat up and touched her face to her drawn-up knees and slightly shook her head. "I can't believe this is me," she said. It *sounded* honest.

I looked at her as coldly and objectively as possible. She was lovely and gentle, and I was swayed again. The night was as vast and deep as the cavern of childhood. The fact, sure as the huge rocks that waited below the unrippled lake, was that I was going to make love to her, that she too was hollow with desire. Just the same, I tried to think. It was true that she was beautiful, and it was true that "by a certain system of morality," as Lykourgos would say, she was good. She'd been a loving and faithful wife to Dorkis all the years of their marriage. I knew that, without her telling me, without any evidence whatever, or none of the kind mere scientists understand. Yet like me, perhaps, she was toying in the back of her mind with throwing all she had been away. It was a thought that, once entertained for an instant, could never be dismissed. She would live the rest of her life knowing that loyalties are moment-to-moment things, even those one clings to till one dies.

Or was she toying with me?

I was horrified anew at the violence of my feeling for her. It shook my world like the wrath of Poseidon and left nothing familiar, nothing even recognizable. Why should I be in Sparta? My whole life was meaningless. I was free. Also caught. It wasn't her body I wanted, or not just that. I wanted *her.*

"You've had an adventure," I said.

"God save me from more!" She laughed, but she seemed troubled. Was it true, then, that she too had glimpsed the skull behind the mask?

She lifted her face from her knees to squint at the

water, then smiled suddenly, as if she'd decided to. It was one of many moments with her when I saw in amazement how powerfully she could clamp down on her emotions with her mind. Unless, of course, she'd faked the emotions.

"Now I'll tell you what *I* think," she said. She spoke too loudly, as if the kiss were far behind us, the foolishness of youth. "I think Dorkis takes too shortsighted a view. What we need is full-scale revolution."

"Oh, right!" I said. I wondered briefly if she'd ever seen a field of corpses, and I sensed, more than thought of, some vague connection between revolution and desiring a good friend's wife.

"It's possible, Agathon," she said, "and moral."

"Certainly." I added, "Moral, anyway."

"Possible, too. We've got them. We've had them all along, we just didn't notice." She put her hand on mine. Again the excitement and doubt. "We could burn them out—every storehouse, every field and vineyard—plug the sewage ditches, poison the water with carcasses, wreck their houses. Let's see what the mighty wasps eat when their drones stop work."

"They could eat Helots," I said.

"Reprisals. Ten for one."

I laughed and moved my hand around her back.

"I wonder what Spartans taste like," she said.

"Stringy and tough, I imagine. Something like baboon."

"We could plow their city to salt," she said. The idea was taking hold. Or the vision. Whatever. She lay back, rolling toward me a little, on my arm. It was as if she was testing me.

"You're untrained," I said. "You haven't got a chance."

"That's what justifies atrocities on our side, and makes theirs all the worse."

I jiggled my head, squeezing my eyes shut. "You better go through that again."

"It's true," she said, hardening to the thought and moving toward me more. "If ten commit atrocities against two, the crime's far worse than if two commit atrocities against ten for the sake of revenge."

"I'll work on that."

"Will you help?" she asked.

"Iona, love—" I looked at her and saw she meant it, meant it with all her heart, at least for the moment. Mainly, though, I saw her mouth. I laughed in alarm. "We'd better get back to the hut."

Her hand closed hard on my wrist. "Agathon, we *need* you." Overtones rang around her words like rings from a buoy. She made me feel, more than I'd felt for a long time, manly, stronger than Herakles, beyond all mortal or divine intimidation. *We need you.* The earth calling to the sun, the sea crying out to the land. Because the Helots weren't men? Big-muscled Dorkis not a man? I wasn't thinking all this. My mind was inside it, like a building standing in a wind. It was as if for an instant we'd fallen back to the first hour, archetypal woman clawing up from her castrated mate to the new male. But was I less eunuch in my own secret bed? My mind struggled clumsily, drowning in the primal scent, straining toward logic, genesis-old defense, desperate and needful as the myth that no Helot can fight. All this in one brief pang of sensation. Damn her, did she love me or not?

"I can hear the historians now," I said. " 'The leader of the Helots, infatuated with an Athenian visitor and wishing to devise some means of seeing him frequently without rousing the suspicions of their respective spouses, conceived the plan of organizing a revolution. But on learning, later—"

"Stop that!" she said, and made a face. "Revolutions don't start because some dumb female . . ." She let it trail off, maybe concentrating on the movement of my hand on her back. She grinned. "Now I *have* to do it.

You've given me a reason." She drew away, sat up, fixed her hair.

"Tell me one thing," I said, watching her. The moment had passed. I could feel it yawning away, and I was filled with anguish. "Did you just now make all that up on the spot—the revolution business? Or is it something you've been working on?" Light, flip. But I was drowning.

"On the spot," she said, mock-innocent. "Would I spend days on such a morbid idea?"

"It's pretty clever. If the Helots weren't people I cared about, I'd advise them to give it a try."

"You think we won't, don't you? That's really dumb."

"You might, from pure stubbornness. Most things people do is mere stubbornness—a sort of proof to themselves that they exist."

"Boy, that's really dumb," she said again. "Believing the things you do, how come you don't kill yourself?"

"I do," I said. "Second by second."

She smiled wryly, shaking her head so that the hair she'd just gotten neat flew out. "I'm beginning to understand you. You're on some drug."

I stood up and gave her my hand. When she was standing I closed my arms around her and kissed her, pulling her body tight to mine. But the moment had passed; I believed in neither of us. After a time she pulled her mouth away and kissed my shoulder. "I really don't believe this," she said. "This can't be me."

In the aerie, Tuka was lying naked on the bed. Dorkis was out somewhere, walking. I wondered, cowardly, whether he'd seen us. I listened to Iona undressing beyond the screen and looked at Tuka. My mind couldn't separate them. She was beautiful, white as old stone by moonlight. It filled me with self-hate—sexual desire and impotence of soul.

Tuka said, "Agathon, we really have to talk about all this. Not tonight, but sometime." I laughed. I undressed and made rough love to her. When she climaxed she growled, for the benefit of Iona.

After that I lay awake for a long time, listening, sweating and remorseful, for Spartan boys with daggers. I heard Dorkis pass in front of the hut, then behind it. He too, it came to me, was expecting Spartans. That was why he'd come. When I got up and crept to the door to look out, he was hunkering in the shadow of a rock pile, a little up the hill, behind the hut. His bow lay on the rocks beside him; his knife lay unsheathed across his knees. The feeling came over me again: *This is it.*

I woke up in bright sunlight. Dorkis was already up, beaming, getting our breakfast ready. His thought of fleeing Sparta, killing Lykourgos, all the rest, seemed to have evaporated. I watched his huge, muscular arms, his wide hairy chest, and wondered if he'd had my wife. He'd had his, I knew. She looked pummeled to limpness, and joyful. She blew me a kiss as she came from behind the screen.

"How's the revolution?" I said.

"Oh, that was *yes*terday!" She laughed.

Tuka said later, "I don't understand them. They laugh and screw around and drink, and the soldiers kill them off like mice. What's the *matter* with them?"

"Second by second," I said. "One hour at a time."

She looked at her hands. "He really *was* good, you know." She shot a glance at me.

It wasn't true, I learned later, that she'd slept with him, though she could have. He was tentative, impotent for all his fondling (or so she decided), and in the end he was embarrassed. She thought it was funny. Tuka has a curious mind.

16   Peeker:

The tall ephor was here again. I'm more convinced than ever of his honest concern. It's all very well for idealists to howl that Sparta's rotten to the core, as my master does, but the fact remains, it's the greatest city in the whole world, not only because of its size and beauty and natural wealth—the fertile plains stretching out all around it—and not only because of its army either, but also because of, so to speak, its vision. No place is perfect—anyone knows that—but where except Sparta have kings and commoners united behind the ideals Equality and Justice, and fought with all their might against corrupting forces like wealth and laziness? You'll notice the god doesn't hit Sparta with plagues and pestilences, the way he does places like Pylos and Methone. I've heard about the seaport plague from people that have seen it, and it's something. It starts with fainting and stomach trouble, and then fever develops and terrible, terrible pain. It comes and goes in waves. You think you're getting better and suddenly it's worse than before and at last it kills you. ("That's life," my master says.) Anyway, we don't get such things here in Sparta. My father fought and died for Sparta, even though he was a Helot. I think I'd do the same. Lykourgos's vision's not achieved yet, true, and it's true that some of his methods are questionable. Nevertheless, it's a great experiment—as Agathon says in his mocking voice. And however bad a few Spartans here and there may be, there are still men like the tall ephor, devoted to making the vision into reality. I feel as if I've been blind, all this time with old Agathon. He's a good man, I still say that, for all his boring self-centeredness; and men like him served a purpose once: no matter how faithful to his vision a man like Lykourgos may be, he can always use a critic. Lykourgos must have known that all along. If he were here in Sparta, Agathon would be free in a minute, putrid old husk though he is.

Still, I look at the tall ephor, standing erect and mild at the door, asking in his dignified soft-spoken way about Agathon's health, inquiring whether something might not be done about the rats (there are always rats in prison; getting rid of them for good would take a god's intervention), and then I look over at Agathon, sitting on his bed with his skirt above his knees and his pupils rolled up and that leer on his face, and I feel as if scales have fallen from my eyes. While the ephor was quietly, determinedly working for the power that sits on him now like a casual cloak, the power that will sooner or later make Sparta the moral torch for the whole world, where was Agathon? I was there: I can tell you. He was sneaking up alleys to peek through windows at people making love. He was shinnying up columns and whispring back at me, "Peeker! Peeker! The jug!" He was sitting on his ass in the onion patch, peeling onions with his dirty thumbs and crying—"for all mankind," he said. Or he was strutting with the soldiers, making fools of them, or mimicking feeble King Kharilaus, so that no one afterward who looked at the king could feel any proper respect for his position. You call that healthy? "If you don't want to be criticized, don't criticize," my mother says. He brought the whole thing on himself. I don't mean I abandon him. He's a sort of national monument, you might say, but just the same . . .

I told the ephor everything I could, and he listened. I explained how Agathon had been driven out of his mind by women, how that gave him compassion for

everyone and everything and made him see through
everything the way a lover sees through both himself
and his love but forgives himself and forgives the love
and goes on and on in his hopeless pursuit, and how,
also, the same things that turned him into a Seer are
the causes of his looks and actions—his ungodly singing, for instance, things like:

> Nobody loves a drunkard
> and nobody loves a whore,
> but nobody loves Their Majesties
> more! Much more, oh,
> nobody loves Their Majesties more!

"What does that mean, exactly?" the ephor said.
"Who knows?" I said.

Or his peeking through windows, for instance, not
because he's really got a dirty mind but because seeing
people in love, especially ugly people, old people, or
best of all cripples, fills his heart with joy. But people
get the wrong idea, I said. Once late at night we saw a
fat old lady eliminating behind a house, trying to hide
in some azalea bushes, and it was holy to him—the
human spirit's struggle to keep its baseness private—
and he couldn't contain himself; he went right up to her
shoulder and whispered, "God bless you!" The old lady
was mad as hell, and she started throwing stones at us.
I understood, but how could you ask some ignorant old
Spartan lady to comprehend a thing like that? We ran,
Agathon giggling and vaulting along on his crutch, and
people came to the doors in their loincloths and saw
the old lady throwing stones and screaming, and they
grabbed some stones and joined in with her. I didn't
blame them, I could see their point of view; he looked
like any other old drunk to them. But I could understand Agathon's side too, not that I wasn't ashamed,
of course. In fact, when he wasn't looking I lobbed a
stone at him myself. It clipped him in the ear. But it

was beautiful to him: it was a vision of the gap between ideal and real, a thing nobody but a lover could understand.

The ephor looked steadily over my head, not showing anything because of course he had to judge these things impartially. "Was this incident recent?" he said.

I told him about the time he caused that uproar in the bullring. One minute he's sitting beside me in the stands, banging his crutch from time to time, the way he does when he's a little cross, and the next minute he's down there in the ring, holding this stupid little square of cloth that he uses for his nose, holding it up like a bullfighter's cape. The bull comes at him and plows right through him. I had to nurse him for six months. "What in hell did you prove?" I howl at him when he's able to talk. *"That bulls are smarter than people,"* he says. I'd like to have killed him—who wouldn't?—but I could understand. As a lover, he lives his whole life by trickery and deceit, and he can't stand it. Any fool can see the poor bull's got no chance, the whole thing's rigged. So Agathon has to show how things really are. He can't stop himself. I admire him for it, up to a point. But naturally people don't understand. They think it's political, they think he's making fun of Spartan courage.

The ephor said, "The bullfight was part of a religious festival?"

I was glad he asked it right out. "Yes. But Agathon's deeply devoted to the gods, in his way. It wasn't that."

He looked over my head, weighing it. The ephors standing a little behind him looked uneasy, the fat one smiling nervously, wringing his hands, the stolid one looking at the ground. They were sweating rivers from hurrying to keep up with the tall one's stride and then standing all this time in the sun. The tall one only had a drop or two over his eyebrows.

I said, "Whatever the charges against him are, I can prove they're all lies. He's got a lot of enemies, but I've been following him for three years and I can guarantee you he never did anything illegal. Especially, he's got political enemies. But he loves this city. He worked with politicians for years. If you investigate—"

The ephor's eyes dropped down from over my head to meet mine, and he was listening more closely than ever.

"If you investigate, you'll find his accusers are the enemies of the state."

"A full investigation may well be necessary," the ephor said. He meant it, and he would see to it. He tried to talk then to Agathon, but the old man was hopeless.

After they'd left I asked Agathon what he thought. He rolled the pupils back down into sight, then closed his eyes and rubbed the lids with his fingertips. "I'm glad you asked," he said. "Peeker, my boy, I've been rethinking the philosophical positions of my youth."

I had a feeling he was at it again, but I waited, hoping against hope.

"It's recently struck me that the fundamental material of the world is not earth or fire or water or even air, as people like Thales maintain, but *wind.*"

I sighed.

"The precise distinction between wind and air is not yet perfectly clear to me, but I'm working on it; and in any case, as I used to tell Tuka, what matters in natural philosophy is not so much what is true as what is interesting." He puckered up his lips. "*Wind* I tentatively define as the Poseidonic essence: that which moves whatever moves (as for example, air, water, fire, or earth). The implications are staggering, my boy."

"I bet," I said.

"Movement can only be perceived *within time,* so that without time (if my theory is right) there can be nothing. I am forced to conclude, reluctantly, that time is space. Or to convert the terms, matter is the breath of God for a certain span of time. I am of course perfectly aware that all this is absolute rubbish, but I tolerate that. It takes care of Zeno's arrow, anyway. So it comes to this: Every event, every adventure, is a ripple in God's exhalation. Or should I say His fart? Maybe Solon from one end, Lykourgos from the other. He he he!"

I did not choose to comment. He told a story.

17   Agathon:

I have just made up a marvelous story that, if Peeker's
credulity does not fail me, will go down through History:

It is said that Solon, when he was old, once visited
Kroesos at Sardis. They say that when he went into
Kroesos's palace he was like an inland man when he
first goes to see the ocean. As the inland man thinks
every river he comes upon must be the sea, so Solon,
passing through Kroesos's court and seeing a great
many nobles in rich attire and surrounded by atten-
dants, supposed every nobleman he met must be the
king. When he came to Kroesos, who was seated, so
fat he couldn't move a finger, high on a throne of gold
and ivory and silver, gloriously decked with every possible rarity and spangle, in ornaments of jewels, purple, gold, scarlet, and surrounded by an army of terra-
cotta statues, he seemed not especially impressed and,
in fact, failed to give King Kroesos the compliments he
expected. Kroesos commanded his men to open all his
treasure houses and take Solon to look at his sump-
tuous furniture and luxuries—his superb black-figure
jugs, cups, bowls, his perfume flasks and ivories,
seraboidal seal amulets with pictures of sphinxes, his
seal stones, carpets, Phoenikian jewelry, Skythian carv-
ings, Phrygian figures, his fine painted chariots, horses,
ibexes, lions. When Solon came back from viewing the
treasures, puffing and huffing and blinking like an owl,
trembling like an earthquake from all that exertion,

Kroesos asked him if ever he had known a happier man than he. Solon, after he'd got his wind, stretched his cheeks with his fingertips and pursed his lips and finally answered, softly and gently, that he'd known a man named Tellos once, a fellow citizen of his, and he told the king that this Tellos had been an honest man, had had good children and a competent estate, and had died bravely in battle for his country. Kroesos, staring down from his seven hundred pounds like an angry whale, took him for an ill-bred fool, but he kept his temper and asked if he knew, besides Tellos, any other man more happy than himself. Solon nodded like an Indian sage. "Two," he said. "Kloebis and Biton. They were loving brothers, and extremely dutiful sons to their mother. One famous day when the oxen delayed her, they hitched themselves to the wagon and drew her to Hera's temple for worship. Everyone there called her fortunate indeed to have such sons, and she agreed that it was so. Later, after the sacrifice and feast, they went to their beds and rose no more. They died in the midst of their honor a painless and tranquil death. We named a road for them."

Kroesos was furious. "Look here," he said, "do you figure we're not among the happy men at all?"

Solon, unwilling to exasperate him more, replied with great and gentle formality: "The gods, O king, have given the Greeks all other gifts in moderate degree; and so our wisdom, too, is cheerful and homely, not kingly wisdom. Our humble understanding, observing the numerous misfortunes that attend upon all conditions, forbids us to grow overconfident of our present enjoyments, or to admire any man's happiness that may yet, in the course of time, suffer alteration. To salute as happy a man who is still in the midst of life's hazard we think as unwise as crowning a wrestler still honking and blowing in the ring."

After this, he was dismissed, having given Kroesos

some pain but not much instruction, as it seemed to Kroesos.

Aesop, the man who writes the fables, was in Sardis at the time on Kroesos's invitation—an old friend of Solon's—and he was troubled that Solon was so ill received as a result of his own mulishness. "Solon," said he, "when a man gives advice to kings he should make it pert and seasonable."

Solon nodded as if abashed and said softly, feebly, for he was well up in years: "Or short and reasonable. Or curt and treasonable. Or tart and please-him-able."

Aesop sighed. Though a person of the greatest sobriety, he was always unmanned by a jest.

Why I made the story up I'm not exactly sure, except that it has of course things to do with my demon Lykourgos. Has to do with Time and Scorn. Solon—realist, pragmatist, democrat—scorns in moderation. Lykourgos's scorn is absolute, like a god's. ("Moderation in all things including moderation," Dorkis used to say.) Solon babbles, filling the air and suffocating his enemies with "humble wisdom" or else comforting noise; Lykourgos hardly speaks and, when he does, speaks in aphorisms or rebukes as quick and short as Spartan daggers or, say, thunderbolts. Solon, in his prime, would fall in love with ten women and five or six boys a years; Lykourgos turns women into men. His marriage laws, for instance. He's set it up so that the husband carries his bride off by a sort of force. The woman who supervises the wedding clips the bride's hair off close around her head and dresses her up in man's clothes and leaves her on a mattress in the dark. The bridegroom comes in in his everyday clothes, unties her virgin zone, and takes her. When he's finished he returns to his own dormitory, to sleep as usual with the other young men. So it continues night after night, year after year, so that sometimes a man may have several children before he has ever seen his wife's face by daylight. If a man falls in love with another man's wife —which happens fairly often where women walk naked—the law allows him to ask the husband for her company; and it forbids the husband to refuse him except if the lover or the wife is sickly or a weakling. Lykourgos goes further. He orders that children not be begotten by the first comer but by the best man that can be found. I suggested to him once that the law was perhaps a little inhuman. "The reverse," he said. "Is it human to breed better horses and cows than men?" When a child is born, they carry it to the judges, and if the child looks sickly, they kill it, throw it from a cliff as they would a runt pig.

He was baffled when Solon repealed all Draco's laws. We were alone in his chamber, except for the omnipresent Alkander—his servant, the boy who put his eye out. According to Solon, the laws were too severe, the punishments too great. Lykourgos quoted me Draco's own comment on why nearly all crimes were punishable by death: "Even small crimes deserve death," he said. "As for greater crimes, well, death is the worst I've got." Lykourgos sat with his chin pulled in, gloomy and distant. His rabbinical nose commanded the room like a battlement against a night sky.

"But why?" I said. It was in the days when I still tried to reason with him. "Why death for, say, loitering?"

"It purifies the blood," he said. "That's the beginning and end of Law and Order."

"The blood." I pretended to muse on it.

"The blood of the State," he said. His voice was flat as iron. "The criminal nature is a product of bad breeding. It must not survive to another generation."

"Of course!" I said. "You mean people like our friend here, Alkander."

Lykourgos winced. Just a flick of one eyelid. He loves his bodyguard, insofar as a man of ice-cold marble can love anything merely mortal. "You're clever, Agathon. An incisive mind." He always judged my sallies dispassionately, indifferently.

I told him of Solon's jurors. It was a plan he'd worked out before he became arkhon, and I knew the theory of it. I had it in my book. In a counterfeit bid for the support of the rich, Solon refused the poorest class in Athens—the Thetes or hill people—any place in the public assembly, but he let them be jurors. The Thetes were very cross at first, but in time they found out that they'd won a great advantage. Nearly every dispute that came up in Athens would sooner or later come to them. Even in cases he assigned to the arkhon, he allowed an appeal to the courts. Moreover, he was careful to word his laws in a way that was obscure and ambiguous, so that the power of his jurors would balance the power of the rest.

Lykourgos scowled at me, thinking it over. "Where inequality exists, Justice is impossible." He was crosser than usual. He had a headache.

"True," I said. "But when a rich man's treated unjustly, he has his wine cellar to fall back on. A poor man has only his ass."

He closed his one eye and pressed his fingertips to it as if to console it. "Clever but not to the point," he said.

"This then," I said. I leaned toward him—sitting opposite him, six feet away. Alkander watched me with his arms folded. "To get rid of inequality you have to change man's nature—in fact, deny the structure of the universe. It can be done. You're proving it. But some would say—not me, you understand; I take no position —some would say your option's barbaric, even stupid. If laws are to deal with men as they are and reality as it is, they have to provide for unequal men in a world of flux. Say the State is, as the poets say, a ship. If you want to keep it exactly what it is, you have two choices. Either you patch it day by day, replace worn-out boards, reweave old sails, repaint it with tar, or you haul it up onto some smooth stones and carefully protect it from all use, even the weather's."

"Men as they are are not worth building a State for," he said. "Common minds have believed too long that whatever is is necessary. The time has come for a higher belief."

"Bullshit!" I exploded. "What would you know about common minds, or any other kind of human mind, Lykourgos?"

His head shot forward, hands braced on the chair arms. "I have known human feeling."

"Bullshit!"

He was enraged, and it wasn't abstract now. I had blundered onto his heart, and I had nicked it. His jaw worked and his voice had all hell in it. "Agathon," he bellowed, "I have known the affections of a woman."

"Never," I said. I snapped it like a whip. "She faked it!"

He was out of his chair and coming at me, and then Alkander was on him, holding him, yelling at me over his shoulder, "Go! Get out of here! *Maniac!*"

But I hung on one second longer. "Your brothers queen," I said, and laughed. "How stupid of us all!"

Alkander let him go, willing to see me dead for that. But Lykourgos sank to the floor, clenching his fists and moaning, helpless, on fire with self-hate and hatred for me. Alkander knelt by him, touching his back. I left. I heard him pacing, hours later. He paces rapidly, stiff-legged, his chin lifted, moving across the room and back, again and again, exactly like a tiger.

It wouldn't be easy for Lykourgos to forgive me for that discovery, I knew. But the next time I saw him he was calm, stern, and distant, as always. "Nothing in the world is knowable," he said. "Knowledge is unflinching assertion."

"I assert, then, that a man still wants to know." And

Nietzche

then, recklessly, with a glance at Alkander: "Perhaps, in fact, she loved you."

"Perhaps the eagles love me, or the gods."

It's a terrible thing to hear Lykourgos laugh.

18 Peeker:

We found one of our rats dead this morning. Some disease. Agathon turned it over and over, thinking, saying nothing. It makes me uneasy.

19   Agathon:

Dorkis and Iona were of course not the only people we ever saw in Sparta. We had various friends we partied with or went riding with or went with to things like the festivals of Orthia and Orestes or, when autumn came, the bullfights. One can hardly help having friends in a vast and sprawling city, even a reactionary city like this one. A hermetic soul may get by well enough in the mountains, with no one to talk to but his god; but here the sheer press of population is against it—and more: the nature of the population. At festival time, or during the games, mankind stands thick as a field of wheat, a mixed and mingled half-breed or many-breed humanity that by its diverse character threatens all that any one man may stand for. The Spartans, first. Naked as tombstones except for their crude iron neck rings and bracelets. Fierce, austere people who laugh at no joke more than six words long, who breed by contract and kill non-Spartans as casually as they'd kill a horse with spavins. Then there were Egyptians and Sardinians, immodestly dressed, by comparison, in toe-length robes and jewelry and spangles, who lay one another, male or female, as casually as Athenians drink wine. Then Greeks of the Perioikoi, born of every Hellenic city, some puritanical as Homer himself, some more licentious than Sardinians. Then Helots, the humble majority, weighed down like donkeys, some of them, and others—like Dorkis and Iona—gilded like Mesopotamian gods. What is a man to make of himself, or of his father's codes, in such confusion? In Athens, the sexual code (for instance) was simple. A man should be faithful, and if he couldn't—and many couldn't—he should view his breach with reasonable shame. If he slept with a slavegirl, and everyone did, he should dislike himself for forcing upon her the shame of prostitution. (In Sparta, the rape of a Helot was called an act of patriotism. In Sardis it was called a snack.) Who could survive, in such a city, except by supporting what was best in himself—or whatever was worst, what cried out in anguish for nemesis—by the sleight-of-hand of friendship, the buttress of some similar nature, bad or good?

Some of our friends—the friends of whom Tuka was usually fondest—were rich fellow expatriates from Athens. These, in general, didn't get on very well with Dorkis and Iona, mainly because of Dorkis's way of fondling women, I suspect. He petted them in public, but in the dark he was stubbornly loyal to his wife. The Athenians were, in public, more discreet.

I was not, in general, fond of Athenians in Sparta. I can tolerate watching a bull murdered with one man as well as with the next. It's better, I suppose, than the old Minoan cult in which the god-bull was always victorious, his victims mere children. And when festival drinking and dancing get thoroughly out of hand, I can sneak off with one man's wife as well as with another's. Nevertheless, there were few Athenians in Sparta who weren't fat parasites, men whom the State's isolationist laws hadn't driven away but had turned to genteel outlaws—heavily moustached, scented, oil-bathed, weighted with semiprecious stones. They were cultured, some of them even refined—when Tuka played her harp they knew what to praise—but I am not, myself, as amused as I might be by culture and refinement. The crudest men I have ever known were gawky old Klinias, my beloved master, and Solon, my beloved employer,

whom some poet once called "The Father of Athens
and Mother of All the Hogs."

We lived what is known as a rich life, badly hung-
over three mornings out of five, hiding our heads from
the sunlight in rooms draped with purple cloth and
thickly padded with Oriental rugs, so that no sandal's
click might cleave our skulls. We were sealed off from
the ordinary work of the world, and virtually sealed off
from our children too, except when we made a point of
seeing them, Tuka instructing Diana on the harp, I
struggling to make poor Kleon a horseman. I was impatient of the same gentleness and timidity I admired
in him on all other occasions, and intolerant of his
fear's beclouding of his mind. I was, myself, a man
absolutely without fear on a horse. Though I'm a gentle
person, in most respects, I have ridden horses men
swore were bewitched; bedeviled, mad creatures that I
think would as soon have eaten me as borne me. A
week after my brother's funeral I rode the chicken-
brained stallion that killed him. Later, on a winter rabbit hunt, I rode that same horse to his grave. —In any
case, Kleon was afraid of the plodding brown mare I'd
given him—a lovely horse dark as a roasted chestnut—
and for reasons too shadowy for me to fathom, I was
beside myself. I would shout at him, calling him stupid,
brainless, and when Kleon wept, struggling to do what
I demanded—think clearly—I would clench my teeth
and swear. "I'm scared," he would say. "Daddy, Daddy,
I'm scared!"—crying, clinging to the horse's neck. I
would reason with him, tense with anger, explaining to
him what fun he would have with the other boys if he
learned to ride, explaining to him how ashamed he
was (and it was true) when friends younger than himself—a boy named Markapor, for instance—went casually thundering off. "Please, please, please, Daddy.
Please!" he would wail, and at last I would say, "Get
off then, damn you, and walk," and I would ride off. I
would talk to him later, telling him that what I had

done was inexcusable, even though his fear was, of course, annoying and frustrating. I had never treated anyone that way until now—and I did this kind of thing more than once, turning the whole force of my rage on a child. And yet I loved him more than I'd ever loved anyone else. Were Tuka's rages at Kleon the same? Or Iona's rages at her children? Tuka hit Kleon in the stomach once—he'd broken something that belonged to her, and destruction, the world's mutability really, was intolerable to Tuka. She hit him—not a slap but an angry punch with her fist—and I jumped to her, caught her shoulder, and slapped her face so hard she went flying across the room. (I wasn't angry then. I was collected but outraged. I slapped her as I would have spanked Kleon for throwing a stone at Diana.) "Don't ever do that again," I said. Righteous, true; righteous as a drunken god. But she never tried it again, at least in my presence. Tuka would reach the same frustration I reached with Kleon when she worked with Diana at the harp. Diana didn't want to play the harp, she said. I insisted that she must. It's hard, in the beginning, I told her; everything you try you fail at. But it gets easier later, and eventually it can be a pleasure. We knew that for a fact, Tuka and I, though Diana couldn't, and so we asserted the natural right of superior knowledge and forced her. Diana wept, letting her hands fall away from the strings, and Tuka would shriek at her, and Diana would lift her hands and play again, weeping. Unlike Kleon—he may never learn to ride a horse, though he knows all the secrets of my grammata—Diana learned quickly, and soon she was playing with sheepish pride for friends.

But except for the time we righteously set aside for their instruction, or for play with them—somewhat better times than the times of instruction, but also less frequent—we saw very little of our children. We had various circles: some friends we "sat up with," as Tuka put it, meaning that I talked philosophy or politics with the husband while Tuka gossiped with the wife; other friends with whom, as she put it, we cavorted. With a curious, obscurely destinal regularity we got into difficulties with the latter. I must reluctantly set down some facts.

First, though no one would believe it who has seen me ranting in the Spartan hills in my later years, winking and sneering and spelling dark spells, prophesying plagues and trepidations of the earth and stars, my hair flying wildly, my eyes like a frog's, my arms stretched out as Lykourgos stretches his, forming with the fingers of each hand V's for Victory, I was once a handsome and sweetly poetic young man. Weak-chinned, admittedly, and given to grand pontifications, but lovable, all in all. I was, moreover, an ambitious person, but ambitious in ways still uncertain, undirected. I'd taken a few students and was gaining a reputation of sorts; but my heart wasn't in it. I was employed off and on by Lykourgos and the ephors, sometimes as a sort of informal adviser, sometimes (by Lykourgos, not the ephors) as an envoy in delicate matters where messages transmitted or discussions held were not to be mistaken for official positions of Sparta. I was, in effect, a high-class odd-jobs man with a company horse; I was the voice of all things tentative or tendentious. "Do so-and-so," I was instructed to say, "or, between you and me, Sparta will have—in my personal opinion—no possible course but war." It was stupid work, though at times dead serious. Those I talked to—after the endless preliminaries (the boat ride, the tour, the entertainment by the poet-harper and his acrobats)—those I talked to understood as well as I did that we were playing a perhaps meaningless game: the ephors do all official diplomatic work for Sparta. Even the kings have no final say in foreign affairs, except as generals in war. Yet I'd been sent at state expense, with the seal of Lykourgos on my introduction, which meant that something might conceivably be possible, a meeting with the ephors in

the future, perhaps, or some secret, gentleman's agreement; and on my side I knew that, though they knew I
meant nothing, they were talking with me, so the game
we were playing might at any moment turn earnest.
There was a further complication. At the heart of the
game, we all knew, lay one question: would Sparta's
role in and around Lakonia be defensive or aggressive?
The ephors favored aggression—extend the borders and
establish a buffer of subject city-states. Lykourgos
favored a defensive, isolationist posture. One meant
immoral imperialism, an extension of suppression like
that which had already deracinated all Helot pride;
the other would produce a city of warriors, state-
supported killers, spoiling like overtrained watchdogs
for a fight. They would have no choice but to occupy
their time as warriors do, fighting one another or murdering scapegoats, some passing Helot drudge. I'd have
chosen neither, if that choice were possible; but Sparta
has always been the plum, with her wheat and cattle
and beautiful hills of olive trees and vineyards—a city
the gods created to entertain them with endless in-
vasions. So I favored Lykourgos's view, the lesser evil.
I was morally bound to it hand and foot, in fact, as
Lykourgos understood. Why else would he send his
most obstinate critic, "pet democrat," as he used to say,
on missions aimed at thwarting the will of the ephors
and imposing his own despotic will? Not, of course,
that I was ever out of sight of his secret police (but
neither were the ephors), and not that, if I had made
some mistake, he would have troubled to rescue me.
Nevertheless, for almost four years the curious partner-
ship of enemies worked. I was born, no doubt, to be
caught, my whole life long, in double binds. But enough
of all that. The game I played with those I met in the
cities of the sons of Hellen was a tricky, devious free-
for-all, in which Lykourgos, through unofficial agents
like myself, worked every city against every other, and
all of them against the ephors. Except for allies I

could win in the playing, my only ally on earth was
Lykourgos, whose values I detested and whose power
gave me no sanction. There are doubtless envoys who
would have scorned the canescent unrealities I manipu-
lated like Sardinian pieces on a playing board, but I
have always clowned and mocked, played games, in
the hope of discovering the real. While we toyed with
fictions, picking our way through the vague potentiali-
ties that littered our path like shadowy rocks and moray
eels, my hands and armpits ran with sweat, and my
hind end went numb from sitting still to dramatize my
indifference.

When I returned from these missions, I would, after
copying what I'd gotten for my book (this was before
Klinias's book arrived and I began adding to it), drink
myself to stone for a week, then plunge with renewed
vigor into the idiocy of parties, wild night rides through
the countryside with friends, or, sometimes, pointless
verbal duels with Lykourgos. Invariably, when we went
to expatriate Athenian parties, I would deliberately,
solemnly get drunk. Occasionally scenes ensued.

One night, very drunk, Tuka and I stayed late at a
party given by a young Athenian couple we'd been
seeing off and on for a year or two. The man, Hamrah, a man of Egyptian stock and comically proud of
his Athenian citizenship, was a black-market king who
dealt in Asian ornaments and jewels, especially ivory
figurines of gods and goddesses. He was a very tall,
stern-minded man who had curiously direct and simple
theories. All life, he said, was based on the principle of
advertising pressure and response—a phrase he'd
picked up from some Phoenikian peddler. That was the
basis of his financial success, his perfect understanding
of his wife, his success with young ladies of heretofore
impeccable morals, and so forth. I rarely troubled to
argue with him. He had a fine sense of humor, at least
about everything except himself, and he was an excellent horseman. I couldn't afford to be too fussy. There

were few enough in Sparta who rode as I rode, hell-bent, indifferent to arm or skull. Also, he seemed a good father—jovial and rowdy with his sons. His wife, unluckily, was a gentle, sensitive girl who could easily be raped (and eventually was) by music or poetry, who cared for moment-to-moment feeling, and whose friendships—with Tuka, for instance—were as close and oblivious to purpose as the friendship of the earth and sun.

And so, as I was saying, one night we stayed late. For me, the party was murderously dull. Tuka's wit was, as usual, flashy, but I knew the stories. Hamrah drank heavily, as usual, and as usual showed no sign of drunkenness. He talked with his Athenian friends of the "art of business." It was characteristic of all of them to abstract real transactions to theory: even among fellow maggots it would have been awkward to talk of what they really sold, or where, or how. They all talked in the same way, holding forth loudly while they had the floor, gazing off into the corners of the room like ill-arranged statues when they had to give way to some other's oratory. I listened absently, moving my eyes from group to group, picking up without interest, like shopworn trinkets, bits of their inflated language— "customer extinction," "impetus diffusion"—and I drank. On the wide stone terrace opening out toward Hamrah's large pond, a group of Helot instrumentalists played lugubrious dances, and couples drifted past the open doorway embracing, moving vaguely in time with the music.

Hamrah's wife came with a pitcher to offer more wine. She was small, buxom, with a face like a child's —pretty mouth, a slightly turned up nose, shy eyes. I held up my cup and she filled it.

"I'm Thalia," she said. "Remember?"

I grinned. "It's beginning to come back to me."

She laughed, holding off. "Wonderful."

"Come sit," I said.

She glanced around the room. There were plenty of empty wine cups, but there was nobody there not able to serve himself. She set the pitcher on the carved center table, came back with her cup, and sat down on the floor beside my cushion. When she'd arranged herself, feet tucked under her to one side, chiton flowing smoothly over her knees, she looked up, smiling, as if for some new command. Since I had none to give, she said with pleasantly childlike irony, "You look like you're having a wonderful time."

"I've been listening and learning," I said solemnly.

"Wonderful!" She looked over at the group around her husband. A short, thick man like a sawed-off column with a black, short beard and eyes large as hen's eggs was talking about market-seizure modalities. She looked back at me, serious. "I hear you write poetry."

"At times. I'm a degenerate."

She drank and thought about it. "Really?" she asked.

I understood all this, of course. The womanly flirtation, the hostessly flattery, and, alas, the serious child peeking out behind.

"Very, very degenerate," I said. I glanced at her husband, clean cut, erect as a general. "Now Solon's poetry is something else. It's public, rhetorical, designed to sway the community to good. But mine—" I shook my head in mock despair. "Pure anarchy. If I had any character I'd burn it."

Thalia lifted her head and laughed, self-conscious but also amused, curious. "Are you serious, Agathon?"

I slid off the cushion, pushed it away, and sat beside her on the floor. Tuka and someone I didn't know drifted past the doorway, dancing. ("Nice enough, yes," Tuka was saying. "You know the kind. Sex makes her seasick.") "Never more serious in my life," I said. "All poetry, good or evil, works by the same process. Solon writes good good poetry, I write good evil poetry."

"You must let me see it sometime. Is it naughty?"

"Alas, no. Aseptic."

She smiled and glanced over at her husband. "What's the process? —What you were talking about."

"You want the whole lecture?"

She nodded happily. "While we dance."

"Good idea," I said, "but unluckily—"

"Oh." She glanced at my bad leg. "How stupid!"

"How about I lecture while we go for a walk?"

"Wonderful!" she said.

I set down my cup, labored to my feet, and held out my hand. We walked, and I gave her the lecture I used to dazzle students with, about philosophy by exclusion (logic) and philosophy by inclusion (poetry), and poetry for the common good (Solon's) and poetry for sickly self-congratulation (mine). We ended up sitting in the tall, soft grass by the pond, holding hands. Looking at the wide, unmoving pond, you couldn't tell whether the water or the shore was more still. I put my arm around her. Her back was softer than Tuka's, less sharply cleft at the spine. She told me about her father. Once when he was drunk and she was bringing him home, he tried to push her in front of a carriage team. All her life she'd been afraid to go to sleep at night. I moved my hand on her back. It was very unusual for her to talk seriously with anyone, she said. She felt like a prisoner sometimes. Life seemed huge when you were sitting out here by the water, looking up at the stars, and it made her feel cheated not to be able to see everything, know everything there was. I thought fleetingly about my old book—a thing I rarely mentioned to anyone—and moved my hand on the far side of her back, slowly. I was thinking now of Iona. "Will you show me your poetry?" she asked. I said nothing, and when she turned to look at me I kissed her. She didn't exactly return the kiss, but she didn't pull away either.

I said, "Let's swim."

"Here?" she said, incredulous. But it wasn't the pond's stagnation she was thinking of.

Quite casually—because, though my tongue was glib, I was too drunk for any ghost of inhibition—I stripped and dove in. I hit my head on a stump but hardly noticed. The water was warm as soup. After a moment she too was in the water, laughing, calling out to me about the water's warmth. She swam beautifully, as graceful as an athlete, and after a time I crawled out on the bank to sit and watch her. Blood ran down into my eyes from where I'd hit myself on the sunken stump. At last she too came out, shyly, her body white in the moonlight—hips and breasts far sweeter, it seemed to me, than those of any casually, habitually naked Spartan girl. She sat down beside me, shook her hair, and laughed. "Marvelous!" she said. I put my arm around her, laid her down, and kissed her. Blood fell on her from my banged-up forehead. She was smiling, and whispered, "Marvelous." It was, but I could do nothing, my body wine-logged. And perhaps something else. Wine doesn't usually defeat me at such moments. "We'd better go back," I said. She nodded. After a while, still not speaking, we got up, dressed, and, holding hands, went back up to the house. Hamrah and Tuka sat on the terrace, in the shadow of the cypresses, talking. (". . . is, there's no such thing as a grown-up," Tuka was saying. "I imagine it's especially sad to people who are really, really old.") Thalia and I went inside, refilled our cups, and drank. Not long after that, I fell asleep. I slept like a boulder.

A week later, Hamrah told me solemnly, his big hands closing and opening around each other, that his marriage was on the rocks because of "what happened the other night." I was astonished. "Hamrah," I asked, "do you think I made love to your wife?" He tipped his head down and rolled up his eyes, full of gloomy guilt. "No," he said, "but maybe it would have been better if you had, because I did with yours, and now Thalia hates me." "But that's absurd!" I said. His news surprised me, to say the least, partly because it came

from such a fine, antiseptic, military-looking man, but I
wasn't shocked, certainly not wounded. I was partly
surprised that Tuka had failed to mention it, and partly
I was surprised at Thalia, if what he said was true. I
could understand well enough why they'd done it.
They'd thought we had. It was mere chance that we
hadn't. I remembered what Thalia had said about the
hugeness of life and her feeling cheated. I could have
laughed, now, but I didn't. "It's ridiculous," I said. I
sounded to myself like Solon, filling the air with noises
while he thought about his next move. "I could have
had her," I said. "I suppose it was stupid of me not
to." He looked mournfully toward the house, like a
warrior surveying the ground of his defeat. Inside,
Tuka and Thalia were talking. "I wouldn't know," he
said. And so that night I went swimming again with
Thalia, pristine Athenian girl, and our naked bodies
would brush together from time to time and she would
raise her arms, reaching for her stroke, so that her
breasts moved against my chest, and afterward (goose
pimples rising on my skin, my teeth chattering) we
made love on the bank where we'd sat looking up at
the stars. When we went to the house, Tuka and Hamrah were in bed. Hamrah pretended not to see us at
the door. I took Thalia's hand and led her to the second
bedroom. Toward daylight, Tuka came to our bed.

All this happened more than once. I understood,
well enough, that it was destructive. Hamrah was a
good lover (Tuka told me in great detail), and I, as a
matter of fact, was far from spectacular in bed, especially with Thalia. Nearly always, in fact, I was impotent with her, and she would say things like "Agathon, Agathon, what have I done wrong? Why can't
you love me?" and would talk of suicide. Hamrah,
meanwhile, would be firm as a rock for hours, mum-
bling, "Tuka, Tuka, I love you, I love you," to which
Tuka would answer, sensibly, "Don't be silly, dear, it's
just a friendly fuck." And they would laugh. But for all

his physical superiority, I had him cold: I loved his
wife better than he did—or, anyway, I understood her
better than he did, cared more about what she thought.
I could offer her pieces of this huge life that Hamrah
had never heard of. What had started, between me and
Thalia, as a friendly fuck became something else.
Though I liked being in bed with her, even when I was
impotent, what I liked best was walking and talking
with her, telling her about politics and philosophy and
poetry, or listening to her stories about her childhood.
I wrote poems for her, degenerate, of course. But whatever of the degenerate there may have been in the
poems, it was mine, not hers. She was the gentlest girl
I'd ever known. Certainly gentler than Tuka, gentler
than Iona. When Tuka was angry she would cut with
her tongue, lash out with her fists, at last go rigid with
fury. As for Iona, she had the mask of gentleness, but I
guessed from the beginning that it was a mask. She
almost never raised her voice at her children, but once
when she was slightly drunk and her second oldest son
was screeching, shivering the night with his pointless,
now merry, now cantankerous noise, I watched her
smash a cup on his skull (almost without expression).
Another time, when I stood behind her and bacon
grease spattered on her arm—no fault of mine—she
turned and meant to brain me, merely because I was
handy, then thought better of it. Thalia, when she was
offended, withdrew or wept. The best of them all, perhaps. Yet Thalia never possessed me, body and soul.
For her, as for them, I felt tenderness, respect, admiration. Like theirs, her unexpected appearance in a room
gave my heart a sudden leap of pleasure and, needless
to say, desire. But she was never inside me like an in-
cubus bent on my destruction. It was like the difference
between a reflection in a clean pool and a reflection
seized by a water spirit as a mask for her deadly court-
ship. What it was that made the difference I don't know.
—In any case, Thalia stopped loving her husband.

Tuka, for her part, loved me more than ever, it seemed. She had never been awed by Hamrah's intellect or his worldly aplomb, and I was a gentler, though not a more robust, bedfellow. But while her nights with Hamrah intensified her love for me, they also had on her an effect she had never expected, though I could have warned her of it. Sometimes when we were talking happily about this or that, her eyes would move away, and I knew she was thinking of him. I was sorry for her, as I was for Hamrah and Thalia, but I said nothing.

And so at last, inevitably, Hamrah looked at me in rage and said, "All you've left me is a piece of ass that wants no piece of me."

"I'm sorry," I said. I could see it was a little inadequate.

He lifted his fists, not as if to hit me, as if looking for something somewhere to hit. "Get out of here," he yelled. "You're evil. *All* of you! Buzz off!"

Tuka cried. We left.

Two hours later, Thalia came. Tuka was asleep. We went for a walk and, for the last time, made love. I neglected to mention her visit to Tuka. Thalia told Hamrah, and he was aflame with moral indignation. He ordered her out of the house forever, then changed his mind and ordered her out for a week. (He took in a girl friend while Thalia was away. A man needs comfort at a time like that.) She was never to see either one of us again. She came to Tuka to apologize for her sin and weep, and Tuka, aflame with, possibly, moral indignation, raged and swore and ordered poor Thalia from her sight. Then she—Tuka—called me from my work and demanded an explanation. I evaded, then finally made something up, heavy, heavy with weariness.

Later I told Iona that I had slept with Thalia. She wept. She shook violently, holding me and weeping, as if her pain went into the ground below her feet and made the earth shake. I felt no guilt, felt victimized by other people's foolishness, or anyway their self-made traps, but it wasn't comforting. Thalia, from that day on, was Hamrah's slave. It was senseless, but I could do nothing for either of them. Tuka went to bed for three days. As she'd done with her brother years ago, she'd passed all human limits in her outburst at Thalia, and now, because Thalia had made herself Hamrah's prisoner, Tuka couldn't take it all back. She would sit very still, looking out the window, with tears on her cheeks, remembering the friendship as a woman remembers her childhood. I couldn't help her either. I went once to Hamrah's house when I knew he was out. Thalia came to the door and opened it partway. Her face was puffy, remote. The room behind her was full of shadows. "Are you all right, Thalia?" I said. She nodded. "Is there anything we can do?" I asked. Without thinking, as if she were past all thinking, she shook her head. I looked at my feet, trying to think what else to say. The door closed softly.

Soon after that—I went on a trip for Lykourgos in the meanwhile—Iona began to joke, from time to time, about leaving Dorkis. Her oldest son, Miletos, watched her uneasily. I too watched. I had drifted into a strange indifference about my life. It was not, I thought, that I no longer loved Tuka—whatever that might mean. But I couldn't help her. The lethargy she'd fallen into wasn't guilt—she knew that all of us and none of us were guilty—and not anger except at the injustice of life itself. Something had snapped, in all of us; whatever it was that had held things together—some illusion upon which we'd agreed—had lost its power. For hours at a time I would wander vaguely about my business, entertaining the thought of going away somewhere, turning to philosophy or poetry or simply observing the seasons, maybe at Krete. Iona knew. When I mentioned the feeling, she spoke obliquely of thinking of going away somewhere herself. We tempted each other toward the idea that we'd go together, without hope of joy or permanence, merely seizing the moment without demanding much; but neither of us would express the temptation in words. Dorkis observed us, while playing with his children or tallying his accounts, and waited. Hamrah became a new man. While we drifted outward, slipping from each other, each of our selves breaking up like old floatage, Hamrah dug in like an anchor, became his own man. When we met at large parties, as we sometimes couldn't avoid doing, I found him a man profoundly convinced of all he said, all of which was wrong. "People do two things," he said, and raised two fingers. (I was across the room, half turned away.) "They *think* and they *feel*. When what people think goes against what they feel, feeling should be slapped unconscious. That's humanness. Think of wily Odysseus! That's what's made me what I am." He lifted his brown marble chin.

"And what do *you* do?" the lady at my elbow said.

"I'm a Seer," I said.

"Ah!" She raised her eyebrows. "Do you have visions?"

"Never," I said. "That's the difference between you common people and us Seers."

But I was lying, of course. I had a vision of old Klinias with his scraggly, yellow-red speckled beard and his sharp Adam's apple and his hairy, skinny legs, pausing on the mountain path to look myopically upward at the boulders beetling over us, and drawing their morality down for me. His eyes twinkled as he teased and lectured and comforted me. He loved me. And so, once, Solon had loved me, smiling at my youthful rigidity, boundlessly confident of my talent, it seemed, and as pleased by my faults as by my virtues. And effortlessly, without a flicker of thought, I had returned their love. Could I ever love anyone as simply and clearly as that again? Was it mere self-love—my unspeakable pleasure in happening to be myself—a pleasure I'd lost? The question was arrogant, of course. A man must study to make himself more like boulders or, say, garbage.

20   Peeker:

Everything's going from bad to worse. I begin to suspect that my master was right in abandoning hope long since. New divisions move out to the war every day—it's broken out on all sides of us now, north, south, east, west. We watch them lumber past in the valley, riding along the river, caravans stretching out mile on mile, the hoplites in front riding four abreast, naked except for their armor, their plumes, their streaming hair, and then after them the foot soldiers, the archers, the company of runners, and then the mulecarts and handcarts, the cooks, weaponsmiths, carriers, the pack animals, the herders with their wide herds of sheep and goats. The caravan's there when we look out in the morning, and it takes all day to pass. Who would have believed that the city could pull together such forces? Sometimes when a caravan's moving out it meets with another one moving in, wagon on wagon of wounded and dead, sick men shuffling and limping behind them, gashed, limping horses, and lines of half-starved men in chains. The two armies pass without a word, as far as you can tell from here, as remote as living men and ghosts. Meanwhile in the city there are fires day and night, and sporadic noises of rioting. Some god must have gone mad. There was an earth tremor day before yesterday. Perhaps it's Poseidon himself, master of all things that thunder and shake, who's gone mad. But I haven't told the worst of it. The Spartans have introduced a new horror: mass executions. According to

Agathon, no man has ever been executed for a political crime in the whole history of Athens. Here in Sparta they herd a whole crowd of Helots, gray-faced, bruised, sickly—and there are women and children and old people among the crowd—herd them into a sloping field and shower them with arrows, and then when none of them are moving anymore, a few soldiers walk among the corpses with swords and finish off any they find still breathing. We can't see it from here, and no one tells us about it, of course, but Agathon says it's happening, and he seems to know. There's a look he gets—as if his spirit has abandoned his body, leaving it old and indifferent as a mountain. He's going to make me a Seer, he says. I've believed it sometimes, but not at those times when that thing comes over him, that deadly, heatless clarity of Apollo's light. There's some secret he's forgotten, some trick to it, something maybe that he found in that book he used to have, or says he had: I never saw it, and it's a hard thing to believe. Who would ever have lost such a thing if he had it? He stands at the door with his hands behind his back and his legs aspraddle, watching the guards lead another crowd of prisoners away—to their death, I finally understand; that much you can see in the guards' eyes— and his stance, his face, have no expression, not pity or disgust or fear or anything: he's like a man at a play he's seen five hundred times. "What do the gods think?" I asked him once. He tipped his head. A tic came over him, or two of them, one on each cheek, trembling like two different zones of lightning in a night sky, and he gave a sort of apologetic, fearful smile. "The gods never die," he said. "It makes a difference." It was evening—twilight—when the earthquake came. Agathon was in bed. He hasn't been feeling up to snuff lately. As soon as the table began to shake and the noise started—a terrible, vaguely human noise like the whole world groaning—the old man popped up on one elbow quick as a puppet, eyes wide, mouth open, ears cocked

—I swear it—like a dog's. "It's an earthquake," I said.
But I'd misunderstood his look. It wasn't fear, or not
merely that. "It's come," he said. "What's come?" He
said, "The plague." He was crazy. It sent a shiver
through me to see him staring there, out of his mind.
He couldn't explain to me later what he meant. When I
pressed him he said only—crossly, impatiently—
"Plagues are Apollo's doing. Go ask him." He wanted
to get back to his writing. That's all he does these days,
write and write. I can't even read what he puts down,
though he says it's all for my benefit. He's fallen into
using some obscure grammata I can't make heads nor
tails of. I said, "But earthquakes come from Poseidon."
He refused to think about it. "Tuka," he said, eyeing
me narrowly, "suppose I was wrong from the beginning. Suppose I misread, exaggerated trifles. . . ." I realized he was once more out of his mind. Senile. My
grandmother used to flick on and off like that. He
shouted, "Look out!" I ducked. But there was nothing
visible to duck from. He did that once before, when he
was having a nightmare. He told me afterward that he'd
had some friend or something that was killed by a
horse. It scared me, this time, hearing him yell, "Look
out," when he was supposedly awake. I called for the
guard, but no one came. It took him about five minutes
to come back to himself.

And then today—from bad to worse, as I was saying
—the ephors came to collect our writing. I gave them a
list of enemies of Agathon's; it was all I could think of
that might be of any use. There were four ephors this
time, but I had no chance to talk to them, because of a
circumstance. They brought my mother. I can hardly
stand to describe it. Her hair has turned as white as
snow and she can hardly walk, her knees are so bad.
She could hardly talk, either. She just stood at the bars
hanging onto them, crying and crying. It came over me
like a spring avalanche that Agathon and I are doomed
and my mother knows it. They may have told her, who

knows? Anyway, all she said was, "Oh, Demodokos, poor Demodokos! What's this world coming to?" Sorrow rushed up in me and flooded my chest, hearing my own name, my own mother's way of saying it. I've been an idiot, hating her all these years, or anyway resenting her, or whatever. A boy's mother is the most precious thing in his life. People should tell people about that when they're young, so that when their parents get old and poorly they don't have to be full of remorse at having thrown away the most precious thing the gods have ever given them. "Poor Mama," I said, over and over, patting her fingers. I couldn't even put my arms around her, though I tried maybe three different times to reach through the bars and back in around her shoulders. I couldn't even see her, in fact, because tears were streaming from my eyes like waterfalls from caves. I felt as if my heart would break, the way all she could say was my name and "What's this world coming to?" All her life she's been telling people all these useful sayings like "A penny saved is a penny earned" and "Nobody loves a sluggard" and "Zeus helps them that helps theirselves." She was a nuisance, a chain snarled around my feet, but she was something you could lean on, solid as a wall. But now here I was, sobbing and sobbing and patting her fingers, saying, "Now now! Poor Mama! Now now!"

When they asked Agathon for what he'd written he didn't give them anything. He said all he had was some drawings which it would embarrass them to show them. You could see they thought he was playing some prank, and he swore a number of solemn oaths to convince them, which he didn't.

But he learned some news. I didn't hear it at the time, I was so distraught about poor Mother, but he told me after they left. The ephor that hadn't come before was an old man that Agathon used to see often at Lykourgos's house, and because he was a friend and elderly, less rigid than most of Lykourgos's men—so Agathon says—he let my master in on something. Before Lykourgos left for Delphi, he called a meeting of the whole city. In what was for him a very long speech, Lykourgos reviewed all his laws and discussed the extent to which his reformation of the State had proved successful. He told them that he now thought everything reasonably well established, both for the happiness and the virtue of the State, but he said there was still one thing to be done, a thing of the greatest possible importance—a thing so important he thought it not fit to impart until he had consulted the oracle. In the meantime, he asked that they observe all his laws without the slightest alteration, despite all pressures of riot, war, and natural catastrophe, until his return from Delphi, and then he would act as the god directed him. Agathon says the ephor says they all agreed and wished him well, but that wasn't enough. He insisted that the two kings, the senators, and all the commons take an oath that they would abide by and maintain the established form of polity until he, Lykourgos, should return. They did as he asked.

A strange business. What has Lykourgos got up his sleeve? I wonder.

Another strange business, and worse than strange: It appears that we're to rot here in prison until Lykourgos himself either releases or condemns us. Considering the oath he made them take, I have a feeling we may be here longer than we like. It's better than execution, of course. But then, if he himself had us arrested—Lykourgos, who seemed to be our hope . . .

I witnessed the end of the conversation myself. It was so disgusting that even my mama's grief couldn't distract me from it. Agathon thanked the old man for his kindness and said he would gladly pay him—the ephor—if only he had anything to give. "Woe is me," said Agathon, "I have nothing left but my good name!" The ephor took it very soberly, though the other three ephors looked slightly suspicious of Agathon's sincerity, and when the old ephor shook Agathon's hand there were tears in Agathon's eyes. Agathon looked to me a little ashamed of himself, but as usual he blundered on, making it worse. "I only regret that my children are not here to see me in my misery! It would serve as an excellent lesson to them, to trust not in the things of this world, neither power nor position, nor puissance nor pelf, nor property nor politics, nor puberty nor pussy." The ephor looked at him somewhat oddly (Agathon was weeping rivers now) and they shook hands again. The tall ephor—the one I talked to the other times—had his fingertips over his mouth, studying my master.

Dear gods, please in the next life make Agathon a cow.

21 Agathon:

Love poetry, like anything else, is simultaneously a cause and an effect. The lover writes because the emotion that charges every line (if the poetry's decent) will give him no rest until he's set it down—"immortalized it," he likes to think—and when he's set it down the emotion becomes more clear, more pure, than it ever was in Nature. Art is more dignified than life, and, to just that degree, more deathlike. Insofar as it's able, the poet's mind rejects any word, any image or subtlety of rhythm or rhyme less grand than what he's seen in the finest poetry he knows—the flesh-and-blood woman he loves deserves at least the best he can offer her—and so, systematically, he distorts the real experience toward what it perhaps would have been if it had happened between, say, Odysseus and Penelope; and then, rereading, he adopts and remembers the experience in its transmuted form, builds upon it as though it had happened, and, strange to say, becomes a far nobler lover than he was before, still day by day casting his net of words ahead of him to trap some finer vision. He shows the poems to his lady, who sees her admirer in a new light, clearer and paler than heaven itself, and, more important, sees herself too in a new light, and so transcends her humanness, becomes in life the once airy, visionary figure of the poems. All to the good, I am tempted to say. But I do not think the light that illuminates lovers' verse is the light of omniscient Apollo. The lover remains, for all his fine words, a hungry, fallible, dissatisfied child, badly in need of a fallible, all-forgiving mother; and the lady remains, for all her borrowed dignity and green incandescence, a girl child groping in alarm through a forest, in desperate search for a father. The light of Apollo (I give you my word as his official Seer) gives comfort, resignation, perhaps even peace, but not hope. Visions, like humble pack mules, exist in time, continually relapsing, transmogrifying, forever eluding the stretched-out hand as they guide the heart, by subtle, labyrinthine ways, to the chill and mist of the tomb. It's the same, of course, with the poetry of Patriotism. Devotion to one's country, like any other pure emotion, is bloodless art, no healthy business of common mortals!—an affair for gray Phaiakians.

I taught Iona writing. Merely an excuse for almost daily visits. Occasionally when I went there, always around midmorning, Dorkis would be there. He pretended, not only to me but to himself and Iona as well, that nothing was wrong. Nothing was, in a sense. He was a man comfortable with risks. He loved her; we knew that. And he was fond of me; we knew that too. There was nothing more to be said: he laid no claims on life. He told me once that to become an expert swimmer, a man had to try himself sooner or later in deep and dangerous waters. If he survived, it was worth it. If he didn't, well, the gods hand down no guarantees. There are those who are shocked by such opinions. Old men rocking in their grandchildren's gardens, their knees wrapped in comforters, their shawls around their heads—old men who drink herbs and observe the elements like worried sparrows—may cough in horror or squeak like bats in righteous scorn of the idea that taking needless risks is a desirable thing, the bedrock of character. But there are many gods, many truths, as Dorkis used to say. This truth was his, and whether he was worried or not—I couldn't tell—he accepted its demands. I would visit his house and he would welcome me like a favorite brother. We would talk, the three of us—very interesting talks: on neighbors, politics, religion—and then eventually, he would withdraw to the room where he worked his accounts, or he would ride away with his oldest son and an assistant or two to consult with his cooks, repair some breakdown, resolve some dispute, or inspect the farms and storage units which provided the food for the communal halls, and Iona and I would go out to the garden to sit on the secluded, rustic bench overlooking her flowering herbs and roses, and run through our masquerade of education. Sometimes, when I found her alone, we would talk in the house, after the writing lesson. I would sit on the rug with my back against the wall, my crutch on the floor beside me, and she would sit on the pillowed couch with her legs tucked under her, and we would talk about our childhoods. I mentioned, once, my brother's death, how I closed up like a catatonic's fist, and how Tuka later calmed me. And I told her about Konon.

He was, like me, a member of the merchant class. His father pretended to be religious, but Konon saw through it. He himself believed only in substance; if he worshiped anything, he said, it was that. We sat in Klinias's hut once, Klinias over at his table, reading in the book that later came into my hands, Konon and I on the floor. Konon hugged his knees, biceps bulging, his dark eyes narrowed, and stared into the fire. (He was short, square, big-shouldered, very tan. Often he wouldn't say a word for hours, even days; but then something would set him off and he'd talk rapidly and aggressively, asserting the most outlandish things, as it seemed to me—how cloth retained magic as long as wood, how slavery was good because it liberated sex—until suddenly, as if bored, he would break off and sink back into silence.) "My poor old mother," he said, "had a statue of Priapos in our flower garden. I remember how she would kneel there on a spring day with a trowel in her hand and a basket of flowers by her knee. She believed Priapos made things grow." He flashed a grim smile, white as the moon, and popped his knuckles. "If it was true, the god must have had some grudge against my mother. Everything she planted would wither and die as if her fingertips were poison. She'd wring her fingers and try again, praying to old Priapos harder than before." He laughed, as if angrily, like metal striking stone. "She prayed to Pallas Athena too. She prayed that Athena would purify Father's mind and make him faithful to her. But Athena was off fucking Hermes."

Klinias glanced over at us but said nothing. He hadn't quite heard.

"So do you believe in the gods," I said, "or don't you?"

He kept staring at the fire. "I believe in the stars," he said, sententious. "They seem to be honest and reasonable. I believe in rivers, mountains, sheep, cattle, horses, gold, and silver. If there are gods ruling them, those gods are no doubt decent enough. But if there are gods directing human affairs, they're either vicious or insane. It's better to believe there are no gods, be satisfied with substance." His eyes were bright as a madman's. "Listen! The gods give you hope—they tantalize you with it, and then they step on your neck. Crunch! The last time I prayed was to Zeus, the night my mother died. My father prayed too, full of pompous moaning and hooting, but he knew she was dying. He expected it. It may be he wasn't too sorry. She was a nag. So my hope is substance. You ever notice a rich man invoking the gods? Who needs the gods if he's rich? He's got gold, slaves to count it for him, and flatterers to tell him how happy he is. If he's a whoremonger, his wife stays with him, for the fattening food and the bows people give her. Listen. Everything on earth is substance. All the rest is drunkenness and illusion. Even ideas, they're things grown into the brain like warts, or they're scratches made on a scroll by somebody's stylus. You know what death is? An abandoned body, you think—the soul flown to Hades? Shit! Death is a broken machine. Some muscle quits, the heart, say, and the rest of the muscles go limp, including the eyes." He was rigid now, staring like a statue. "And religion, that's a machine too: a mechanical system of words and howls and lifted arms that you start up to comfort some fool and abandon as soon as he's comforted. Politics, honor, loyalty—all machines."

Klinias looked up, roughly in Konon's direction. "How do you account for the universe, boy?"

"Like the Akropolis," Konon said. "Somebody built it. Some dead man."

There was a time when he meant to take Tuka from me. He meant all his life to marry money, the shining hope of his corpuscular world. He might have gotten her. He was handsome enough, and his bitterness made him attractive, in a way, though moroseness and remorse, my special gifts, have always beaten bitterness in the end. But Konon was rough, too eager for Tuka's substance in the clinches.

"What ever happened to him?" Iona asked. Like all her questions, it had some overtone meaning in it I couldn't penetrate.

"He turned completely to substance," I said. "He died."

She waited, frowning a little. She had something to say. I could feel the pressure of it in her drawn lips, the muscles of her jaw, her tightly pulled-back hair.

"He tried to assassinate Solon," I said. "He was a grown man then. He thought it would be his in with the Athenian rich. It might have been, if he'd succeeded. They'd given Solon more power than they ever meant to, and they couldn't get it back except by ripping him off and throwing the country into civil war. There were some who believed it was worth it, and they supported Konon's plan. When he failed they joined the others in condemning him. You never saw such looks of righteousness!"

Iona looked over my head, thinking, charged like a sky full of thunderclouds. "How come he failed?"

"He made a mistake," I said. "He told some friend."

I could see her mind coming to it—flashing to it, drawing back, at last accepting it. She asked, "You?"

I nodded.

That, too, she thought about, her mind racing. I couldn't tell whether she was racing over her own life or mine or something else entirely, and I couldn't tell whether or not she was going to forgive me for it. I hung on her judgment like a child on its mother's, the ominous father in the background, threatening or harmless, depending on her. She said:

"But what made him tell you? Didn't he know how you felt about Solon?"

"Oh, he knew, all right. But we were friends. We'd grown up together, more or less. We'd had fights and things—sometimes bitter ones—but . . ." I stopped, watching her. The look of intense concentration, some curious excitement and perhaps suffering, distracted me, made me feel I was missing something. Did she *want* me to be guilty, unforgivably wicked? "How can I explain it? We were like brothers. Closer. We'd talked all night many times, lying in our bunk in Klinias's hut, looking at the dying embers of the fire. We knew things nobody living knew, except Klinias—things from the book. We'd run away together once. I stole something once, and he lied for me. We'd slept with girls together. Konon *knew* me. He knew me as well as I knew myself. I tried to talk him out of his treason—I *told* him that was what it was—but Konon had made his mind up. He asked me to swear I wouldn't tell. If I wouldn't swear, he'd change his plan, do the thing some other way. I racked my brains for a way out, and finally I gave him my word. He knew what that meant to me, in those days. He felt safe."

Her eyes were still intense, tearing at me. "But why did he *insist on telling you?*"

"Because," I said. And then understood with a jolt. "Because he wanted me to love him no matter what, love him absolutely, like a one-man dog, and prove it."

"And yet you told."

I nodded.

She closed her eyes. "Poor Agathon." After a long time she smiled and met my eyes steadily, as if to say more than her words could tell me. "You were right."

I shook my head, looking away, panicky. I'd seen how she talked to men at parties, as if each man she talked to was the finest man in the world. I'd seen how she could fall in with strangers, make them open up their lives to her in minutes. I'd seen her dance with men at parties. ("I only let other men kiss me on the cheek," she said once. "You know that." But how could I? I wasn't at all the parties.) She'd had brothers. She knew a man's pulse from across the room.

"I was 'right,'" I said. "It would be pleasant to think so. But I did it by impulse. Who knows what the reasons were? It may easily have been jealousy—of Tuka, even Klinias. It may have been resentment: I could never beat his damned arguments about substance, but here I could beat him once and for all, making Patriotism or loyalty to Solon or God knows what the answer to all his materialism. Or maybe it was ego. I could make my character into something by behaving as if I were it. Or the will to power. I would strike down the traitor and win the applause of Athens."

"That's all dumb." I'd made her uneasy, missed the point.

"So you say. Maybe so. All I know is, I gave the warning by impulse, and instantly regretted it, though for two whole days I didn't tell him I'd warned them. When the time he'd decided on came, the guards appeared out of nowhere and disarmed him. Konon looked at me and his face twisted like a monkey's, trying to smile."

The room became still. She looked at me, full of some feeling I couldn't read. I tried to think what I really felt about my betrayal of Konon and found I felt nothing. She seemed to love me: love, or else the joy of conquest, shone on her clear as an aureole. If she loved me, was it as an amused mother, or as my own soul's image, or as an infinitely tolerant, weary goddess? A queer image passed through my mind, of locking her up in a room someplace as Sardinians lock up their gold.

"What are you thinking?" I said.

She laughed, an explosion of the churning thought I couldn't guess. She swung her legs off the couch and leaned forward, elbows on her knees. "I think we're incredibly different people," she said, "and incredibly similar."

"How?" I said.

"Have you got about nine million years?"

I, too, laughed. But what I wanted was an answer, final and sure as a thunderbolt. "How are we different?"

Iona retreated to the ironic mask she knew how to work so well. "All ways," she said, turning the corners of her mouth down. "Do you collect chickens' feet?"

"Do you?" I said.

She laughed, turning down her mouth again, then relenting, smiling and frowning. "We'd better not talk about it," she said. She came down to the floor beside me and kissed my cheek.

But I was thinking about the brothers she rarely talked about, and the father. She knew all the tricks. I was jelly. She knew how men long to be superior, masculine; knew how timid they are about advances, how shattered by a No. She could tease me to the limit she wanted to go and could ease me away so that I felt not rejected but mighty as a god. It was too perfect. I wasn't worth it. I was her toy. But my God how

I loved her and wished it were real! But what if it *was?*

"What was your father like?" I said.

She sat on her feet and thought, then began talking softly. In the mountain village where they lived there was a river with a strong current. There were large, sharp rocks. They swam there, and he looked on with stern approval. He was fierce as a lion all his life, but he wasn't bitter until after Iona's mother had left him, when the children were grown, to go off with some prophet from the far northern hills. Iona's father had become, then, an angry, misanthropic old man.

I put my hand on hers. "Are you like him?" I asked.

"Ridiculous!" she said, laughing.

Perhaps she wasn't, I couldn't be sure, but she carried his image like a carved stone in her heart.

"I have to go," I said.

After a moment she nodded, a little stiffly.

I climbed up my crutch into the room. "I've stayed too long," I said. "Forgive me." I offered her my hand to help her up and, after a second's hesitation, she accepted it. She walked with me to the door, saying nothing. Was she angry? I leaned on the doorframe as I always did when leaving her, my hand on the door but my chest undecided, and I watched her face, wondering if I would kiss her. She did the same, though perhaps thinking about something different, leaning on the other doorframe. She watched my face as I watched hers. It would have been better if we'd worked out some ritual, I thought, or settled the matter by going to bed. But our metaphysics or something was against it. At last she came to me and put her arms around me. "You *are* a good man, Agathon."

"Who knows?" I kissed her. As usual, it wasn't enough. I held her close, moving my hands on her smooth small back and then her hips. Then, as usual, I paused and we waited for the sign that neither of us would give alone, true democrats, and it was over for another day. As always when I left her, the streets were beautiful. The flowers, the birds, the sunlight were out of their minds.

It was a terrible time, for Tuka. I never told her of my visits to Iona, not so much from cowardice, I think, though I never deny my cowardice, as from a wish to spare her unnecessary grief. But she knew about them, or some of them. When our families were together Iona would sometimes show knowledge of things she ought not to have known, and Tuka would ask questions, casually, lightly, and Iona, as casually as possible, looking guilty as hell, would mention that I had dropped by. It made Tuka furious and a little frightened, though she wouldn't show that to Dorkis or Iona. "Agathon, they're practically *slaves*," she said. It was the worst she could say, and my total indifference to their accidental and irrelevant condition frustrated Tuka to the edge of violence. "What do you think people are *saying* about you?" she said. "You must be insane!" But she knew, too, my indifference to the nonsense people say. She loved society, the conversation of her own kind, as the saying goes; as for me, Sparta was my hermitage from all that. There were none of her own kind here, or mine. The Spartans, whom I thought less than human, were our supposed superiors. The few Athenians in town were black-market pigs. She blinked all that, playing aristocratic lady in a dung heap she changed by her imagination to elegant old Athens. Why she'd come with me in the first place I couldn't say. She almost didn't. When the carriage arrived to take us away from Athens, she sat in her room and refused to move. I gave her ten minutes and went out to the carriage to wait. At last she came, still furious, weeping. But in time she accepted her life in Sparta. She made our three rooms in the palace a fair imitation of Athens, and she created, in them, with the help of her culinary skill and her harp, an imitation of Athenian society. It was temporary, she understood. What stories we'd have to tell when we went home! Even my consort with Helots was acceptable in those terms. And she did not actively dislike the friends I made among the Helots. In her generous moments—that is, when she felt secure in her total possession of me—she could understand that they were merely victims: she herself might be a slave, if Sparta were ever to capture Athens. And she, as an Athenian, had known Korinthian slaves who had once been aristocratic masters. In fact, she had very much liked Iona and Dorkis, at first. Iona might have been her closest friend, if I hadn't gotten involved. Now she was afraid to leave the house, for fear Iona might appear; afraid to let me go off by myself in the morning, for fear I might go visit her.

It was a strange, irrational hatred, and she knew it. I did not love Tuka less than I had before. When I woke up in the morning and looked at her, with sunlight falling over her shoulders and glittering in her blue-black hair, she seemed the most valuable thing in the world to me. I'd press closer to her warmth, nestling up to her firm, broad-beamed buttocks and sliding my hand around her waist to her breast. Then for a long time I'd lie half awake and half asleep, all our lives since childhood closed together, secure and safe, as if the room we lay in were not mere physical space but a bubble of time. We would hear the children's voices in the next room, and the bubble of time stretched outward to include them: my son, absent-minded and quiet and gentle as myself (or gentle as I liked to imagine myself), kneeling by the seashore shaping huge figures out of sand and stone; our daughter, clever and sly and as beautiful as Tuka, hoarding her treasures in Tuka's cast-off woolen purse, or climbing some tree to branches higher than any of the boys had nerve for. It was absurd that Tuka should doubt that I loved her—loved all of them.

Sometimes we'd ride to the hills north of Sparta and would sit on some cliff looking down while the horses grazed behind us. On a clear day you could see for a hundred miles.

She said, once, "Do you ever think of Thaletes?"

I smiled to keep her from seriousness. "Never."

"He was never happy except when he was facing death. *That* was existence, he thought."

"This is existence," I said. I nodded toward the city far below us, miles away.

"I know. Standing back from things. Seeing where you are."

I glanced at her strong, fine legs. "I meant beauty," I said.

"That too, I suppose." She put her hand on mine. "But you can't see that either unless you're back from it." She looked at me sideways for a moment. "You, for instance. I forget I love you until someone starts stealing you from me."

"Nobody's stealing me," I said.

She squeezed my hand. "Damn right."

After a while she said, "Poor old horse." It was our word for Lykourgos. "What does he do for pleasure?"

"Bites himself, I guess."

She laughed. "And other people, yes. And yet I admire him. He knows what he wants."

"Like you," I said.

Her fingers drew away from my hand to pull some grass. "Little good it does me."

Him either, I could have said. I tried to imagine Lykourgos in love, mournfully, hopelessly in love with his brother's wife and convinced that she was merely toying with him, a woman everybody knew was loose, and as beautiful, people say, as he was ugly. Was Kharilaus his son? No matter, of course. It was all a long long time ago, irrelevant.

Her face was drawn, as if someone had stolen her earring. She continued pulling grass, casually, grimly, as though it were the dead Iona's hair.

I sighed, faintly grieved and weary of broodings. "One must try to want what's possible, Tuka."

"I know." She wouldn't look up. "Is she better than me in bed?"

"Tuka, Tuka," I said, growing wearier and wearier. "Whatever people may say in Athens, the world is not made exclusively of beds."

"But tell me. I have a right to know. Is she better?"

"I haven't slept with her."

"You're a liar." She glanced at me, and I shook my head. She closed her fist hard on a pebble beside her knee, as if to hurl it at me, but she didn't. "All the worse, then. How can mere human flesh compete with some glorious airy vision?"

"Tuka, I swear by all the gods—"

"Don't bother, boy." She stood up abruptly and started for her horse. She walked like a Spartan soldier girl, her whole body hard as nails except for her lips, her belly, her breasts. I loved her. Why was she blind to it?

"Do you want the truth or don't you?" I yelled.

She stopped, turned, put her hands on her hips. "If you sleep with her, I'll kill you."

I raised my hand slowly and kissed the fingertips, Solon's gesture, saying good-bye to life. She sank to her knees suddenly, as if the strength had gone out of her legs, and covered her face, crying. I only half believed it. "Why can't you ever *talk* to me?" she screamed. "Why can't you see when I *need* you?"

"So I see it. You need me. Everybody needs me, even Lykourgos. It's absurd."

But she was crying, her muscles growing tight, and I was worried: it was a thing I'd seen before. I went to her and put my arms around her, but her muscles stayed tight. Her face was as stiff as a mask.

"Tuka, listen. I love you. Listen!" It was Konon's word: *Listen.* The recognition checked me for a second. Everything I said, everything I ever did was somebody else's, not mine. An empty ritual, nothingness. But I said, "Listen, Tuka, *please*. I love you." It was true, probably, yet I knew I could have said it as easily, and as honestly—and *would* say it, if the need arose—to Iona, or Dorkis, or my children, or Konon. And I could have said it as convincingly to Lykourgos's stooge Alkander if ever some still-warm ember of humanness in him cried out in need of me. And yet I did love her, so far as I could see. Was I unfit, or was it the world that was? But she was rigid as stone, and all the time my mind played games I was rubbing her back and arms, kissing her temples, whispering to her, like an actor. I summoned up tears. At last, all at once, as if something had broken, she relaxed, crying again. I went on whispering a while longer, wondering how I was going to get both her and the horses home, since Tuka was in no shape to ride. "I love you, love you, love you," I said. I would stake the horses, I decided, and send someone back for them.

I told Iona I could see no more of her, it was unhealthy. Luckily, I had work to occupy me. Lykourgos had a stack of documents for me to copy, his new labor and reprisals code. He used me, I suppose, not because he lacked scribes of his own but because, as always when the thing he proposed lacked humanness, he wanted my flaccid Ionian reaction. (In those days he still put his laws on parchment.) Not that I would be likely to change his mind; I knew that by now. I played out my role of righteous indignation not for righteousness' sake anymore, but for art's. To tell the grim truth, I could see no dignified alternative. I might stomp and bray and disembogue for Athens in a great show of outrage, but it would be un empty gesture: I would change nothing in Sparta that way either, and I knew I couldn't face without a sneer or an obscene giggle the people at home who praised my righteous noise. I might strike out at Lykourgos—kill him, say, or make seditious speeches in the marketplace—but who but a fool would believe me if I struck out now, after years of silence, even bootlicking? I wouldn't believe myself. I could do it, I was sure. I could as easily shuck off my dignity as Solon does his, but I would know all the while that I was acting not from noble principle but to appear a man of principle, or to please my old mother, or to break the dull routine of life, or for some other silly reason. There was, it seemed to me, a certain moronic virtue in giving Lykourgos my honest reactions to his monstrous ideas. Until one thinks of something better to do, one should do what one is doing. "Carry on!" as Solon would say. "Love, carry on!"

Two weeks later, I met Iona by accident on the street. She looked shocked, horrified, when she saw me, and she instantly turned away with a squeezed-shut, wounded, stubborn look, as though my face were a wolfish attack on her. I had known that my breaking off with her would hurt her, but I hadn't guessed that the pain would last so long. Her look filled me with confusion. I did love her; she knew that. And not seeing her was right; she knew that too. I was not to blame for her misery: life itself was. Apollo's seduction. Poseidon's stupid restlessness. Yet she was miserable, so that I, too, was miserable. To continue the separation was empty righteousness—love reduced to arithmetic: Tuka's love minus Iona's love equals Virtue, three dead crows wired to a fence. But to end the separation was nonsense too. Tuka would be hurt and eventually, no doubt, Dorkis. I walked half the day, trying to make up some kind of reason for action. Around midafternoon I saw a donkey beaten by a screaming slave. A troop of Spartan soldiers walked past, eyes steadily front. Were such things omens? I concluded that the world was insane.

I went to her house that night. The door was unbolted. I went in. She was sitting on the floor, laboriously copying from a scroll, a page of Solon's opinions that I'd given her weeks ago. She looked up in alarm, opened her mouth to speak, then closed it again. I tried to think of something I might say I'd left at her house and had come for, but nothing came to me. I stood.

"I thought I'd never see you again," she said.

"Not possible," I said. I realized for the first time that my bad leg was on fire from all that walking.

"Is Dorkis home?" I asked absurdly, maybe pretending I'd come to see him.

"He's in there, working." She moved her head in the direction of his workroom, prepared to lead me there.

"He works too hard," I said.

There was a silence. I went over to her and, with difficulty, got down on the floor beside her and studied the scroll. I made no comment. She expected none. At last, after a deep breath, she said, "Well!"

I smiled.

"How's Tuka?"

"Fine."

"You still get along with Lykourgos?"

"Like brothers."

"Good. I'm so happy for you."

Another long silence. Dorkis came in from his workroom and, when he saw me, smiled, holding out his arms. "Agathon!" The lamplight played over his shoulders and head as if he'd brought it with him.

"You've been working late again," I said. "You'll ruin your goddamn eyes."

"You're right." He laughed and rubbed his hands like an innkeeper. "It's time for wine. —Iona?"

She nodded, and he ran in place, the way athletes do before a meet, showing his eagerness to serve, then went, bent over like a sprinter, to the next room for wine and cups. When he came back, swooping in with the cups all in one hand, the pitcher in the other, he poured wine for each of us—his own puissant, meticulously cured honey brew—then sat down on the couch with his cup, beaming. He talked of Lykourgos's latest scheme, the brotherhoods. From now on each table at the eating halls would be made up of a company of "brothers," four older men, six younger men, chosen by the vote of the whole company. The old men would train the young men's wits, teaching them sententious discourse and seemly humor. A bad joke would be punished by a bite on the thumb.

We laughed, all three of us, but Dorkis was looking above our heads, like a contestant assessing a vault while he jokes with admirers. The Spartans were getting to him more and more. It was not exactly that they shook his calm, you would have said, but they were there; increasingly there, like omens.

"All this will pass," I said.

He smiled. "In five hundred years."

"Nonsense," Iona said. "Don't be pessimistic!"

"Ah well," he said, and smiled again. He fell silent.

"It's a great adventure, Solon used to say," I said. He looked vague, so I added: "Sparta. Who would have thought human nature would let it get so far?"

"We overestimate human nature," he said. "I think about it sometimes, in horror." He smiled. Horror, like everything else, he had learned to duck, shrug off, accept in peace. "You get in the habit of thinking you do things for certain reasons, but you don't. All you can do is act, somehow, and pray."

"You think the gods hear you?" I asked him, non-committal.

He grinned again. "*Some*body has to be listening!"

"But suppose they're not," Iona said, curiously feisty.

He gave a laugh and stretched out his hand toward her, palm up, his sharp black eyes on her face. "Are *you* ready to take life on without them?"

She said nothing—pouting, it seemed to me.

I looked at the ceiling, philosophical, maybe a trifle

woozy from the wine. "But what do the gods *do* exactly, Dorkis?"

He thought. "Did you ever do anything in your life that wasn't by impulse?" he asked.

I frowned, troubled by where he was going to lead me. "Never," I said. Thinking: *Don't say it, Dorkis. For God's sake!* Solon's kind of indignity I could take.

"And where do you think impulses come from?" he asked, gently triumphant. His absolute and simple faith filled the room like autumn light, like a sea breeze. Even when his ideas were crazy, the man had sophrosyne, as they used to call it in the old days. There are men in this world—wizards, witches, people like Lykourgos—who spread anger, or doubt, or self-pity, or the cold stink of cynicism, wherever they walk: the sky darkens over their heads, the grass withers under their feet, and, downwind of them, ships perish at sea. And then there are men, here and there, like Dorkis. God only knows what to make of them. Their ideas are ludicrous, when you look at them. Peasant ideas. Childlike. But what tranquility!

"That's very interesting," I said, resisting his mysterious effect on me—from guilt, maybe; my lust for his wife—and I pretended to think about it. "Do bad impulses come from the gods, or just good ones?"

He wasn't put off. Benevolent. "There's a sense in which there are many many gods," he said, "and they're not all in agreement. But what we call good, with our little minds . . ." His eyes snapped away. "There's a sense in which nothing is evil," he said, calm as spring. "To certain people, everything that happens in the world is holy."

"Nonsense," Iona said. It was her favorite word. "Is slavery holy? Is Lykourgos?"

He shrugged and looked down, unable to argue with her, but not because he was beaten.

"It's not as easy as you think, Iona," I said. "Dorkis could be right. Suffering's bad, but sometimes the effects of suffering . . ." Why did I say that? Guilt again? Defense of his thought because his wife's smile filled my mind from wall to wall?

"That's dumb," she said. "Tell me that after you've ended people's suffering. *Then* I'll believe you." She drained her cup and held it out to Dorkis. He filled it for her. I too took more, though I shouldn't. She said, "What people like us need in Sparta is men. All we get is pious philosophers. If you were men you'd act first and then make up theories."

"You sound like Lykourgos," I said.

"But it's true." She was petulant. In fact angry. She even looked like Lykourgos now.

"Maybe," Dorkis said. "But dead men don't make up theories." He grinned, palms up in a helpless gesture, as if accepting human impotence along with the gods' other gifts.

"Better a living fool than a dead philosopher," I said. A dullard's observation, needless to say. Did I sound ironic, shifting loyalties?

She ignored me. "It *is* practical. We could overthrow them. You personally, Dorkis. We control all the food, all the clothes, all the work—everything that supports their life—and you have all the contacts."

And why, I wondered, was *she* suddenly so full of revolution? It was a thing she hadn't mentioned for a long time. Did his calm force her to thoughtless opposition? Because of me? Because of guilt?

His eyes widened and he laughed. "Iona, you're crazy!"

It hit me that this was the first time she'd mentioned her theory to Dorkis. I wished she hadn't.

"Do you realize what would happen to us if we failed?" he said. "You're simply crazy." His eyes were full of light, a husband's pleasure in the girlish foolishness of a now more than ever precious wife. Yes, she could work men. He would have second thoughts on the scheme. Inevitable as sunset.

"It's true," I said. "Crazy as a loon. A pity."

She said nothing. We drank. It was late now. I should have left long ago. At last Dorkis got up, grinned, and announced he was going to bed.

"I'll be along," Iona said.

I sat still, rubbing my sore leg and casting about for reasons to go or stay. He waved and left us.

We both sat in silence for a long time after that. At last she rolled up the scroll and her copy and tossed them up onto the couch. She lay on her side with her head on her hand and looked at me. Nothing moved but the lamp flame, flitting in and out through the wall paintings, making the stiff leaves and artificial flowers of Iona's decorations quiver and stir as if alive. No sound came in from the street. "I never knew two weeks could be so long," she said. "Was it long for you?"

"I kept busy, helping Lykourgos."

She laughed. A fine laugh like a girl's. "I really believe it."

I put my hand on hers and she smiled, shaking her head as if in disbelief. "You dear, good man," she said.

"Not necessarily good," I said.

"Everything's good—holy, in fact. I just learned."

"And you believe it?"

She lay back and looked at the ceiling. "It's sad to find that a relationship you thought was very close and beautiful is not what you . . . imagined. I ached a lot, this last two weeks, and Dorkis never had an inkling. I thought we always knew each other's feelings." She was aching now. We'd switched again: I the father, she the little girl.

"He knew, all right," I said.

She shook her head.

"What could he have done? Of course he knew!"

"No." There were tears in her eyes, and I was

startled. She loved him more than I'd admitted to myself, and I was jealous.

"So he missed it," I said. "So he's only another damn human."

She reached up to touch my face and then, as if by impulse, drew me down to her, kissing me. "I know."

I'd had too much wine. I could hardly focus her face. Even so, she was beautiful—as beautiful, in her separate way, as Tuka was. I had some vague thought about Dorkis's conflicting gods, but I was too foggy to concentrate. I'd stayed too late, yes. There was no possibility now of hiding the visit from Tuka. I no longer cared. It was impossible to serve all the gods. Ride it out like a bird. I remembered the strange madness that had come over Tuka, the rigidity of every muscle, and I was grieved, hopeless. But Iona's mouth tasted of wine, and the flesh of her hip under my fingertips was soft, naked under the loose robe.

"It's strange that I can do this to Dorkis," I said, brushing my lips across her cheek. "In theory, I'm an honorable man."

"You don't understand him," she said very softly. She said nothing after that for a long time. Then, wistfully, "Do you think he's lying awake, full of jealousy, suffering?"

"I don't know," I said.

"Would you, in his place?" A whisper.

"No," I said, but doubtfully. Then: "Maybe."

"Tuka would," she said. She kissed my cheek. "You're her life. I wonder if you can call it love at all, what she feels for you."

"I don't know." I tried to think. Lying in her arms was like lying half asleep and half awake in the bottom of a big, safe boat. Her low, soft voice was as comforting as the click of oars or the thud of small waves against the hull, quiet as a heartbeat. It was not just the wine, this sensation of endless peaceful floating, fathoms of dark sea yawning below me, bottomless kingdom. I'd often felt the same with Tuka, the strange peace of the child in its first calm sea, or the peace of the grave. Could this, more than what Tuka felt, be called love? But I had never been afraid of Iona. I had been startled, now and then, by her temper, but I had never been, even for an instant, afraid of her. Now, because I had stayed too long, had come to Iona and abandoned hope, so that I was no longer afraid of Tuka's wrath—wearily indifferent—I saw the fear I had felt before clearly. I've been afraid of my wife, I thought, surprised. And was Tuka also afraid of me? Maybe love, like the Just Life, was a mythological beast. But for all my questions, I floated on, serene. Despite her deeper love for her husband, I could love Iona's gentleness and goodness. I was satisfied. I lay almost over her, her bosom my pillow. When I started to slide my hand under the robe to her breast she touched my hand lightly.

"I'm sorry, that was stupid," I said.

She was silent, not disapproving, but she had decided, and she was right. I felt like an ikon thief.

I kissed her one last time, long and gentle, then got up. Without speaking, I picked up my crutch and went to the door. My leg was throbbing, but I observed the fact indifferently. My own pain was the least of my troubles. Once, when I was younger, playing in the yard with a friend's small child, I swung the child around and around, holding onto his feet. The child laughed, frightened and joyful, but I realized after I'd set him down that, much closer than I'd realized, there was a tree. If the child's head had struck it, I'd have killed him. I remembered it now. To live at all is to be a threat.

She came to the door and took me in her arms and kissed me again. "I love you, Agathon."

"I know."

I walked home. It was a long way. When I arrived, there were friends there, childhood friends of Tuka's, visiting from Athens for three or four days. They were all high on wine, hardly aware of what time it was, and whatever lie I made up to explain my lateness they accepted casually. We talked—Tuka, the friends, and I—until sunrise. Just like old times.

Three days later, Tuka learned that a year or so after our marriage I'd slept with a girl friend of hers, named Klytia. It was nothing, a meaningless night of "good friendship," as we say in Athens. But Tuka was outraged, as much at the cruelly false friend as at me. She came into the room where I was talking with Lykourgos and three of his ephors and said, "Agathon, I need to talk with you. Now."

I excused myself and we went to our room. She closed the door and told me what she'd learned. She was white. "How *could* you?" she hissed.

The hopelessness came back, the incredible weariness. "Nonsense, Tuka. It was years ago."

" 'Nonsense,' " she mimicked. "That's *her* word. Find your own!"

"I have no words of my own. Do you?"

"How *could* you?" she said again, and began to cry. "Every friend I ever had is another piece of ass to you. 'Love,' you say! You don't know the meaning of the word!"

"That's true. If you're finished—"

"I'm not! Explain it to me! Explain how your fancy metaphysics teaches you to screw every goddamned whore that comes after you. *Explain* it!"

"They're not whores. They don't come after me. If you'll quit ranting and think a minute—"

"Ranting!" She seized the pitcher by the bed and hurled it.

I let it hit. It bounced off my shoulder and smashed. "I'll talk with you when you're calm," I said. I went to the door, went out, and closed it behind me. When I returned to the room where Lykourgos and the others sat, they fell silent a moment, glancing up. "It's nothing," I said. "Nothing serious."

We talked. I teased Lykourgos a little more sharply than usual, but otherwise it was as if, in truth, nothing had happened. When I went back to our room, perhaps two hours later, Tuka was sitting motionless on the bed, staring at the wall. I spoke to her. She didn't move. I touched her. No response. It struck me that maybe she'd taken some poison. I couldn't believe it, and I knew that it was more likely that this was the end of the thing I'd seen the start of several times before, the odd rigidity. But I was scared. "Tuka, are you all right?" I asked. No response. I pushed at her shoulder. She fell backward onto the bed. I straightened out her legs and looked at her, trying to think. I was convinced now that she'd taken poison. She lay still as a corpse, staring at the ceiling, and even when I slapped her face hard there was no response. A machine, I thought. Some muscle quits, the heart, say, and the rest of the muscles go limp, including the eyes. I knew I should call a doctor—the thing was beyond my knowledge of medicine—but I was afraid. "Tuka!" I said. "Come back! Wake up!" I tugged at her shoulders, shaking her. Nothing. I tried her pulse. It was faster than my own, but I couldn't remember what that meant. "Tuka, Tuka, Tuka," I whispered. But her mind was far away, sealed up like a grave. She farted, or defecated—I couldn't tell which and was afraid to look—but that too brought nothing human to her face. At last, with the same weary hopelessness I'd felt before, when I abandoned her, I sent a servant for a doctor. He came in half an hour—a lean, middle-aged, bearded man with a long pointed nose—and examined her without speaking. "Shock," he said at last. He bled her and forced a liquid down her throat. When he finished he turned his head to look at me, quizzical. "I've seen this in cases or rape. Was she raped?" "Not physically," I said. He said she'd be like this for two days. He left.

Later, when the servant brought the children home from school, I took Kleon in to see her. He was ten, a thoughtful, moody child, and it was better that he see her than wonder.

"Is she dead?" he asked.

I shook my head. "She's all right. She just can't move right now. She'll be herself in a day or so."

He sat down on the edge of the bed, watching me to see if it was all right.

"Touch her hand if you want," I said. "She knows you're here. She just can't talk."

It was true that she knew he was there. There were tears in her eyes. He touched her hand. "What's wrong with her?" he asked.

I thought. "She's unhappy. So unhappy she can't move. She doesn't believe I love her, though I do."

"Will she know in a day or so, when she gets well?"

A logician, poor child. A philosopher. His life was going to be hell. "No," I said. "Once you ask that question—does he love me?—you ask it forever."

He patted her hand, full of sadness. I believe he understood.

I stayed with her, watching for a sign. When I woke up in the morning, two days later, she had turned her face toward me and was looking at me. When I realized what it meant, I kissed her. She returned the kiss, gentle, full of sorrow.

"I do know you love me," she said. "But I have to go. I'll go back to Athens, with the children."

"Don't talk," I said. "Later."

She was quiet for a while, and I lay with my cheek on her shoulder. At last she said, "No one should have as much power over another person as you have over me. There's nothing I can do to you. If I sleep with another man, it doesn't bother you. If I ever tried to fight you, you'd break my neck. I'm helpless. You have no feelings."

"I do," I said.

She rolled her head back and forth on the pillow. "No. I'm not criticizing. It's just a fact. There's nothing I can do to hurt you the way you hurt me. It's not fair."

"Don't think about it," I said. I kissed her shoulder. "Go to sleep."

She did. She slept until late afternoon, and when she awakened she looked as if she hadn't slept in days. She looked old. "Agathon," she said, "I can't stand leaving you."

"Then don't."

"I have to. But not Athens."

"Whatever you say."

"You have to help me. I'm too tired to think. Where should we go?"

I shook my head. "Why should I help you do what I don't want you to do? Work it out yourself."

She stayed that night, putting it off until tomorrow, and I made love to her. The next morning I said, "Put it off for a week. If it's serious it will still be serious a week from now."

She looked frightened. "You know what will happen. I'll stay."

"Maybe. But try it. One day at a time, second by second."

She put if off for a week and decided to stay.

I visited Iona and told her what had happened. Iona said nothing when I told her, merely, "Strange." I couldn't tell whether she was alarmed or grieved or what: her face was wood. She asked me questions about Tuka, and I told her all I could—her childhood, her father, her friends, her music. She kissed me when I left—clung to me, her cheek against mine, but she looked past me, her mind far away. A few days later I visited her again. We sat in the garden behind her house, where she'd been collecting flowers for one of her decorations. She said, cold-eyed, smiling like ice, "I've figured out why I love you, Agathon."

"Good," I said.

"It's a kind of revolt. I've cleaned house, cooked meals, borne children, all without stopping to think about it—obeying the laws of Nature and Society. I'm tired of it. I want to *be* something."

"Commendable," I said.

"Don't mock. I mean it. If it weren't you, it might have been someone else. When I fell in love with Dorkis it was because the time had come for me to break free. From my parents, that time. From childhood. Now it's from the drudgery of a wife."

"Maybe that's so," I said, though it wasn't. She knew it wasn't. I looked up into the bare branches of the tree arching above us. I was very tired. The chilly air seemed heavy on my arms and legs and chest. My bad leg, asleep, was heavy as a log.

After a long time, Iona said, "Do you suppose everyone in Sparta knows about us?"

"I suppose," I said.

"Then we should stop, shouldn't we?" She pursed her lips, seriously considering it, or pretending to, peering into the cup of the dark-red flower in her hand as if the answer might be hidden there, written on the petals.

"It would be a terrific idea, if it were possible."

She started to nod, then checked herself, still studying the flower. "Anything's possible, Agathon." Her smile could bring an early winter.

I shrugged. "Sure." So break it off, I thought.

She leaned forward, clasping her knees in her arms. All I thought, all I was, disgusted her. I couldn't miss it. "You really believe that no one can ever change anything, don't you?"

"No," I said. "One can change things. One can stab people. One can break up people's homes. One can throw out one tyrannical government and put in a new one for somebody else to throw out."

"Solon's?" she asked. "Is that tyrannical?"

"Not at the moment," I said. "Not fully."

She sighed, then smiled like alum in your teeth. "Thank God I'm no philosopher."

"Oh, you're a philosopher, all right. You'll no more start a revolution than"—I hesitated, then went wearily on—"than Dorkis."

"Wait and see," she said.

Her tone grieved me. At least for now, she meant it.

"Second by second," I said.

"Oh, nonsense. You say that too often. 'Second by second.' You're like a machine." Her annoyance was not seductive now. It was withering. I felt a queer flash of panic.

"It's true," I said, clownishly morose. "Except that I don't say it. I just open my mouth and it comes out— an impulse from the gods."

"There are no gods," she said.

I looked up into the trees.

When we parted, that day, we didn't kiss, though she gave me one of her flowers, breaking a petal off as she dropped the flower in my hand. No doubt she had her mind on the revolution.

Tuka said, "You were there?"

I nodded. "I was there."

I spent the afternoon with the children, telling them the glorious story of Herakles.

"Tell them the story of Akhilles," Tuka said, "how the poor boy died for love."

I smiled and shook my head. "An idle tale."

22 Peeker:

I can't get the picture of my mother out of my mind.
The white hair, the tremble of the knobby fingers. I've
got to get out of here. And yet how can I? Even if I
could escape some way, or get the tall ephor to do
something, as I'm convinced he wants to, even then
could I go back to my mother and help her, now when
she needs me, and not help poor Agathon? I think
of taking care of them together, feeding them and waiting on them in the same house, and I laugh. It would
be safer putting a tiger and a smart old snake together in a cage. Yet I've got to do something. No
choice.

I told Agathon the problem and he went on writing, scratch on scratch, leaking out the obscenity of his
life. "She's old," he said. "Everybody dies eventually."

"I could say the same of you," I said.

He paused and glanced up, leering. "You're beginning to catch on!"

Smart-ass old bastard. I should brain him with the
chamberpot. But I was only mad for a second or two.
I understand him better and better. He's philosophical
about death. Good. But I hear how he groans and
whimpers in his sleep, and I see how goddamn scared
he is when he peeks out through the cell door, watching the fires. He jokes about how when they drag
him away he'll bawl like a baby the ephors have decided to throw from a cliff for its sickliness, but I
see through the jokes: he really will bawl, and stupidly,

hopelessly, he'll try to bribe them, and when they lift the execution rods over his head he'll die of terror. So would I, maybe, though I don't think so. The difference between us is that he hates himself for it, hates himself for everything, and hates everybody else that shares his faults. As simple as that. Agathon, the great lover, hates people.

He told me a story once. I didn't believe it at the time—I thought he made it up to convince me that he really used to have the famous book—but I'm not sure now. It could be true.

There was an empty crypt in the graveyard next to the shrine of Poseidon—a very old crypt that he learned about from a man in Korinth. The bodies had been removed a long time ago, maybe a hundred years or more, and the door had been sealed. But the crypt had a secret entrance, the man in Korinth told him, a large movable stone half buried in vines, and when Agathon went to look where the man said the entrance was, he found it. The crypt was the perfect place to hide the book. So night after night Agathon would sneak out to the graveyard, taking a few scrolls at a time and ducking from tombstone to tombstone and tree to tree till he reached the crypt, and at last, after weeks of this, his treasure was hidden. He could go there when he pleased and close the secret door behind him, and he could read with no crack of light showing until the air became too thin to breathe; then he'd blow out the lamps and open the secret door until morning and then close it and steal away home to bed before anyone was up. Not a soul in all Sparta knew about the place, not even his wife.

Then came the revolution. He had friends that were up to their ears in it, especially the woman he keeps prattling about, Iona. (I saw her twice: small, shrunken, rolling-eyed as a wolf. The grass wherever she touches it turns to dust. It may be true that she was beautiful once. You might even say that she's beautiful now, if you like your beauties old as Time, and violent, and crazy.) One night she and her husband and their people burned up the hall of ephors. By morning it was nothing but stone walls and window holes. (They've rebuilt it since, though not the way it was before. It used to be carved columns, beautiful hangings, statues, the works. The inner supports are now planed timbers, and the only decoration, if you can call it that, is Poseidon's iron trident. Statues encourage hero cults, Lykourgos says.)

Anyway, someone saw them and recognized one or two Helot faces. So the Civic Guard was after them, and Iona, or else Dorkis, one of them, went to Agathon. She knew he had some secret hiding place for his book. He'd bragged about having one, no doubt. They put on pressure. (Iona, it must have been. Both of them must have known that sooner or later, even when the book was involved, he'd succumb to her.) And at last poor miserable Agathon showed them the secret entrance and the revolutionists—all but the leaders: Dorkis, Iona, and one or two others—went in. They bored air holes and closed the entrance behind them. No one knows for sure what happened then. Some Spartan saw them going in, or some informer revealed their hiding place. Within hours the Civic Guard had cracked open the front door and thrown in oil and lit it. Those who tried to escape by the secret entrance or the open front door were struck down like pigs at a slaughterhouse; those who didn't flee died in the fire. The Guard waited until it was certain that no one had survived, then left. Until then, the Helot crowd watching could do nothing. But as soon as the Guard left, the crowd rushed to the smoldering crypt to see the horror and reclaim their dead.

Agathon was one of the first. No one noticed, in the beginning, what he was doing. While the others were dragging out bodies, hunting in the maniacal way people will at such times for some sign of life, and grieving when they found none—old men tearing their clothes and hair, women beating the ground, screaming—Agathon was rescuing the charred remains of his scrolls of dead knowledge, hurriedly stepping over bodies, as indifferently as he'd have stepped over stones, snatching up the parchment husks and running with them, weeping and moaning, to the torchlight where the others were examining their dead. Cruelly, like a sow driving through children to her litter, he pushed past mourners, trampled dead men's outstretched hands, till he came to the center of the torch's influence and threw himself on the ground to peel blackened page from blackened page, searching for some remaining scribble. He would howl, finding nothing, and would tear out locks of his hair and beard; then, with a wild look, remembering the crypt, he would charge back through the mourning crowd, indifferent to their lives and sorrows as a battering ram, and would search the blackened room again. Long after he knew there was nothing there he kept returning to the place, searching and whimpering like a bitch who's lost her pups.

They saw it, at last: separated their grief from his and reacted like a single heart to the outrage. It was the women first. Some woman, pushed over as Agathon ran past, looked up from the corpse she futilely soothed, and saw, and understood, and screamed. They seized him by the hair and clothes, pulled him to the ground, began beating him and scratching at his face. Then the men and children understood and started kicking him and throwing sticks and stones. They would have killed him except for Dorkis, his friend.

He appeared out of nowhere, as if shot down by lightning, shielding Agathon's body with his own and howling, "Wait!" In the dim light no one recognized him. He caught stones as they came and hurled them back, snatching up stones from the ground with his free hand. "Wait!" he kept yelling, hurling stones with the aim of an infantryman. Whether his barrage checked them, or whether they finally recognized him, Agathon couldn't say, telling me the story. They paused, anyway, and Dorkis rose to a crouch. "What's the matter with you people?" he yelled. The women told him, sobbing, all of them speaking at once. (Agathon got this all at second hand. He was out cold. They'd fractured his skull.) Who knows whether Dorkis understood their jumbled noise or simply knew, knowing his friend? "Go away!" he said. "You have no idea how this man loved his book. You're fools! Idiots! Go away! Mourn your corpses!"

They were swayed, or shamed. Who knows? They backed away, and then Iona was there, and the other leaders, and they began the process of carrying away the dead. Dorkis threw Agathon over his shoulders and carried him the mile and a half to Dorkis's and Iona's house. Dorkis worked on him all that night and all the following day—Agathon remained unconscious —joining broken bones, forcing in the mysterious Asiatic medicines he'd learned in his father's house in Hydrea. For six days Agathon remained a breathing corpse. When he awakened Dorkis was sitting above him, upright, unsupported by his chair but fast asleep. Agathon asked for water, and Dorkis was awake in an instant.

It was months later—a week before Dorkis was executed—that Dorkis said to him, almost pityingly, as Agathon tells it, "You care more for knowledge than for people."

"No," Agathon said.

Dorkis smiled. It was a terrible smile, as Agathon reports it. Dorkis was blind, at this time, and he'd been beaten till he was a mass of raw meat. "Don't fret," he said. "I haven't said I don't love you for it."

—Something has dawned on me. Agathon's friend Dorkis was the man the revolutionists called Snake— the man I saw die. The mutilation, the blindness. Yes. He died like a god. Inexpressible. When the Spartans killed him, they killed him at the first blow—an extraordinary mark of respect.

Everything I think is confusion! Crazy old Agathon's best friend in Sparta was Snake! They called him "The Mind of the Revolution." Famous for his wisdom, his gentleness in private life, his deadly efficiency—until the time of his great mistake, the night he showed up with the sympathizers at the crypt. They had evidence before that. Documents. But no one believed, no one could connect him with the revolution. Then why? Why throw away his safety for Agathon? If he was wise, as everyone says he was, he must have known Agathon's thing for his wife. And he must have known that Agathon would never do the same for him.

"You haven't suffered," Agathon tells me. "That's the problem." Not like him, thank God, not by betraying everything I ever loved without lifting a goddamn finger. He made his beautiful Iona ugly, and drove his wife Tuka home to Athens, and all by mere Nature, without a malicious thought. He'll wreck me too, if his luck holds out. I should strangle him, and save the whole human race!

23   Agathon:

Curious how my mind wanders, these last few days.

I watched a terrible thing once. Why it should come back to me so forcefully now is not exactly clear. A man sees horrors enough in Sparta. Nevertheless—

I was up near the shrine with the children—Kleon and Diana—exploring. Kleon was about nine, I think; Diana something like seven. It was before the revolution—if you can really date the beginning of such things. We'd been climbing the ancient stone path all morning, a path just wide enough for a cart. (We saw one on the path, far below and behind us. It did not occur to me to wonder, at the time, at its coming *up* toward the trees with its load of sticks.) The stones of the path had been worn smooth as old coins by generations of Helot laborers, donkeys, cows, and goats. Here and there tufts of grass and bright blue flowers pushed up between the stones. The bluffs soared up to our left, rising from the edge of the winding path and cluttered with huge boulders that looked like wolves' heads, sleeping bears, the bones of giants. It reminded me a little of Athens. Between the boulders there were patches of short, brittle grass and twisted, dwarfish trees. Beyond the wall to the right of the path—where the wall itself had not fallen away—the bluffs rushed down toward a chasm where one of the streams that feeds the Eurotas rattles over little falls, pauses a moment in deep still pools, then swirls away past stones and the roots of trees. I held Diana's hand, Kleon walking to the left of me and a little ahead, his heels just out of reach of my crutch. All the way up we'd seen almost no one—only four old Helot peasants fishing in the stream below.

We came around a sharp turn in the path, and there, high above us, stood Menelaos's shrine. It was clean and white and solemn as a ghost on its cliff overlooking dark-green wooded slopes, its four front pillars set against the chasm like fists. Beyond the pillars, below the wide roof, the shrine sank away into darkness. We paused, startled by the suddenness of the shrine's appearance. It seemed that the place might indeed be the home of a god. Then we hurried on, climbing toward it.

When we reached the place there was no one there, only the rows of darkening columns, the torch rests (but there were no torches), and at the center of it all, the sculptured altar. The fire was out, and there was no priest. The children talked in whispers as we moved through the place; as for me, I talked hardly at all. It was as if the air were filled with omens I couldn't read. And it was, maybe, though the coincidence of place and event was accidental.

Diana said, "Daddy, listen."

We stopped walking. Nothing but the wind in the trees above the shrine. We took a few more steps. I was aware of the floor's hollow boom. We listened again.

She said, "There's somebody coming."

And now I too heard it, children's voices, chatting, casual, coming from somewhere in the trees to the north, beyond the outer row of columns. For some reason—it may have been something I heard without knowing I heard it—I took their hands and quickly led them away from the altar and out into the sunlight and through it to the trees to the east of the shrine, and there we stopped to see what would happen.

"Is something wrong?" Kleon asked.

I shook my head. But something was. I couldn't put my finger on it.

A group of Helot children broke out of the trees and ran laughing and talking toward the shrine as though it were a place where they played often. There were—I don't know—maybe ten of them, all very young, ragged and dirty, children of the lowest class of semislaves. Most of them were girls, and one of them, I remember, carried a handful of limp wild flowers. As they ran through the sunlight toward the shrine, the hackles of my neck rose and I knew before I saw them that there were others besides ourselves watching. I knelt down, in the shadow of the trees, and laid down my crutch and pulled Kleon and Diana to the mossy ground beside me, motioning for silence. They watched in fright, and I knew that in a moment Diana would scream. I closed a hand over each child's mouth and held on relentlessly. Four Spartan boys, dressed in the loincloths of their war exercises, came out of the trees stealthily and ran in a crouch toward where the children played. They were smiling, the Spartans. It was unbelievable, nightmarish: not human. I heard the screams of the Helot children as the Spartans reached them, and the same instant I saw the Helot men coming out of the trees and from under the altar. One of the Helot children lay in a pool of blood—dead, I was certain. But now the Spartan boys had seen the men and understood. Ambushed. The Spartans could have run, but they turned and faced the Helots, witlessly brave, as usual. The Helot men surrounded them and killed them with their clubs and work knives. And now the cart we had seen on the path came up to the shrine as if casually, and the Helots lifted out the sticks —their children silent now, terrified and numb—and lifted in the dead Spartans, bright red with blood, and put the dead Helot child in with them, and covered the bodies with sticks. They splashed water on the blood-spattered floor of the shrine and worked quickly, efficiently with rags, cleaning up all signs. After that they vanished into the trees. The whole thing had taken perhaps ten minutes. I listened to the rumble of the cartwheels on the stones of the path, going down again to the valley, slowly, slowly. The driver looked asleep. Kleon vomited.

That night the children lay wide-eyed, shivering. Two servants carried in the harp for us, and Tuka played.

Lightly, at a Helot party later, I mentioned the incident to Iona.

"Horrible!" she said, then whispered, "but what do you expect?"

24 Agathon:

Also this:

One night at a party at Dorkis's—a dark, ugly party, cloying funereal roses and ferns, because the revolution was on now, the laughter and chatter rang hollow and thick as the jokes of trapped miners—Tuka told Iona's oldest boy that Iona was in love with me, that she was leaving Dorkis, and that Iona's basic problem—the reason for her drunks, her indifference to her family, her bold activity in the senseless rebellion—was that Iona was insane. All this came out very casually, I understand. Casual as the blue-black welt, the fire-scarred fingers of the testy little man who sat in the corner of the room, never speaking, starting wildly whenever a new guest knocked at the door or a cup fell to the polished stone floor and shattered. The boy, Miletos, was fifteen: a beautiful, curly-headed innocent. It was his first adult party, the first time he'd drunk wine with his parents' strange friends. (There were no Spartans there that night, and no Athenians but ourselves.) He was in the kitchen cutting cheese to take in to the others, and Tuka was helping him. She'd always been fonder of him than of all the rest of Dorkis's family put together, because he was the gentlest and, she thought, the wisest of them all, and handsome besides: he made her remember her own youth, her own ideals. She wanted to protect him, save him from pain and disillusionment like her own. He must have understood that as plainly as I did. He must have understood everything, in a way. If he was baffled by what he felt around him—the emptied, silent streets outside, and here in the charged dimness of the room, the hothouse closeness of his mother's feeling for me and mine for her, his father's wise preference for noninterference (watching the party with an absentminded smile and thoughtful eyes), and Tuka's jealousy—baffled or not he nevertheless understood it all, and if he were older he would have accepted the bafflement, as the rest of us did, as one of life's conditions. But he was young and did not know about that, and he knew Tuka's feeling for him, which he could not help but return because she, too, was beautiful, and he knew that she was, besides that, brilliant: she spoke, always, with keen wit and absolute authority, and everyone listened to her. He knew by her every gesture now —her sailing over to help him with the cheese, her flashing of the special dimpled smile reserved for the few she really loved, and her teasing ("Miletos, hand over that weapon before you saw your arm off")—that he could ask in safety about the thing that was troubling him more than anything out in the larger, more dangerous world of stealth and war. Perhaps he was troubled more than usual that moment, and less inhibited; he wasn't used to wine in such doses.

He said, looking at the plate and smiling as if the question were possibly silly, "Tuka, what's going on between Mom and Dad?"

"Nothing," she said, too quick-witted. "That's the problem." The knife slipped through the cheese as if through butter.

He smiled, not showing he was weighing the answer. "Mom's acting really strange," he said. "Sometimes she leaves me with the kids and she doesn't come home all night. I wonder where she goes."

Did Tuka suffer a twinge of alarm? We hadn't known, Tuka and I, that Iona sometimes slept away from home. I don't know yet where she went, or why

—assuming Miletos was right about her absences. Revolution, no doubt. The news worried me when I heard it later. But Tuka was not thinking about the rebellion. Did she quickly search her mind for times I too had been missing? I don't know, of course. I know only that Miletos asked it, or anyway that Tuka said later that he asked it, and that Tuka told him that Dorkis and Iona were breaking up, that Iona had, oh, a "crush" on me. "Lots of women do, from time to time," she said. "You get used to it." (I can imagine the lightness with which she must have said it, the false bravado of securely loved wife forever having to pick up the pieces for heartbroken women, and I can imagine the pain she did not see in the boy whose mother had been reduced to another poor helpless infatuate whore.) Did she go on to talk about middle age, the feeling Thalia talked about, that life is huge and everyone is cheated? I know why, if she did. Because she loved Miletos and confused her own troubled nature with his, and wanted to ease with her brittle quick tongue the pain he too must sooner or later come to, like all who live.

But whatever they said, the boy did not show that he was hurt. I talked with him briefly as we left the house, and he was cheerful, eagerly looking forward to a job he was starting in the morning, out at the stables on one of the farms.

Two nights later I received a message from Iona, saying she was staying at an inn and wanted me away tomorrow so that she could talk with Tuka. I could hear the exact tone of her voice in the flatly recited message: it was husky; sorrowing and drunk. She mentioned, in a single obscure sentence, that Tuka had said terrible things about us, and about Iona and Dorkis, to Miletos. I was frightened, frustrated by the span of time and space between the human voice that had dictated the message and the mechanical echo on my stoop. It was late—near midnight—and the message, delivered by a dark-faced boy who spoke the words twice over, then vanished in the darkness, had, it seemed to me, the character of a summons. She named the inn, and all her phrases had a checked violence in them, like tornado weather, that I couldn't shrug off until morning. I knew for sure that she'd been drinking. The tremor of anger is always there, just edging the surface like a crocodile snout, when Iona's had too much wine. And I guessed that it was not entirely her son's pain that enraged her. She could have defended herself (and wouldn't have needed to) against a direct attack from Tuka. But she had no defense against Miletos's innocent grief, in which, whether she admitted it or not, her own guilt—not as he saw it but as she saw it, looking at herself through her son's eyes—shone clear. I was afraid, in a word, that, hurled back into a childhood vision of goodness that even children know for a half-truth—thrown back into memories of family happiness that she seemed to have destroyed by selfish, however unconsummated lust— she would kill herself. I knew well enough that I was probably exaggerating. People rarely commit suicide except to punish loved ones, and though Iona was fond of Tuka, in a way, or had been once, Tuka and she weren't close enough for that. But whatever sense might argue, I was afraid. Fear was in the air, in those days. Worse even than now. There's a kind of healthiness in open violence—scattered fires against the skyline, roars of rioting and looting: the healthiness of a good gust of wind in an electric storm, or an honest heart attack after riddling weeks of mysterious malaise. In those days you were forever waiting, watching for signs that the trouble was over, or else not. Someone had to go to her, I thought, and it obviously couldn't be me. I would sleep with her, and if ever I slept with Dorkis's wife, it was not going to be by chance. And so, incredibly, I sent Tuka.

From the point of view of the omniscient, indif-

ferent gods, it must have been amusing. As Poseidon's
lightning bursts forth between thunderheads, shattering
the darkness and sending down rain like a thousand
swords, driving small animals into their burrows and
birds to the silent depths of trees, so Tuka burst in in
her terrible splendor on the darkness of Iona's room.

"You *bitch!*" she said.

But as the earth spreads wide in the lightning glow
and opens its furrows and seams to the rain, so Iona
rose sweetly wide-eyed from her pillow and stretched
out an arm to her adversary.

"Why, Tuka!" she said.

In short, they were both as reasonable as possible,
given the circumstances. Tuka adopted the point of
view that she'd told Miletos all in a last-ditch effort
to save the two marriages, that she'd warned Iona that
she'd tattle to Miletos if Iona continued to see me
(which may have been true. Who knows?), and that
she'd done it all, to tell the *real* truth, for Iona's good
and Dorkis's. Iona adopted the point of view that she
couldn't understand what on earth made Tuka believe
she had cause for jealousy, that she and Dorkis shared
a love more profound than words could express, there
had never been the slightest question of that! and that
her sole concern in this squalid affair was that Miletos
might now respect Tuka less, Tuka whom he loved as
a sister. They were both, I know without having been
there, simply brilliant, though one couldn't exactly call
what they had together a conversation. Iona wept,
clutching her covers to her bosom, and said, "Tuka,
dearest, dearest Tuka, you're *sick.*" Tuka said (a part-
ing shot), "Lie there and masturbate!"

And so they both won hands down. Iona talked to
me later, briefly, distantly (because Tuka had won).
She was worried about Tuka. There was no problem
now with Miletos or Dorkis: they had talked, she said.
Miletos, when he came home from his first day of work
at the stables, had eaten supper apart from the others

and had gone to his room. She'd pursued him there, and when she'd asked what was wrong he'd come out at last, weeping, with "Mother, why are you leaving us?" She'd answered that she wasn't—an honest answer. (All of us are honest second by second, and she was talking with the son she loved. How could she dream, that instant, that she had ever dreamed of leaving—if she had?) She'd probed further, and he'd told her the rest of what distressed him, and she answered all that honestly too. Considering. They talked about love, and she told him, honestly, of her feelings about me, her feelings about Dorkis, about Tuka. And so it was true, there was no problem with Miletos. He remained our friend. The problem was Tuka. She'd gone again past all human limits, and Iona, who had never seen it before, believed Tuka incapable of love for anyone, certainly indifferent if not hostile to Iona's whole family. Even if that were false, as Iona hoped it might be, Tuka's anger was not a thing you walked into twice. Iona told herself two stories, both half-truths and mutually exclusive but nevertheless as real for her as two large owls in a tree. That Tuka was insane, a physical threat to me and to our children. And that Tuka had acted at my instigation, breaking off a "relationship" that I was too gentle, that is, cowardly, to bring to an end myself. She could be, supported by these theories, fond of me as an aunt is of a nephew who has some terminal disease, but her "crush" on me, as Tuka put it, was done with. Also, ironically, she no longer needed me. Thanks to Tuka (though this was hardly what Tuka had in mind), or thanks directly to Miletos's grief, which first found words that night in the kitchen when Miletos and Tuka were cutting cheese—but sooner or later would have had to find words, with Tuka or without—Iona had fallen in love, once more, with her family.

Tuka also won and lost. The pain of jealousy was over, for the moment anyway, and now, clear-minded, she could see the jealousy and the attack on Iona as they were, and she was depressed. It was true that she had hurt Miletos, and though she wasn't the cause of his grief, she was to blame. And it was true, she knew, that Iona had been fond of her, that they really might have been like sisters, whatever that meant, if it weren't for Dorkis and me. It could have been very good for all of us. But Dorkis was a lover, not only a man with busy hands but a man who did in fact fall in love, though he did nothing about it—and so, alas, was I. So that whenever we came together, the four of us, there was no escape from the heart-swapping game, tiresome and futile, doomed to frustration and anger because of our natures. She understood, now that her attack on Iona had ended it, that we'd had nothing from the start, only a grand potential that was, like all grand potentials, illusion. She walked abstractedly through her days, carrying with her, in everything she did, a dreary sense of loss, the loss of a thing that had never existed. She missed them and wished she had never known them. Secure at last in her possession of me, she wondered what it was that she'd fought so fiercely to possess. We began to have long talks about our childhoods, saying everything that came to mind, talking quietly, almost wearily, as if turning old happiness over and over, hunting for what had seemed so good in it.

"*Do* you love me?" she would say sometimes. "I mean, if you were free to sleep with someone else, would you?"

I would laugh.

I heard, during this period, of Klinias's death. (My first news was the arrival of the book.) I took the whole thing as though I'd been expecting it, and I wondered idly how old Solon was now. I could recall very clearly how happy I had been with Klinias, and how alive he made me feel. Tuka mentioned that she had slept one night with Konon. It was like something

I had read somewhere; interesting, nothing more. Poor Klinias, I said absently. She nodded.

But my lethargy, at least, did not last much longer. I woke up a few mornings later with the thought of Klinias's book. It was mine, it came to me. I owned it. I got up, dressed, and began to read through it, and as I read my fingertips began to tremble. I read faster and faster, excitedly, wildly. What a book it was! I'd forgotten! When, toward noon, Tuka said, "Good morning," interrupting me, I looked up at her in rage.

25 Peeker:

I think something's wrong with Agathon. When he shits
the smell is too horrible to believe—it's like after asparagus or something. And this morning he fell down.
It scared him; I know because when I went over to help
him he hit my hand away. "Let me be!" he yelled.
"Boys should respect their elders!"

"Are you all right?" I said. "Is your hip broken?"

"I'll dance on your grave," he said.

But it wasn't natural, his simply toppling over like
that. It made me think. He's been sleeping late, and
taking naps all the time. He never used to do that. He
has this thing about using every moment. And the rat
bites on his toes and fingers don't heal the way they
should. That may be just his age, I suppose—like the
rat bites themselves. Rats never bite me. I feel their
noses the minute they touch me, and I slap them away,
even in my sleep. But old people's nerves aren't sensitive, and their reactions are slow. His hands and feet
look like something that's been fed to the chickens.

This afternoon when he was at the table writing he
fell asleep without even knowing it was coming on:
just bent his head down and drifted off, sleeping on
his nose. He still had the pen in his hand. I called
the jailer, and after a while he came.

"I think my master's sick," I said.

He looked in, making a face at the smell.

"Dead?" he said.

I shook my head. "He's just asleep. But he never

sleeps in the afternoon, or anyway he never used to. He fell down for no reason this morning."

The jailer looked at me, doubtful. I suppose they tell him a lot of crazy things.

"Listen," I said. "I really think he's sick. Honest. I've got to get him out of here. He'll die or something."

The jailer thought about it, scowling, and at last he shook his head slowly, as if saying it was hopeless. I looked back at Agathon, sleeping on his nose, with his long hair going out on the table in all directions, like ropes from a tent. "Please," I said—because it panicked me: he really did look dead—"you've got to help me. Get a doctor. Make the ephors come." He was shaking his head, slow, hopeless, and, it seemed to me, not quite indifferent. "This then," I said, and glanced at him, wondering if I was right. "Pass the word to the Helots. They know him. *They've* got doctors."

The jailer turned his face away, looking at the mountains.

"He's sick," I hissed. "He may stink like a sewer, but he's human. And he's sick."

26 Agathon:

Life is full of mysteries. I found two more of my rats dead this morning. That's not one of the mysteries, of course. Some simple sickness that terminates in death. The usual business—summer, winter, day and night. The mystery lies in my jailer's reaction. I've underestimated the man. When he came with my breakfast I held up my three dead rats by their tails, putting on, for his benefit, the saddest face possible and granting him the glimpse of a tear. He frowned, at first, disgusted by my feeling for a fellow creature. But when I placed the three corpses beside my plate (it was a means of taking my mind off the food), his frown changed to a thoughtful look. (Coming of spring.) It had no doubt come even to his attention that too many dying rats can be a bad omen. If the disease they have is communicable to man, my situation is not exactly enviable.

"Poor devils," I said. Peeker rolled his eyes up and covered his face. He knows when a speech is coming.

"Alas," I said, "riding the golden chariot of our prosperity, we neglect to give proper attention to the humble rat. Only in miserable circumstances—this cell, for example—do we pause to reflect on their lot. Like us, the poor rat is born into a world he never willed and can only in minimal ways control. He suffers the agonies of youth—the squalling indignity of his first nakedness, the inexplicable rules of harsh parents —he matures into the age of love and saddles himself

209

with some whimpering, nagging, winsome female—he declines into middle-aged sickness and mournful confusion—and at last, bewildered and shivering, he dies, to be forgotten." I clasped my hands and lifted them to my forehead. "Ah, Zeus, what's it all for?"

Peeker banged his fists together on his ears.

Suddenly, miraculously, as the sun in all its splendor breaks from the hood of clouds that encloses the brow of Mount Taygetos, my jailer spoke. "Some disease," he said. My eyes widened, my mouth dropped open. I turned to stare at him.

"They have some disease," he said.

Imagine the mouth of a cave speaking! Imagine sober opinions emitting from a horse!

"God bless you, jailer!" I cried, leaping up. "You can talk!" I walked to the door without my crutch, as if the miracle had cured me.

He glowered at me, deeply offended, but now, seeing that the rules were broken, it was a whole new game, he spoke again. "The dishes," he said, and pointed.

"Of course!" I cried. "God bless you! Of course!" I snatched the dishes from the table.

He took them with lips curled back from his teeth and banged them on the outside wall, getting rid of the few bits of filth we hadn't eaten. He strode away.

"Have a good day, jailer!" I called. "May the gods watch over you! They listen to what I say, you know. I snap my fingers and . . ."

A little after noon (we get no lunch; only breakfast and supper) the jailer reappeared and had someone with him. Without speaking, he unlocked the door of my cell and swung the door open. He waved the other man in, came in behind him, and closed the door.

"Physician," the jailer said.

I bowed The physician grunted and wrinkled his

nose. They do not have toilet facilities here, only a pot, and my control, of late, is not all that it might be. Gingerly still with his nose wrinkled, the physician picked up one of the rats by the tail and examined it. I watched eagerly, bending over my crutch, eyes wide with scientific interest. "Some sickness," I said. "The first one—the one that stinks a little—well, I thought I might have rolled over on it, unwittingly, you know, while I slept. But those other two, there, I found them in the corner. So they were sick."

The jailer glanced at me. No humorist.

The physician threw the rats out the door, one at a time, lifting each one by the tail. Then he turned, put his hands on his hips, and looked at me. He had black, black eyebrows, thick as a hedge, and tiny black eyes like a rat's. He had a nose like someone had twisted it for him, and his gray beard hung to his middle. He said, rather casually, it seemed to me, "You sick?"

"I'm not sure," I said. I felt my forehead. "Am I?" I turned to the jailer for help. He glared at the floor.

"I knew a man once who was never happy unless he was sick, or threatened with execution, or dying. Thaletes was his name. A splendid fellow! How I wish he could be here now!" I laughed, high and wild, like a madman.

The physician winced, then sighed in despair and glanced over at Peeker, who watched it all in gloomy disrespect. Then the physician came over to me. He put his fingertips on my forehead and considered for a moment. At last he nodded.

"I'm sick?" I asked.

"You're still living." He looked at my feculence in the corner.

I laughed. "Small comfort. He he he!"

They went out.

I was sorry, afterward, that I'd played the buffoon. It would be pleasant to know for sure that one is not dying. But I occupy my mind with other thoughts. My jailer likes me, or anyway cares about my health. It's not his duty. When Thaletes got sick in prison, they let him die. He enjoyed it, of course, so it was different. Nevertheless . . .

> Thaletes, wherever you are, you're not forgotten!
> We who live on still cherish your words of truth!
> Happiness is delusion! Life is rotten!
> Reality is a hole in a lady's tooth!

I must pull myself together. This is very unwise. What would Solon do in this saddening situation? That's what I must think of.

He'd write some fool poem.

So would Thaletes, of course. No doubt he was mad.

I visited him once in prison. (Read with both eyes, Peeker! He he!) He knew he was dying. You wouldn't have guessed, to look at him, that he was the happiest of men. He had a single cell that looked down on the river, exactly like this cell of mine. Perhaps I have his same cell, I don't know. When I came to see him, it was late afternoon, and the cell was full of shadows. There was a crude wooden table very much like mine, and some writing materials on it, I think, and a three-legged stool. The floor was covered, unlike mine, with straw. He had no lamp, as far as I remember, but he had a woolen blanket twisted up under him where he lay.

He'd been a famous man, once. He lived in Krete. He was a poet-philosopher, one of the best-known wisemen of his time when Lykourgos landed in Krete, during the period of his travels. I didn't know him then—Thaletes—but I have read what was written of him: " . . . though by his outward appearance and his own profession he seemed to be no other than a lyric poet, in reality he performed the part of one of the ablest lawgivers in the world. The very songs which he composed were exhortations to obedience and concord, and the very measure and cadence of the verse, conveying impressions of order and tranquillity, had so great an influence on the minds of the listeners, that they were insensibly softened and civilized, insomuch that they renounced their private feuds and animosities, and were reunited in a common admiration of virtue." (I quote from memory, but I don't mean that as an apology, boy. I quote with the memory of a professional in these matters.) How much truth there may be in what is written of him, God only knows. I'll admit that I have seen crowds moved by a stirring tale, or tranquilized by stories of childhood love and peace; and I'll admit that the songs attributed to Thaletes are rather moving, in their way, though always overweighty and sometimes coarse and, in my personal opinion, obscene. But if Thaletes ever gave out a law, I never heard of it, and if he ever quieted an angry mob, it must have been a mob of thoughtful old men. What he did, besides make up tediously intellectual songs, was two things: he worked out a strange, difficult theory about what people are, and he fought in the underground at Amyklai. Lykourgos, I forgot to say, brought Thaletes home with him from Krete and set him up in his palace as an "adviser," as he later did myself. Thaletes immediately adopted the customs Lykourgos was busy imposing on his people—hard work, sparse and plain food, a minimum of clothing, a minimum of sex. His masochistic pleasure should have made the horse (Lykourgos, I mean) suspicious at once, but it didn't. Thaletes wrote war songs, hymns to hardship, satires on sex, and when he'd busily helped Lykourgos strip Sparta of all the traditional human freedoms, he turned on Lykourgos and tried to lead the Helots in an uprising. It fizzled, and Thaletes fled to Amyklai. Lykourgos put the city under martial law, and Thaletes helped form and run what came to be called the underground. He wrote, during this period, as never before in his life: tales, songs, philosophy books. He must hardly have slept seven hours, if six, in a week. The theme of all he wrote was the same: *Man truly knows himself only when face to face with death. We in the underground* ... etcetera.

I knew his theories and was not especially interested. I visited only because I had heard he was sick. If he turned out later to be a great man, with opinions worthy of putting in my book, I would be sorry to have missed him.

I stood at the door of his cell. The jailer withdrew. "Thaletes!" I called. No answer. I called out again. For a long time the creature on the straw pallet lay still, but I knew he had heard. He had closed the hand stretched out toward the table, as if angrily resisting me. I called one more time and now the tangled gray mat of hair—all I could see of his miserable head—stirred a little in short, mechanical jerks. At last he brought his face into my line of vision. It was gray as old ashes, and lined like the face of a mummy. There were round holes in his beard and part of one eyebrow was missing. Ringworm. His seeming age was incredible: I knew he could not be over forty-five.

"Thaletes, my name is Agathon," I said. "A fellow philosopher-poet, though the world is not yet aware of it. I come to ask if there's anything I can do."

He made a great effort and stretched his eyes open wider. "Go away!" he said. It was the hiss of an old, old python.

"Be reasonable, Thaletes," I said. "Think! You have no one to talk to, you're too weak to write. All that goes through your famous mind is lost! Yea, lost forever!"

He laughed—hiss, hiss, hiss—and I thought I had overplayed, but it wasn't that. He had no humor in him. The laughter ended in a coughing fit that made him squeeze his eyes tight and clench the one fist I could see. The other fist lay under his crotch and he couldn't get it free, apparently. He would jerk at it fiercely now and then, and then he would quit, with a startled look, and would let his head fall back to the floor with a thud that should have broken his jaw.

"I'm a scribe, Thaletes," I said earnestly. (It's even possible that I meant to be kind.) "I could write for you."

He laughed again, until his mouth stretched open against his will, exactly like the muscle spasm of something dying. "I don't need you," he whispered. "I'm free."

I looked, noncommittally, at the bars. He laughed again.

"Mere facticity," he said, and laughed again. But suddenly he frowned. "No, perhaps I'm mixed up." He wet his lips, straining to think. Then he laughed, startled. "Free!" he said.

I patted the bars with my fingertips. "Perhaps in a certain sense," I began.

"Not in a certain sense! Free!" He was enraged, his whole frail body shaking like a mountainside in an earthquake. He tried to drag himself toward me, snatching at straw and pulling on it, but the straw came to him and his body lay as it was. "What am I?" he hissed. "Am I the It that walks and talks, or am I the Not-It that watches what walks and talks? I am the Not-It! Not-It!"

"That's true," I said, as soberly as possible.

"Precisely, precisely! And what is the world? The world is the It that my Not-It's It is *not!*"

"That probably follows," I said.

"Precisely! Since my Not-It is not It, I am free of It, true? Hopelessly, joyfully *abandoned* to my freedom! Is that not so?"

I rubbed my chin. "It may well be."

"Precisely." He laughed. "Let us say that my body— my everything-except-what-thinks-about-itself—as it functions in the world, is It-within-Itness. Let us say that."

"Good."

"Then what is the nature of my freedom? I cannot choose my Itness itself: it is prior to me. I can choose only the goals of my It, and thus I create my It-as-What-It-Is. I choose to build a house, for example, and I define my It as That-Which-Will-Build-a-House. Excellent! We're progressing! But am I free to build a house? I'm in prison! Ha ha!" He laughed and laughed. I waited. "My freedom," he said softly, slyly, "is contingent: I am free to choose ways of manipulating what I might possibly manipulate, the Itness of the World."

"Of course." I believed I more or less understood, in a certain sense.

"Let us say that I am not in prison, and I choose to ride an elephant which exists. I have chosen a goal, the riding of the elephant, and simultaneously I have chosen a means—an attempt to ride. I now face two problems: First, my free choice indicates that other free choices are possible, for instance the choice *not* to ride the elephant after all: hence, my freedom eats away my freedom. Second, my free choice of a goal may be of one beyond my power: the elephant may be too mean or, if not that, too bumpy for me to stay on!"

"That's true." I did not feel I was contributing much.

"Nevertheless, my Not-It has, we discover, defined more than just my It. It has also defined the *elephant*. This particular elephant, which manifests a profound resistance if I wish to ride it, will on the contrary be a valuable aid if I want to kill my enemy by making *him* ride it. In itself, you see, the elephant is neutral; that is, it waits to be illuminated by an end in order to manifest itself as adverse or helpful. It is, we might say, a *brute existent*. Now pay close attention! We are free when the final term by which we make known to ourselves what we are is an *end:* that is, not a real existent like that which in the supposition which we have made could fulfill our wish, but an object *which does not yet exist*. Only an ensemble of real existents can separate us from this end—in the same way that this end can be conceived only as a state-to-come of the real existents which separate me from it. The resistance which freedom reveals in the existent, far from being a danger to freedom, results only in enabling it to arise as freedom! There can be a free Not-It only as engaged in a resisting world! Outside this engagement, the notions of freedom, determinism, and necessity lose all meaning!"

"I see," I said.

He dropped his head into the straw and panted. At last, with enormous difficulty, he said, "You don't see. Nobody does."

"Perhaps that's so."

A terrible shaking came over him, and I looked away.

"Nevertheless," he said at last, "to be free does not mean to obtain what one has wished, but only to determine one's wish oneself. Success is wholly irrelevant. If I wish to be free of this stinking cell and I cannot achieve it, I illustrate the common case. The history of a man's life is the history of a failure. That is my happiness."

Years later, after I'd reread his writings, it came to me that he was not exactly wrong. At the time, however, I was more interested in his politics. Why had he first supported Lykourgos, taking delight in his inhumanity, then turned on him, stirring up the Helots? I said, "Is it possible that it was your love of failure that attracted you to Lykourgos's scheme—and then, when, against all reason, the scheme began to work, turned you against Lykourgos?"

He lay still. More still, it seemed to me, than the stone walls of his cell. At last—horribly—horribly!— he sighed. "You've understood nothing," he whispered.

"Perhaps that's so."

With a look of terrible sorrow, for all his talk of joy, he raised his head two inches, enough to look at me by rolling his eyes up to almost under the lids. "Freedom is individual," he said. "Lykourgos's antimaterialism established the possibility of personal freedom. But antimateralism is a metaphor, a myth."

I sighed. He was a very difficult person.

"Pay attention!" he hissed. "Lykourgos denies the value of substance, but he exploits. He's a hypocrite! A despot! All government is imposition except the government freely chosen for the moment by one man. Who knows which government a free man would choose? Values leap up before our acts like partridges!"

"But that's absurd!" I broke in. "If every man in Sparta is to choose his own form of government—"

"Never mind," he said, petulant, crabby. "We all fail. Didn't I *tell* you?"

"Thaletes," I said, "is there anyting *practical* I can do for you?"

He lay quiet as a fallen column. Perhaps he was dead. When I visited, the next day, he'd been dead for several hours.

I was not impressed by Thaletes's opinions, I admit. Even after I had reread his work and discovered that his ideas made a kind of sense, I was not particularly impressed. But at least one person in Sparta was deeply moved by all he said. When reading became relatively easy for her—not so much through my influence as through my high-minded (or anyway high-toned) staying away from her, abandoning her, as Thaletes would have said, to her freedom—Iona read all Thaletes wrote in the underground days at Amyklai. Things she'd said clumsily before, she said now with the dangerous conviction one gets from new big words.

I sat with her in the garden once, and after a good deal of talk about nothing, murders and suicides, fires and secret messages, she handed me, timidly, a letter

she'd been working on—a letter on ridiculous cheap
pink parchment, which she intended to send to sympathizers throughout Lakonia. The writing was crude,
each stroke violent, and I was embarrassed for her. But
the ideas were interesting. It went something like this:

One can no more judge the means without the end which
gives it meaning than he can detach the end from the
means which defines it. Murdering a Helot or suppressing
a hundred members of the Opposition are two analogous
acts. Murdering a Helot is an *absolute* evil—it represents
the survival of an obsolete civilization, the perpetuation
of a struggle of races which has to disappear! Suppressing
a hundred opponents may be an outrage, but it can have
meaning and a reason. It is a matter of maintaining or
saving a Power which prevents *the absolute evils of
bigots and despots.*

I read it over twice.

"Well?" she said. The girlish dimples. Puzzling beside what she'd written.

I said, "Hmm." After a while I said, "Iona, you
can't be serious about all this."

"Why not?" she said. No smile now.

"Because it's silly. It's philosophically naïve."

She closed both hands around her cup, wounded,
and I was sorry I'd said it. I should have guessed
she'd taken her philosophizing seriously. (I had, in
fact. Why do I excuse myself?) Her jaw was very
sharp now. "I never claimed to be a philosopher. I just
act."

"I know. But according to Thaletes, the choice and
the action are one."

"I wouldn't know what Thaletes says. Whoever he
is."

I sighed and let it stand. There were two squirrels on
the porch, and I watched them, studying their unrea-
sonably perfect balance. "You send these things to the

troops?" I asked. Ironic, of course. They had only a handful of fighters.

"We don't need to talk about it."

I sighed again. How had we gotten onto these crazy spiderwebs? "You want me out of here, Iona?" I asked.

"Oh . . ." She glanced at me, smiled, touched my hand. "Let's just not talk," she said.

I asked, "Who *do* you talk to, Iona?"

She smiled, fond and distant, this time. "The gods."

I must stop here. I feel curiously weak. It is possible that I am unwell.

27 Peeker:

We have a chance, I think. I fight the temptation to count on it, but I think we may really have a chance.

Not the ephors. That's become clear. They came yesterday, just the usual three, this time, with their usual retinue and pomp. My heart leaped when I saw the tall one striding across the field toward us, almost ahead of the guards who are supposed to precede him. When he arrived at the cell door he smiled at me, unmistakably friendly, his head high, as always, shoulders only slightly stooped, as if from politeness or kindly interest in our welfare. "How've you been?" he said, soft-voiced, very dignified. The others—the fat one and the square, mulish one—tipped their perspiring heads toward me to listen.

"I'm OK," I said, "but Agathon's awful." I drew away from the bars so they could see. He was sprawled on his back in the bed, with his feet up on the wall because he felt faint.

"My goodness," the tall ephor said, and frowned. He met my eyes in the penetrating, attentive way he has. "How long has he been like this?"

"For days," I said. "He gets up sometimes and wanders around like he's looking for something, and sometimes he sits down at the table and—" I was going to say *writes,* but something made me check myself. They would want to see what he'd written. He never gave them the stuff, himself; it would be wrong for me to do it for him. The ephor watched me. He caught the pause and read it, no doubt rightly. "I don't know," I said. "Just sits. Sometimes he comes over here by the door and sits leaning on it, trying to get air. The heat really gets terrible sometimes, and the smell in here . . ." The ephor nodded; he'd registered that already. I said, "His mind's funny. Almost like he's delirious, at times. He's got a really bad fever. I have to keep washing his forehead with cold water the jailer brings. Sometimes Agathon doesn't seem to know me, but then other times he's as lucid as anything. A doctor gave him some medicine, but he's still getting worse. It's serious."

"This is not a good atmosphere for a sick man," the ephor said, looking the cell over, noting details.

"The rats bite his fingers and toes," I said. "That's where he got the disease, I think. A couple of the rats have died. The jailer can tell you."

He turned his head and glanced at the jailer. The jailer nodded.

"Is he eating properly?" the ephor asked, watching me.

I shook my head, serious, though the question seemed odd—stupid. I said, "Hardly at all." While he seemed to reflect on that, I said, "You said there'd be an investigation. Has it come to anything?"

He considered, watching me with his pale eyes. "Is an investigation what Agathon really wants, Demodokos?"

It reeled me. I thought it had been going on for weeks. "You haven't started it?" I said. I hung onto the bars to give help to my knees.

"The question is whether Agathon really wants an investigation," the ephor said gently.

I glanced at the jailer and he looked away. He too was amazed, I had a feeling.

"Let me understand this," I said. "You said there would have to be an investigation—but you haven't even started it?"

He cleared his throat and tipped his head slightly, meeting my eyes as if thinking out what would be best for me. "You realize what's involved here, Demodokos. Before I can move an inch I have to have some reassurance that an investigation is what Agathon himself prefers."

"But that's crazy," I said. "You're an ephor and he's just a sick old man. What's the difference what he wants? Who *knows* what the crazy old bastard wants? He's going to *die* in here. You think that's what he wants?"

The tall ephor continued watching me, not moving at all except for the quiver of one eyelid. "I've assured Agathon that he's perfectly safe as long as I'm around this place. I think he knows that."

I shook my head, jerking the confusion away, and wiped the hair back out of my eyes. "OK," I said, trying to penetrate the talk, the fatherly gentleness—trying to start over. "OK, never mind," I said. "Start all over. Agathon will be dead in a week if he doesn't get out of this stinking cell. Is it possible for you to get him loose?"

The ephor studied me, thinking. He really did have a kind face: I hadn't been wrong about that; and you could see the speed of his thought: I'd been right about that too. And he was honest. Liars can mask their lies, but no man can put on the look of simple honesty. Then what was wrong?

"Is it possible to get him out?" I said again.

The ephor cleared his throat and pursed his lips. At last he said, "No."

"*No?*" I whispered it.

Now the three ephors said it at once, the little fat one wringing his puffy white hands in dismay, the stern one gruffly, as if the decision was nobody's but his. "No." The tall one shook his head decisively. It was entirely out of the question.

I went over to the table and sat down. They talked with the jailer.

"Demodokos?" the tall ephor called. I refused to answer. Eventually they left.

I don't get it. I've given up thinking about it.

But a little before dawn this morning my new hope came. I don't know where the jailer was—sleeping in his hut, probably. Anyway, I woke up with a start when something bumped my arm. I looked down: a clod of dirt. I thought it fell from the ceiling, but then I heard the hiss from the door. It was the boy, the one that brought the letter to Agathon. He waved me toward him. He was scared as hell, his eyes rolling back and forth like a chased dog's. The jailer hadn't put up the planks the boy had hid under last time. Agathon was asleep, half off the bed, whimpering, very sick. I crawled over to the door, jerking my head, trying to shake away sleep.

"Three nights from now. Midnight," the boy whispered. "Have the old man ready."

"What?" I said. "Ready for what?"

But he was gone.

Three nights, then.

If only the perverse old bastard will stay alive. He may. He's almost like normal today, feisty and impish, jabbering about the beautiful glitter of the snow.

28 Agathon:

desperate to finish

The rest in haste. I have certain reasons for believing
I am running out of time.

Late one night I was roughly awakened and summoned to Lykourgos's chamber. I was given no time
to dress but went in my nightgown. Lykourgos sat at
his desk, solemn, as quiet and dangerous as quick-
sand. Six of his ephors were with him, some seated,
some standing, all formal, dangerous. I moved toward
his desk like a man on trial. On his desk he had an
open scroll. I recognized it at once.

He was direct. "You know a Helot by the same of
Dorkis?"

"I may," I said. I pretended to cast about.

"You know him, all right," he said. "Examine this."
He pushed the scroll toward me. "You've seen it before?"

I shook my head.

"It's seditious," he said. "It opposes us."

I shrugged, though frightened, and ventured a joke.
"All life opposes you, Lykourgos. You must learn to
take it in stride."

"Be still," he whispered. I had never heard Lykourgos
whisper. I felt myself trembling, the bones melting in
my legs.

"I forgot my crutch," I said, rather loudly. "I wonder
if I might have a chair?"

"A chair," Lykourgos commanded. One of the ephors
brought one. I sat down. My leg had suddenly and un-

225

accountably begun to give me pain, and I reached under my knee to clamp the place that hurt. Instantly Alkander appeared from somewhere in the shadows behind me and laid his dagger on my shoulder with the blade, light as a hair, along my throat. I glanced at Lykourgos, and he frowned. Alkander stepped back.

"I ask you whether you recognize this writing as that of your Helot friend Dorkis." He tapped the scroll, hard, with two fingers.

"No," I said. "I don't think I've ever seen his writing."

"That's hard to believe." His one-eyed gaze drilled into me, through me. But he changed his tack. "You have served as a professional scribe, have you not?"

I nodded.

"As a scribe, you'd know this writing if you'd seen it before?" He watched, not a muscle moving.

"That's ridiculous," I said, though it wasn't. My whole body was shaking. "Why should I remember every hand I have ever come across?"

Lykourgos waited. He had three tall shadows, two flickering on the wall from the lamps on the desk in front of him, one stretching out on the floor from the lamp on the wall ledge. Below his two shadows on the wall I could see the many shadows of Alkander and the ephors hovering around me. I felt surrounded, the shadows at least as dangerous as the men.

"I have never seen this hand before," I said.

He said, "You're a liar."

Again we waited. I concentrated on the point where the flames of the two desk lamps converged in Lykourgos's eye. At last he said, "Read it."

I read a few lines.

Of any revolution it may be said later that perhaps some atrocity might have been avoided. But few who raise the question are men of goodwill.

Lykourgos said, "You know the style of speech?"

I pretended to search my memory, then shook my head.

His eye still nailed me. Without raising his voice he said, "Bring in the prisoner."

The two guards at the door went out and returned not with Iona but with a man. He'd been whipped badly. His head and torso were a mass of blood and torn flesh. One eye was swollen shut, the other only partly shut. It snapped into focus on something far in the distance.

I glanced back at Lykourgos. "You fool."

"Perhaps." He watched me, thinking. He knew me too well to doubt that I had some reason for calling him a fool when I saw his prisoner. But he showed no emotion. When he signaled, the guards brought Dorkis close to the desk. He looked down at me and faintly smiled. They'd broken his teeth and smashed the powerful cheek muscles, but they hadn't changed him, hadn't even touched him. The wounds were mere facticity. Thaletes was right.

"Agathon," he said, moving his mouth with difficulty. "Bless you." Again the ghostly smile.

"Who wrote this?" Lykourgos said, pointing to the scroll.

Dorkis ducked his head a little, like a boxer moving in, and cocked his brows. "I did."

"Who taught you to write?" Lykourgos said.

"A friend."

Lykourgos looked at me.

"I never taught Dorkis anything," I said. "If I did teach him, which I didn't, I know of no law against it."

"No law against . . . writing," Dorkis said. He tried to talk without touching his swollen and broken lips together.

"*This* writing is against the law," Lykourgos said.

Dorkis actually grinned. "He didn't teach me *this* writing."

I was impressed; in fact, awed. Shackled, beaten, Dorkis seemed more powerful than all of them. It seemed to me for an instant that he had learned something of unspeakable importance, but the next instant I doubted that—it was my silly philosopher's prejudice, that power comes from knowledge. It struck me (God knows what I meant by it) that Something had learned Dorkis. It was as if one of his gods had gotten inside him, had taken over.

But I had no time for abstract speculations. I too could hardly want the real writer of the scroll discovered, but I couldn't let Dorkis throw himself to the Spartans if I could save him without involving her. I said, "Lykourgos, you *know* this man. He's been absolutely faithful, completely dependable, for years. Why should he suddenly turn to sedition now? And if he's turned to sedition, why doesn't he make use of the actual power he's got, because of his position? Why doesn't he, say, organize an army of saboteurs— burn the storehouses, plug the sewage ditches, destroy the herds?"

Lykourgos rubbed his jaw. "Curious that you've hit the details so well."

I looked at Dorkis. Obviously I had not been keeping up. He smiled.

"It's impossible," I said. But my mind had quit. A minute passed.

"The plan was of course discovered," Lykourgos said. "It was a stupid plan. Unworthy of our friend. As for you—" He reflected. "Though I know you to be a liar, I am inclined to doubt that you involved yourself in the plot. It was too bold, too direct, and I believe you to be . . . more timid." He showed his horse's teeth. It was meant to be a smile. He told the guards, "Take the prisoner away."

The guards approached Dorkis but did not touch

him, wishing to give him no more pain. He turned to
go with them. He reached toward my arm with one
shackled hand, but he was too far away to touch me.
"Agathon, look after them, if you can."

I nodded.

He was executed in the public square. He wore only a
loincloth, the usual garb of the condemned. He knelt,
as directed, and the priest he had chosen put water
on his forehead, then backed away, head bowed, and
stood looking religious. The two executioners came up
to stand beside Dorkis, each of them holding his iron
bar in two hands. They waited for the iren's signal.
As for Dorkis, he seemed to be beyond waiting for
anything judgeable by our kind of time. He knelt with
what seemed infinite patience and something I'm almost
embarrassed to give its name: tenderness. He was separate—totally, absolutely—separate from everything
around him. It was as if he had at last, without thinking about it, accepted something, and the choice had
transmuted him. I tried to think, snatching at straws
to keep my feelings dead, what it was that made his
kneeling different from that of a condemned Spartan,
but I couldn't get hold of it. Then the iren went to him
and asked him something, and Dorkis nodded, gently,
as if to a child. And suddenly I knew. He had accepted evil. Not any specific evil, such as hatred, or
suffering, or death, but evil as a necessary principle of
the world—time as a perpetual perishing, space as crea-
tion and wreckage.

The iren gave the signal. They killed him with the
first swing.

29   Peeker:

The old bastard's impossible! I may strangle him yet!
I told him the Helots were going to rescue us, and his
eyes got big as oven lids.

"The hell!" he said. "That's dangerous!"

I told him we had no choice, the place was killing
him, but he wouldn't listen. He whooped to cover up
my voice.

"It's rape!" he yelled. "It's a violation of my civil
rights!"

"You *have* no civil rights," I said.

He thought about it. "That's true." He thought some
more. "Rape!" he yelled. "Rape! Rape!" You could
hear him twenty miles away. I tried to cover his mouth
to keep the jailer from coming, but he bit me. *"Rape!*
Rape! Rape!" I hit him over the head with the lamp.
He passed out.

But what am I to do when the Helots come to rescue
us? If I keep on hitting him on the head I'm liable to
kill him. I might not be exactly sorry, in fact, but how
the hell would I explain it?

The Helots are setting it up even now, if I'm not mistaken. Breakfast was two hours late this morning—it
was a real shit two hours, with Agathon growling and
grumphing around, saying the whole damn thing was
my fault—and when the jailer came he said it was
because the prison was shorthanded. Somebody blew
away the palace guards last night, and the ephors trans-
ferred a group of the prison guards to the palace.

Standard procedure, our jailer says. I suppose they must have known that, or else it was a clever guess. The palace guards and the prison guards are supposed to be the two toughest outfits. While I was talking to the jailer, Agathon ate my food. I am going to kill him.

The guard left without waiting for our plates, and we haven't seen him since. Someone has been watching us all day, across the field. A girl, I think. I only catch a glimpse of her now and then, sticking her head up over the bushes. Whitish blonde hair tight to her head, dirty face, maybe purposely smudged. You'd never see her if you didn't sit staring at the hedge, watching. It occurs to me that a good bowman could pick off our guard with no trouble at all as he stands looking in at us, talking. I'm tempted to warn him, but how can I?

The palace guards. God. Maybe the rebellion really will succeed. The bastards are nervy, anyway. At least the rescue will succeed, I think. I've got a plan. I'll tear up my clothes in strips and then I'll gag the old man and tie his hands and feet.

No. Fuck it. I'll tear up *Agathon's* clothes.

Will the girl come when they rescue us?

Why in hell did I never ask them their names when they smiled at me, swiping my apples? What if I get killed or something, and I never even touched a girl's hand?

30   Agathon:

Socrates ✓

I have whatever the rats have. I can no longer deny it.
Ah well, these pages convince me that I deserve it. The
sickness works slowly, as plagues go—a point I mention merely for its facticity, as Thaletes would say. I've
seen the seaport plague before. And so I am a dead
man. Reflection tells me that death must certainly be
one of two things: either a wonderfully sound sleep, in
which eternity passes like a single night, or else the
soul's journey to another place. Either way, clearly,
death is a gain. What private man—indeed, what king
—ever passed a more pleasant day or night than the
night passed in dreamless slumber? On the other hand,
what would a man not give if he might converse with
Orpheus and Musaeus and Hesiod and Homer? Should
a wise man fear death, then? Emphatically not! A
further proof of my foolishness. I am scared to the
soles of my shoes.

Luckily, I haven't the energy to concentrate on fear. I
can hardly stand up. I haven't even the energy to tease
my jailer.

Her grandson came again last night. Talked mostly
with Peeker, plotting my rescue. Hah! I stayed at the
table, exceedingly unwell, sometimes passing out momentarily—but never mind that. How long has it been
since the first time he came? A week? A month? How
long have I been out of touch with ordinary time?

The revolution drags on. Very close to us now. All
around us. Bah. The boy gave us the latest news with

childish pride. I merely looked at him from my table, leaning on my fists. He must have been hardly more than a baby at the time of his grandfather's abortive revolution—the one that killed him. I might, another time, have worked up mock enthusiasm, my only answer to the optimistic excitement of lunatics.

"The guard will catch you," I said. "You'd better go."

He ignored me, raving on to Peeker in a whisper. "We're hitting the wheat bins to the north. You'll be able to see the glow. Sometime before morning. We're spreading them out, you know. Thinning hell out of the guard ranks."

Peeker nodded.

"After that, we strike at the herds."

"Don't tell us," I said. "Trust no one!" I laughed.

He was silent a moment. I couldn't see him from where I sat, and my legs were shaky. He said, "Grandmother sends her love."

"Tell her thank you. She's very kind."

"We're going to get you out of here," he said.

"Wonderful," I said. Poor old Thalia. Alive or dead? A trembling fit came over me and I covered my face with my hands.

"Are you all right?" he asked.

"A little bit under the weather. He he!"

"You're sick as hell." A mere child and talks like a soldier. His grandfather was a man of noble diction.

"You're sick," he said again.

"So my wife maintained." I gave him a leer.

He seemed comforted. Good old Agathon, always the kidder. "You'll be out of here in a matter of hours," he whispered. "Take my word for it."

"I believe you. Thank you very much."

Another brief faintness came over me, or a memory, which is perhaps the same thing. My son across the table from me in Athens, the one time I visited there after Tuka left with the children. He wanted me to stay.

He was nearly grown now. A handsome devil, with a girl friend who, one of these days, I was sure, would be his wife. He said, *"Why* do you have to go back?"

"I don't know," I said. "To look for something." Then: "No, that's a lie. To escape from something, perhaps. No, that's a lie too."

Kleon said gently, as though he were the father and I the son, "What do you do there, now that Lykourgos no longer trusts you?"

"Nothing," I said. "I teach, a little. Eat roots and berries."

"I believe it." He smiled suddenly, and the smile transformed him to the twelve-year-old I remembered. "I couldn't believe it was you, when you first came. That beard—you look like a Jewish merchant. And that paunch! How'd you get so fat on roots and berries?"

"Berries with cream."

Kleon became serious again, rather lawyerish. Made me defensive. "What do you really do there, Father? Do you ever see Lykourgos at all?"

"I see him, Kleon." Speaking my son's name brought tears to my eyes, my standard reaction to verbal evocations of the past. I folded my hands on the table and looked at them carefully, so I'd remember them later. "I am, I suppose you'd say, a hanger-on. I was not exactly kicked out of the palace. I saw fit to move, and no one objected. I go back, from time to time, and that, too, they accept. I've taken on the character of, you might say, a local Seer."

He watched me with sorrow in his eyes, and I remembered his mother's sorrow.

"Ah, youth!" I said. I kissed my fingertips. Solon's gesture.

He too had folded his hands on the table and was looking at them. It struck me all at once that this handsome boy was the mirror image of what I myself had been as a younger man. I could have giggled.

He said, "You seem unhappy, Father."

"Ah, well." I shrugged. "Not as happy, perhaps, as Tellos, or those fortunate, fortunate brothers Kleobis and Biton."

"Who?" he said.

"Some idle tale." (Poor Akhilles, I thought. Dead these six hundred years.)

I did not see Solon while I was in Athens, though he asked after me. I saw Tuka twice, dressed in black, as stern and grieved as Lykourgos and more beautiful than ever. I said, "You look like a shipwreck, Tuka." She smiled. "Thank you."

I sat with my daughter Diana on the steps. She said, "You really are wonderfully funny. It must be they keep you as a court clown."

"Do my kind of humor in Sparta and they bite your thumb," I said.

She laughed. I wondered if it really was funny or if it was only that she loved me, whatever that meant.

Kleon said soberly, "Stay, Father. For Mother's sake."

I shook my head. "It's not possible."

"Because of——" He worked at it awhile, looking at his hands.

"No, not because of Iona. I rarely see her, though we're friends."

"Why then?"

"You wouldn't understand." An evasion. He knew I knew it. "Destiny," I mumbled.

"What?"

He leaned forward, and this time I shouted it. "Destiny!"

Iona's boy (grandson), crouched outside the bars, whispered at me, "Don't shout! If the jailer hears——"

"Destiny," I said more softly. I knew where I was and yet didn't know. Time had collapsed on me. *Destiny. Destiny.* I tried to make out what it meant. Terror came over me, deeper than anything physical, it seemed, and I tried to face it, embrace it, but it wouldn't come clear. An image of people dying: a faint sound of screams. They were all around me. I see an army moving down from the north. Great God Apollo save . . . I got up, shaky, and, leaning heavily on my crutch, went over to the cell door to be closer to the night. The image was gone.

The jailer was standing behind the boy. The boy's eyes moved, following mine—Peeker saw him the same instant—and when the boy saw the jailer he cringed against the bars.

But the jailer didn't stir. He merely looked at us, and after a while he said hoarsely, "Go away." The boy inched around him, backed away, then turned with a jerk and ran. When I touched the place on the bars where the jailer had laid his fingers, I received an impression. "You are going to be murdered," I said. He looked at me. "Don't doubt me," I said. "You are going to be murdered."

When I woke up briefly, sometime an hour or so before dawn, the sky to the north was red orange. The grain storages were burning.

31 Agathon:

I had chicken for breakfast. It was four hours late. I was too sick to eat it, but I ate it anyway, because I knew it was not my food, it was my jailer's. He stood stiffly erect, watching me eat, and when I thanked him he did not speak.

"I do you good, jailer," I said. I made my face unhappy. "But alas, like the world, I'm perishing."

> Agathon is perishing,
> But hear my second verse:
> If Agathon is perishing,
> He still could be worse!

I could be much worse, if I tell the truth. My stomach is in knots, my bowels run pebbled black water, I have a high fever, intermittently, but my mind is sometimes clear. I worked most of the morning on a piece of writing not related to this series of notes, or lamentations, or whatever—a kind of disquisition on jugs, the relationship between jugs and plants and lower animals and men. I filled several parchments, but I seem to have mislaid them. It seemed to me as I wrote that my brain had never been more alert, for all the civil war of my system. It was perhaps the effect of the powder my physician gave me, a thing that lowers fever and makes the fingertips and toes go quite numb and at times produces a kind of ringing in the ears, not wholly unpleasant. It makes my mind seem detached from my body and nonpartisan, almost spiritual. But whatever the chemistry of the thing, I praise Apollo that my mind is clear again, if only for the moment. I wrote, and read part of what I'd written to Peeker and my jailer, and they listened, though each perhaps with only part of his mind. They showed neither approval nor disapproval of my theories. A group of strangers were behind the jailer, peering in.

I said to my jailer at one point, breaking off in the middle of a sentence, "What makes a man like you a Spartan jailer?"

He shook his head, as if that were the least of his questions. "I'm past the age of fighting for my country," he said.

No doubt he knew I could make that very risible but had decided to bring it out anyway, and so I said nothing. He looked off to the north, where the storage bins still filled the sky with smoke. He shouldn't be standing here, he knows. The prison is desperately shorthanded. —Iona's work, unless I miss my guess. But he's indifferent. He's given up, like me. Perhaps he has accepted the fact I warned him of, his death. Poor soul, he loves this hellhole of a country. So do I. I will finally admit it. For all its sicknesses it has stumbled to certain virtues. It does not have, like Athens, the cancer of slavery. Even a Helot has more humanity than a slave, as I used to try to tell my wife. She couldn't see it; arkhon's daughter, fat-souled with wealth. But then, even Solon couldn't see it. And so I understood my jailer, I think. I have sometimes stood on a hill in summertime, looking over the miles and miles of blowing wheat and barley this fertile land produces, the deep green pastures—specked with goats and cows and sheep, studded here and there with elm and maple trees —the land parted, as if gently, by wandering streams, and split down the middle by the wide, smooth-as-a-mirror Eurotas with its fishing boats and pleasure boats and its children swimming, splashing each other and

laughing. I have gazed at the peaceful old temple to
Orthia rising out of the marshy borderland, its white
reflection motionless in the water (they have no scourg-
ings there, only prayer and calm; the darker temple of
Orthia is hidden in the mountains). And sometimes at
night, on a fast horse, I have ridden that countryside
alone, my head down close to the horse's neck, my
nostrils flaring to suck in his smell. The still night air
would go rushing past my ears and the stars hung
motionless, poised to strike, as if not a mile above me.
I'd gallop down lanes where the smell of grapes rose
from either side like fine perfume, down wide dirt roads
that by day would be filled with Helot wagons piled
high with cabbages or bundles of cloth, and I'd ride
through villages where even the poorest were richer than
most of the world. No such abundance leaps out of the
earth around Athens. You fight the stony ground with
broken knives and get scraggly grain in return, or
thistles thick as fenceposts at the base. No wonder
horde on horde of invaders has seized this Spartan
ground with spears and shovels and temples to propiti-
ate the knocked-down gods. Slaves are slaves, in Athens: the rich stand on the broken heads of the poor,
and Solon's laws are not the laws of nature but a feeble
redress. In Sparta they have no need of slaves, they can
get along on the semicaptive civilization of the Helots.
In times of peace the Helots are even granted their
own society, up to a point. What they need in Sparta—
Lykourgos is right—is men who can hold off next year's
crop of invaders.

My jailer, whom I have scorned as a fool, is the
helpless victim of a dream, an idea. Sparta at peace,
wealthy, aloof, invulnerable.

Did he mean this too, looking off to where the storage bins still smolder: the dream is, like any dream, a
victim of its history? They came down hungrily out of
their mountains and seized the place and made their
captives slaves, because slavery was their way, the way

of all our cultures for centuries, though in fact they had no need of slaves in Sparta. That changed. The situation evolved. But the anger of the Helots did not die, nor the guilty arrogance of the conquerors. It might have been a magnificent State: a group of workers, a group of defenders, and at the head of it all two kings, not one—just rule tempered by another just ruler. But hate was in Sparta's history, irrevocable: the diarchy too had its history: two kings, not one, because of the jealousy of ancient houses whose names we no longer remember except in dim, contradictory legends. And so Lykourgos wrested from Apollo the theory of the ephors, the board of wisemen-priests who ruled both kings and commoners. But every man on the board had his history.

My jailer merely looked off to the north for a long time, saying nothing, solemn, tight-jawed, and, I had a feeling, disheartened. From the instant time began, it has been too late. I clown and rage and lecture the stone-eared universe, but my noise comes too late. As for him, he gazes across the valley, observes the smoke of the impossible ideal, then at last looks down, reflects on his duties, and moves away without a word to attend to whatever prisoner or dreary task he takes into his mind when he puts me out of it. Call him Atlas. His work has no meaning, perhaps, but it has its dignity.

> Agathon is sinking fast
> While standing still.
> The travel of the Universe
> Is all downhill.

How was it? Dorkis was dead, yes. And Iona . . .

It's all escaped me. I did something for them, something generous, even brave, perhaps.

Gone.

Incredible! This once fine mind, well, decent mind . . . I could commit long speeches to memory on a single hearing. I could read ten pages and remember them for years. Gone.

> Poor Agathon has lost his wits
> And is too sick to dance;
> But still he has his dignity,
> He hides his dirty pants.

Dorkis was dead.

I was in a room: the palace, I think. It was night, because when I looked up—I remember now, yes—the tops of the columns were in darkness like a heavy black fog. Footsteps—guards—and then lighter, slower footsteps: the feebleminded, prematurely old man, Kharilaus, the King. He raises his arm, a signal for me to approach, and I . . .

I've lost it.

Tuka said, "Do you want her? You can have her now, you know."

"You know who I want for my wife."

"Not really. I know you love me, and I know you have a sort of investment in me—twenty years of your life."

"Isn't that enough?"

"It's nothing at all. I wouldn't have believed it, but it's true. I even understand. I might have felt the same, if I'd met the right man."

"Not Dorkis?" I asked.

She looked out the window, with one hand on the sill, as if for balance. "Almost," she said. "If he'd been what he was that last few minutes—

A troop marched by outside, clicking their heels out. After they'd passed I said, "What was it that changed him?"

"Certainty," she said. She bent forward a little, as if from some pain, then half turned her face to look at me. She said, "Death."

I thought: *I love you, Tuka. Come back. Wake up.*

Wait. Yes.

Dorkis was dead.

The King raised his hand, and I went to him. I knelt. I said, formal and sober as Solon with Kroesos, "Whatever this woman's husband may have been guilty of, the woman and her children were not involved. Dorkis was a loyal and faithful servant for many years, and a loyal freeman after that. He was given concessions—a good house, provisions, the freedom to come and go as he pleased—and he valued them, as his family did. I speak as a friend who knew him well. Toward the last, he must have gone mad. Why would a sane man turn on all who had been good to him? Your majesty saw the execution. The man was not himself. He was admirable, perhaps, in a certain sense. Even noble. But I give you my solemn word he was not himself. If your majesty's favorite dog went mad, would you punish the bitch and whelps?"

Both Iona and Tuka were white with rage at my degradation of his martyrdom. I could have mocked them. I remained solemn.

The King waved at me feebly, or waved in my general direction. His eyes were bad. "What is it you ask us?"

I bowed lower. "Let them keep their house. Let them live as they've lived in the past, honored by the community. They've done Sparta no wrong."

The Joy of the People looked over to Lykourgos for help.

Lykourgos said nothing, watching me.

Kharilaus said, "Is this man, here . . ." His mind wandered.

Lykourgos showed no emotion. "As far as we know," he said, "the man is trustworthy."

Kharilaus was not exactly satisfied. Also, he was uncomfortable standing up, and clearly I was to blame for his having to put up with it. "He has gall, this man," he said. "He has his gall making us listen to pleas about Helots!"

Lykourgos said nothing.

Kharilaus scowled and closed his eyes. "Very well, let him have what he asks for, whatever it is."

Lykourgos nodded again. "As your majesty wishes."

Though the King's judgment was not binding, the ephors assented.

Kharilaus retired.

When Lykourgos turned to go, I said, "Thank you, horse."

He paused, brooding. "You played it well," he said. Then left.

Tuka said, "Do you want her? You can have her now, you know."

"You know who I want for my wife," I said.

"Not really," she said. "I know you love me, and I know you have a sort of investment in me—twenty years of your life."

"Isn't that enough?"

"It's nothing."

"Let us say I am riding an elephant," Kleon said. "I have chosen a goal, the riding of an elephant, and simultaneously I have chosen a means." He smiled, gentle, infinitely distant.

For some reason we are in our room. There's a terrible fight. Tuka is violently angry, but whatever it is that bothers her is a matter of indifference to me. She throws things. I dodge them like the coward I am, but this time I do not leave in scorn, because the last time I did she went into shock. We are naked, and I think, for all my anger or boredom or whatever, *I love you, Tuka. Come back.* She hurls herself at me and scratches my face, trying to reach my eyes. "Stop it!" I yell. "If you make me lose my temper, I could kill you." I push her, to show her the absurdity of her pitting her woman's strength against mine. But she's there again, and I can feel the cool blood running down my chest, washing down my cheek like tears, though she still hasn't reached my eyes. I seize her in a lover's embrace, and while I hold her with my left hand I pull punches into her back with my right. She gasps, falls away, and I hit her in the face, then the stomach. She lies still, her nose bleeding.

"I told you!" I yell at her. "I *warned* you!"

She lies still. I hold her, move my hands on her back as I used to do when she went rigid with anger, but she's not rigid now, merely unconscious, beaten. I tell her of my love.

The following morning, Tuka and the children were gone.

I have lost track of time completely. It may have been yesterday that I last worked on this sordid tale. It may have been last week. In any case, I'm feeling splendid this afternoon, relatively speaking. My friendly jailer's physician does not look optimistic, but a man knows how he feels. And God knows it must be physical. It can't be what's been happening.

Iona came. Her grandson had told her I was deathly sick and recalcitrant about accepting their version of liberty; and though she long ago gave up love of me for love of war, she had to come see for herself, try her arts of persuasion. She walked up to my cell door in broad daylight. She shouldn't do that, for more reasons than one. War has made her ugly. The jailer must certainly have seen her, but no one was around to force him to the duty he has no respect for, and so he allowed the visit. Or else he's dead.

No. It's not true that war has made her ugly. It's changed her, merely; moved her toward the universal wreckage. Her slanted eyes, once charming, seductive, have grown cunning, smoldering like lava pits. Her language, once stumbling, girlish, self-conscious, has become professional, incisive, the language of one who has grown accustomed to giving cruel orders. In her presence, I become poor old Kronos. I understand her, love her, pity her, and pretend not to notice that she looks on me as a kindly, once potent and beneficent old god, now half dead.

She talked with Peeker for a long time. Then with me. She said, "We're getting you out of here tonight."

"Iona, you look so lovely!" I wrung my hands.

"Lay off, Agathon. I haven't much time."

"I saw the glow of the fires. It was wonderful. Wonderful!"

"Agathon, stop it."

"You see through me. That's your way." I shook with delight.

"For the love of God!" exclaimed Iona.

"Behind all those masks I'm serious, you know."

She clenched her fists. "Stick your face up close to the bars and I'll ruin you!"

"You would! You really would! That's what I love about you!"

Iona looked at the bars. I could still beat her.

"Look," she said. "You're sick. You have to get out of here. So we're freeing you, Agathon. Tonight. —No, don't interrupt, don't clown, just this once."

"I'm sorry," I said. I wrung my hands.

She bit her lips and said nothing for a minute, and I knew why. She did love me, whatever that means, and she was waiting out her frustration. —No, that's too simple. She remembered that she once had loved me, and that, however destructive it was, it was good. But it wasn't, now, good; my degeneration disgusted her, and she was trying to think back to what I had been before. I had her, because I am simpler than she, even though I am, quote, a philosopher. I said, "Iona, you should have left. I told you to run. Don't you trust me?"

"I couldn't," she said.

"Because of Dorkis's martyrdom," I said. "Right.

But he didn't choose it, you know. It landed on him."

"Agathon, stop it."

"I know," I said. "Nevertheless, even though it's reasonable, it's true."

"Listen," she said. (I tried to remember if I'd told her about Konon. *Listen. Listen.*) She said, "Let's say I killed Dorkis."

"Child, dreary child," I said.

"No, I'm tougher than I used to be. Let's say I did—and I don't mean merely by the scroll. That part's easy, you know—dying to protect someone you love. It went beyond that. He'd accepted the plan. He'd begun to act, and it was because of his actions that they believed he wrote the scroll. Each thing made them believe the other, the scroll and the actions. So if I was to blame for his dying, it was this way: I pushed him too fast, refused to allow him his own nature. He acted hastily, unlike himself, and because I pushed him into making mistakes I killed him."

"Surely Dorkis deserves a little of the credit," I said pleasantly.

"Nonsense," she snapped. "I killed him. I loved him, of course. Irrelevant. I accept what I did, because *he* accepted it. You saw him die. He was proud, Agathon. Even though he'd acted too quickly, clumsily, he was glad he'd acted. It was as if he'd finally discovered his depths. And so listen. I have to finish it for him. If I don't, it's meaningless. And so I *will* finish it. This time the plan's better. It won't fail."

"Ah, optimism," I said.

"No. Care."

"Possibly."

"It is."

"Conceivably." Then: "Take advice from a sly old Seer. You plan for the future, but what you don't understand is, there *is* no future. Thaletes's words, but the voice of the universe as well. I have seen the future of the Helots, Iona. Doom. Fire and torture and decimation."

"Agathon," she said. She tightened her fists on the bars. The knuckles went white.

"The world in its Itness," I said merrily, interlacing my fingers, "is a bunch of gears. You move them by their own laws, not by the laws, much less the desires, inside you. To plan for the future you expect is, alas, to plan for a time that will never exist. Even if you mysteriously succeed, by the time you achieve your glorious plan, the world will have changed, and the plan will be irrelevant. You know what everything's about?"

"Stop it, Agathon! Just for one second in your life, stop it and *look* at yourself. Those filthy clothes, that tangled hair, those wasted eyes, wasted gestures, wasted ideas! *Be* something!"

I did stop, because her commands even now had power over me. I studied her, eyes narrowed.

"We're going to make you well; as soon as you're well you'll help us. We need your mind, your knowledge of them, your way of swaying people." She paused, searching my face. *"Will* you come with us?"

I rubbed my mouth. Her neck was creased like an eroded hill and age had enlarged her knuckles. I thought her more beautiful than ever.

At last I said slowly, " 'Be something,' you tell me."

I would not have said, the first time it happened, that my spirit was seized by a god. I dislike the terminology, though I use it myself at times, for the sake of convenience or obfuscation. I was filled, merely, with an overwhelming sense of the boundless stupidity of things. Tuka had left me—I'd thrown her away as if her beauty, her goodness, her artistry—that above all —were nothing. Now when I heard some Helot lyre I was not softened by it but stirred to scorn by the crudeness of the instrument, the vulgarity of the technique, compared to Tuka's on the harp. Because of some animal force in me, or animal rigidity of brain, I had let all that go. And for what? Dorkis was dead, Iona full of sulfurous smoke. And leaving the palace because the place was bitter to me now, I had lost even whatever chance I might have had to influence Lykourgos. If I ever had it in the back of my mind that I'd come here to Sparta in search of some kind of Destiny, I could see now that I'd blasted it to atoms. In the months following Dorkis's death, I'd let myself go to seed, had taken pride, in fact, in how quickly and thoroughly I went. When I stood on a hill in a good breeze my rags flew around me like blackbirds and my smell laid vineyards waste. Any man so bold as to speak to me got back such babble, such lunatic clowning, such mock weeping, such preening, such mock flattering, above all, mock philosophizing, that he left walking sideways, cautiously eyeing my crutch.

And then one day, in the main square of the city—it was the first of May—I watched the Spartans marching. It was the opening of Lykourgos's ugly festival of Orthia, goddess of the hunt—the festival in which, nowadays, the maidens dance naked and sing scornful songs about those who have been cowards, and teasing songs to those who are bachelors, and hymns of praise to butchers. After that they go up to Orthia's mountain temple, twelve miles north, for the barbaric ritual scourging of young men. Sometimes they kill one or two. The soldiers' flutes went through me like heart pains, and their festival capes, the painted round shields, the raised swords of the second rank, blinding in the sun, assaulted my eyes like glaring ice and snow. They came wave on wave, the hoplites in front, bearded, overgrown, deadly efficient from many wars, and after them the younger troops—the archers, the company of javelinists with their white capes, the clean-up troops, naked and terrible, their daggers stretched forward and upward, rigid, as if to scrape open the bellies of the high, still clouds. I thought all at once, watching the precision of their murderous march, of Tuka's fingers moving precisely, at lightning speed, on the lyre; and I saw, in the same motion of mind, Iona's fingers constructing one of her enormous decorations. As if in a daydream I saw an underground room full of corpses —a room much larger than the crypt where I used to keep my book: the vault of some mountain shrine. I saw, clear as day, Iona's head on a pikestaff, and soldiers laughing. And as the phantom or impression passed over my eyes, I felt something new coming over me, a rage so black and indifferent to life that my natural cowardice left me. I could feel my eyes widening, bugging, and a tremble coming over my lips. Then suddenly, as if part of the dream, I found myself strutting majestically beside the troops, whistling with their flutes. No one laughed, of course. The irens glanced over from the fronts of their ranks, but they were baffled: there were no rules for how to deal with this. The spectators, too, were looking at me, some frowning, some glaring, bursting with indignation. I mocked their frowns, their glares. We came to a corner where a group of young Helots were sitting on the wide stone steps of an ephor's majestic old house, and they pointed at me and laughed. I pointed and laughed back. Then, in front of the chief gate of the two kings' palace, the procession stopped. The kings came down, Arkhelaus stern, effeminately pompous, as usual, Kharilaus vague, miserably wishing for a chair. I mimicked them too. Even kings were not above my law. Lykourgos stood to the left of them and slightly in front of them. I mocked the mighty Lawgiver.

"Who *is* that person?" Kharilaus said.

"A messenger and friend," I said, and looked obsequious, panting in short breaths that went *ssew, ssew*.

"Who?" he said.

Arkhelaus raised his hand and said, "Be still, brother."

I put my finger to my lips and winked.

Lykourgos glanced at the saner of the kings and got a nod. "Leave, Agathon," he said.

"Ah, woe!" I said. *Ssew, ssew*. "Poor Agathon is no longer with us. His soul was snatched at the pinprick of midnight, and now, praise heaven, his leastmost fart is a wind from the great god Apollo." I clutched my chest and panted harder. It burned my throat.

"Agathon," Lykourgos said quietly, "leave us."

"Apollo?" Kharilaus said.

"He's mad, your majesty," Lykourgos said.

But Kharilaus was uneasy. "Have him come nearer." I hurried close.

Kharilaus looked more uneasy yet. "He smells, this man."

"Odors deceive us," I said, and wagged my finger at him. "A thing which is unusual may seem at first unsavory, as, for example, a child's first olive, or a lady's bush, or idiocy in a monarch. But on closer inspection and greater familiarity, we learn that olives are fashionable food, however disgusting, and even one's own blessed mother has a bush, and idiocy in a king gives the ship of state ballast."

"Get him away," Kharilaus said. "He stinks."

Lykourgos's jaw was working. "Go," he said.

I stood before them, smiling, wringing my hands, puffing, looking pitiful.

"Arrest that man," Arkhelaus said. But Kharilaus said, "Is it true that he's a god?"

I bobbed my head. "Sure as day," I said. "I'll prove it. I'll cause an earthquake." I raised my arms.

"No, no, no!" Kharilaus cried. "No earthquake, please!" His tiny eyes widened to roughly the size of a pig's.

I grinned. "I was just kidding."

Two guards stood beside me, waiting to arrest me. They didn't smell so heavenly themselves.

I said, "I don't want to keep you from your naked

girls or your whip games, so I'll give you my message at once, and then I'll be gone."

Arkhelaus waited and poor fool Kharilaus bit his soft lips.

"O Kings, O mighty Lawgiver, I stink to teach you the smell of your mortal flesh. I hobble on a crutch to teach you the awful arrogance of your soldiers' strutting. I cower and tremble like a new-caught slave to teach you the emptiness of puissance and power. And now, worst of all, I shall reason with you, to teach you the perfect foolishness of reason." I began to hobble back and forth in front of them, gesticulating, winking, twitching. "Why does a man become a lawgiver? For fear that, if somebody else does it, he may be given laws which run counter to his nature. And what is the nature of a man who becomes a lawgiver? It is the act of giving out laws. But ah! Here's the hideous problem, then!" I stopped and cowered, as if pressed down by the weight of the towering sky. "What is the nature of the laws a lawgiver gives out?" I pretended to wrestle fiercely with the question, pointing my toes in, knee against knee, and counting off the difficulties on my fingers. "Are they the laws of somebody else's nature? No! Otherwise somebody else could give them out. Are they the laws, then, of *anybody* else's nature? No again, for if anybody else could give out the laws, we would have no discreet and official position called Lawgiver. But then we're forced to a terrible dilemma! Either the laws which a lawgiver gives force all men to be lawgivers, which is ridiculous, or else the laws which a lawgiver gives are the expression of a nature foreign to all but the lawgiver himself, which is unthinkable. For if the latter were true, the lawgiver's laws would force all men into the nature of the lawgiver, each man sadly abnegating his real nature, that being outlawed, and all men would be lawgivers, which situation we call by the name of anarchy. Terrible! Repulsive! How do we resolve this dreadful dilemma? Ah! I see light in your

majesties' eyes. You have solved it—and rightly, I may
as well mention, for as a god, I know your thoughts!
The strongest lawgiver in the country gives laws to the
next strongest, yes! and he gives laws to the next, and
so on, down to the least and feeblest of all men. Yes,
yes!" I clapped my hands, delighted. "And who does
the least and feeblest give laws to, since by law he must
be a lawgiver? Of course! Obvious!" I leaped to
Kharilaus as though he'd thought of it. "He reverses the
chain and gives laws to the man just above him. Wonderful! Wonderful! And this reversal we call *by the
name of Revolution.* I bid you adieu. Dance prettily!
Whip stingingly. Tra la!"

I left them abruptly, moving as quickly as I could,
listening in pounding terror for the footsteps of the
guards behind me, but no one followed. When I glanced
over my shoulder they were standing, undecided,
watching my retreat, frowning like crocodiles. That
night I lay in my hut sick with fear, sick to the point
of vomiting, but no one came to get me. I thought myself a very lucky man and resolved to flee at once to the
safety of Athens. Yet I didn't leave. Within three weeks
I was at it again, wheedling, grimacing, banging my
crutch on the pavement. It was like some kind of addic-
tion. I couldn't help myself: I would see some new
absurdity—now from the Spartans, now from the Helots—and an impression would come, and the clowning
despair would rush over me, the total indifference to
anything but the monstrous foolishness of human be-
ings, and in a flash—or a giggle—I was at them. As my
idiocy became familiar, it became safe. Children began
to mock my eccentricities, or follow after me, mimicking my hobble. At last I had taught them something.

So it was that, for better or worse, I had found my
Destiny. I picked at my clothes with my fingers, as if
nervously, and winked at my beloved Iona. " 'Be something,' " I said. "Maddening as it is, love—to you and,
ah! to me as well—I am Sparta's Seer. I've called myself

a silly fool, a coward, and I am. But I'm also something more, and conceivably better. I'm the absolute
idea of *No*. No, I will not come and help you murder
Spartans, and with me or without me you'll fail, die in
blood, as even the Spartans will eventually fail, and as
we all will die, eventually, become dinner for worms.
But I will die with a certain worthless dignity: I did
not simplify."

"Pompous, pompous, pompous!" she screeched.
"You'd mock it in anyone else."

"I *am* pompous. It's true! O miserable, miserable
beast! I *hate* myself!" I stamped my foot.

"In the name of the gods," she hissed. She was
clutching the bars as if to snatch the door off.

"But you see how it is," I said, funereal. "I told you
to run. It's your only decent choice, but you refuse to
run, because you're dead set on killing—because of
guilt about Dorkis, or hunger for revenge, or because
you're caught up in Thaletes's ideas, or anyway your
version of them. You think like a Spartan: it's filthy,
vulgar to submit. You must rule them, destroy them.
I understand. I understand! Creative destruction is the
first law of the universe. But I say *No* to the universe.
'Fuck it!' saith angry Agathon. I'll have no truck with
it. And so I refuse to be rescued from my cell."

She shook her head, tight-lipped, and there were tears
in her eyes. "You don't know what you're saying. Agathon, you're *dying*."

Peeker was watching me. Solemn, strangely good-
looking, I thought, with those deep sad eyes of his.

"So kiss me good-bye, Iona," I said. "Come, come!"
I pushed my face into the bars and leered.

She shut her eyes tight, and I could see her thinking,
hanging terribly suspended between the choices. Or
maybe she was thinking of the smell. She kissed me.
My heart filled with pain. "I love you, Agathon," she
said.

And so she left.

Night, but I must continue. Time almost out.

My jailer has dropped all feigned indifference. He told me the news himself. Lykourgos is dead.

It happened at Delphi. Suicide. He sacrificed to Apollo, and asked him whether the laws he had established were good, and sufficient for the people's happiness and virtue. The oracle answered that the laws were excellent, and that the people, as long as they observed them, should live in the height of renown. A fake Rhetra, but never mind that. Lykourgos took down the oracle in writing and sent it by a messenger to Sparta. Then, having sacrificed a second time to Apollo, and having taken leave of his few friends, he made an end of his life by a total abstinence from food. He is said to have told his beloved Alkander that it seemed to him a statesman's duty to make his very death, if possible, an act of service to the State. I'm not certain whether he meant by that, as I hope he did, that he was saving the State the cost of his food, or merely that by dying at Delphi, having forced the people to swear they'd abide by his laws till his return, he forced them now to perpetual obedience. No matter. As usual, no one in Sparta laughed. Even I forgot to laugh. Solon, I suppose, can now call him a happy man.

It occurred to me—and I mentioned the fact to my dear apistill—that Lykourgos had it already planned before he left that I should rot for years in prison and finally die, sick, miserable, ugly, like Thaletes. I understand, of course, that he couldn't very well leave me out on the streets, forever criticizing. My dear Peeker, however, saw more. He looked at me and at length nodded. "People make too much of hate," he said. He's growing up. I'm forced to confess it.

Also, I was startled. Peeker was right, of course. Lykourgos must have hated me all these years, hated me so devotedly that tyrannizing me in life was not enough. The discovery, or my sickness, or the two to-

gether, made me woozy. When I came to myself Peeker
had gone away. (No, that's not possible.)

Sickness, discovery. There it is again in a new dis-
guise, the old opposition, or conspiracy, I'm not sure
which, that's plagued my life: brute adventure, the brutality of idea.

There's an ancient theory—unless I myself made it
up at some time—that the Earth and Moon are enormous balls that fall endlessly in the mind of God, turning around and around each other, as if at arm's
length, like Helot dancers using each other as pivots.

Very sick. Troubled by nightmares, visions. Unable
to write.

32 Peeker:

How many years have I lived in this one deadly summer? I feel older than Akhilles's ghost, and more filled
with sorrow, despair. Agathon told me once, long ago,
of a dream he had, or a vision; he couldn't say. He
stood on a dark and smoky island that had long ago
suffered some mysterious storm—deracinated trees,
wind-worn skeletons of birds and fish. The island had
never recovered. On all sides, there were only rocks,
fallen timber gradually disintegrating; and nowhere a
trace of green. The heavy brume that lay over the island
was motionless, like the surrounding sea. It was the island of Persephone, it came to him: the country of the
dead. His heart jumped. He'd be brought, like Odysseus, Tieresias, and the rest, to be given conversation
with shades. "There's no other way to get the Answer,
you know," he told me. Carefully, feeling his way in
the dimness, furtively glancing to left and right in case
he'd been brought here by mistake, he inched with his
crutch toward the center of the island. He came to a
great black mountain, and in its side, like the stiffly
open mouth of a drowned man, he found a cave. It
was the entrance to the Underworld. With a prayer to
Apollo, and one last shudder, he ducked in. Blackness
and silence. He felt his way along the cave walls and
came at last to a wide stone stairway curving down as
if to the core of the earth. He descended. The stairway
drew him down for hours, until he'd lost all track of
time, all sense of direction. He came to a wide stone

256

descent into psyche

floor. "At last!" he thought, and rubbed his hands together. He couldn't tell how far the floor stretched or what the room contained. There was a squeak of bats; nothing else.

Agathon scratched himself, cocked his eyebrow, and at last made his decision. He called out in a loud voice, trying not to sound too grandiose: "I am Agathon the Seer! I have come to the Underworld to learn from the dead!" Only echoes answered. He waited, biting his lip and feeling sheepish. Hours passed. Perhaps you have to do it three times, he thought; so he did it three times. No answer. A bat snarled in his hair and he caught it and broke its neck by way of sacrifice. Still no one came. There was only the darkness and stillness. There was no one there. Nothing. World without end. Agathon sat down to tighten his sandals, then started back up the stairs.

I will set down the details of our stupid escape.

It was midnight. The sky over the city was red with the glow of a dozen huge fires, distractions for the Spartans, to cover our escape. Agathon was in a deep, unhealthy sleep. I would have no trouble with him, I saw. I'd almost have welcomed the sound of his crabby, mocking voice or the noise he makes tasting his lips. I lay in front of the door, watching the open field for movement, ready to snap my eyes shut if I heard the guard. The rescue time was long gone, it seemed to me; but I had to judge by guess—I've never paid proper attention to the stars—and maybe anxiety hurried the clock inside me. I went through a thousand doubts. Maybe Iona had dropped the plan, because Agathon wanted her to and, old and ugly as they were, they were still lovers. Maybe the Spartans had caught some Helot at one of those fires they'd set as distractions, and had found out about the plot. Maybe they'd changed their mind about the night. There was a full moon—stupidest possible time for a rescue—and the fires from the city made night even more like day.

Then they appeared, out of nowhere. The old woman stood at the bars looking in with eyes like ice, her white hair knotted tight, her nose like an arrowhead. The ghastly face vanished the instant it appeared, and there were two men, one huge and slow, as silent as a whale coasting, the other wiry, bald as the moon and quick as a frenzied lunatic, also silent. The air was hot and still. The only sound was the crunch of the iron bar drilling in at the side of the doorframe, forced in not by hammer blows but by the steady drive and twist of the big man's hands. The end of the rod came through, and I touched it. "It's through," I whispered. The rod was hot. The big man leaned on the rod, and others, four or five of them, arms, legs, and faces smudged with black earth, seized the bars at the bottom of the door and pulled, straining outward and upward. A little earth fell from the side of the door, and you could hear the grate of the hinge grinding on its pin. They kept pulling and suddenly, like a bone breaking, the hinge gave way and the bottom of the door swung out. Faster than a snake, the little bald-headed man was in. He went over me and around the table to Agathon.

"He's dead," he whispered.

"No he's not," I said. I wasn't sure.

The little man grabbed Agathon's feet and pulled him off the bed like a corpse of no value and dragged him across to the door.

"Move, God damn it," he whispered.

I jerked out of his way. He crammed Agathon's feet through the space they'd opened up.

"It's not wide enough," I said.

The men on the outside began pulling at his feet, the little man pushing at his shoulders and head. Agathon looked dead as hell. His eyes were open. His belly caught on the underside of the door, and in a second he was wedged solid. The big man leaned all his weight on the rod but the door wouldn't lift. The old woman bent to help pull. "Kneel on his stomach," she said. It horrified me. I was sure he was dead. But I was afraid of them and I did it. When I pressed my knee close to the edge of the door base and shoved down hard, his body jerked loose and he slid out. He groaned when I jabbed my knee in, whether the groan of a live man or some sound left over I couldn't tell, but the old woman said, "He's alive."

While the bald man snatched our possessions from the cell, the big man set the rod down and, slowly, the way a mountain would move if it decided to, knelt down beside Agathon. He slid his hands under and picked the old man up the way you'd lift a child. "This way, Ox," the old woman hissed. I glanced at his face, guessing from her tone. He was blind. We started across the open field, all of us crouching except the big man who was carrying Agathon. I turned to look back along the prison walls, one last fleeting look at home—old stone walls gray as pottery shards from a refuse heap, pitted with windows and doors—and I saw the body of our jailer. He sat against the wall as if he'd fallen asleep. I looked at the boy beside me, the one who'd brought the messages. He grinned and nodded. He looked crazy.

And so we made it across the field and down a thousand wandering alleys where in the days of our innocence Agathon snatched food from garbage tubs or giggled, peeking in at elderly lovers, and so by devious paths of sorrow we arrived at the shrine of Menelaos, where we hid. In the wide, cool vault below the shrine —the whole space lit by only two dim lamps—there were pallets waiting, and a physician for Agathon (and for others as well, because more than a few were sick here), and women with tubs of green water and oil to give us baths. I sank into the water half asleep, my mind littered with images, and a middle-aged woman bent over me to massage my shoulders and back. One of the men who had saved us was not a man after all but a girl, maybe the one I'd seen watching that day across the field. She glanced at me, unself-conscious as a Spartan girl. The woman bathing me turned my head away, gently, firmly, like a barber. They must have carried me to my pallet, because in the morning that's where I awakened.

We had breakfast. Cold mutton and beef and goat. They couldn't risk using fires here, except sometimes to burn sulfur over in the corner where the sick were, to cleanse it. No one could go outside the vault but the guards. There must have been fifty or sixty people, sealed up high on the bluff across from Mount Taygetos, under the ground. The old woman moved through the camp, as they called it, like a queen—giving orders to the women, talking softly with this man or that, at times withdrawing to a small room opening off from the vault, apparently her private chamber. One knew it was morning or afternoon or midnight only because people said it was. (Often they disagreed.) Day and night had the same dimness, the same light fog of lamp smoke. The people talked quietly or not at all, laughing occasionally at nothing.

I slept, most of the first day, and when I finally came out of it I was not refreshed, merely sore from lying on the pallet. Seeing me stir, an old man with no teeth came over to me. There were very few old people in the camp. He must have had some useful skill, but I never found out what.

"Hungry?" he said, and smiled.

"I had breakfast," I said. It still lay on my stomach cold as sea fog.

"That was hours ago. The rest of us have had lunch since then. I'll get you something."

He left, soundlessly, as all of them move, crouched over. He came back immediately with a bowl of cold greasy soup. I made a show of drinking it.

"You've been in prison a long time?" he said.

"Couple months," I said.

He shook his head, disappointed. "A nasty place."

I nodded. I sipped at the soup again. It was awful, worse than the prison food. I said, "Is Agathon alive?"

He looked blank.

"The fat old man," I said. "The Seer."

"Ah!" He didn't know. No one knew except "her." He pointed toward the old woman's chamber. "He's in there."

"Can I see him?" I asked.

He smiled. *"No* one goes in there." Then: "Well, the doctor goes in."

"He still goes in?" I said.

He nodded.

"Then Agathon must be alive."

"Maybe so," he said. He looked doubtful.

But I was convinced. You couldn't kill the old bastard as easy as that. He'd promised to dance on my grave. I was going to hold him to it.

The relief his news gave me made me sociable, I guess. I said, "Is she the leader—Iona?"

He shot me a look. No doubt she had some stupid code name, like the others. The whole world is this crazy children's game.

"One of the leaders," he said at last.

"I imagine she's really something," I said. "My master used to tell me about her."

He nodded, and went on nodding for a long time. I knew his kind. One of those people that make you think they're very deep because they always keep you waiting. My own suspicion is they're counting seconds, like actors. "Takes after her dad," he said at last, and nodded. I nodded too. "Man of stone, he was. Whole world was his war." He smiled, crafty, as if what he said was code. He raised his finger slowly, counting seconds, then wagged it slyly. "They tell how he had a foot race once with his ten-year-old son. Kid thought he was big enough to beat the old man. So they raced barefoot half a mile, sharp rocks all the way, and the old man had the poor kid whipped from the start. But you think he'd let up, let the little fellow beat him? No, sir! Whipped him by every inch he could, and afterward, when the little boy's feet were all tore up, the old man carried him home." He smiled and nodded.

"A real statue of a man," I said politely.

He nodded. "Lived up in the mountains."

I was ready to drop the thing. Knowing looks sicken me. But the old man hung around, so I asked, "Was he really a fighter—in wars and things?"

"Wasn't nobody in the world he agreed with enough to fight on the same side with. He was still living under the laws they had in the mountains nine hundred years ago, every man an equal." He shook his head. "Yes, sir, that man was his own one-man rebellion."

She had come from her room while he was talking and was moving among the groups, telling them something. He saw her now—he'd had his back to her—and became silent. She looked a little like a statue herself. After a minute the man took my bowl and went away. When the old woman had talked with the last group— the sick ones—she turned again—you could almost hear the grind of stone—and moved back to her room.

I lay on my elbow and watched the people. They sat doing nothing, merely talking a little. They'd been living this way for a long time, and no end of it was in sight, unless it was the sickness. Their dejection filled the vault like the smoke of the lamps. Those who went out on the expeditions—the younger, crazier-looking ones—kept to themselves. The others wanted stories, tales of murder or near-capture, and they would say as one of the fighters went past, "How was it, Spider, that night at the bins?" The man would smile, shake his head, keep moving. That too was like a game: I had an evil temptation to mimic them. Only the huge blind man would talk, and it wasn't tales of war. He would sit on his crude low wooden bench, his hands on his knees and his shaggy head tipped, looming over those around him like a bear, and he would talk about his childhood. The people would sit on the stone floor, smiling thoughtfully, nodding. I only half listened, thinking of my own ridiculous childhood, running along behind my mother, stumbling sometimes, sending my basket of apples rolling, my heart mourning after Spartan girls' convexities. Someone said, "Tell about Snake." The code name for Dorkis. People in the group to my right were talking softly, so that I couldn't quite catch what the giant was saying. I got up and moved closer to his group.

"That Snake!" he said, and shook his head slowly, smiling. He looked at the ceiling, grew serious. "He was the only religious man I ever knew," he said. "He loved God with all his heart and soul, and he also loved man." He let it sink in, something of a preacher. It was a language none of them understood, children of the revolution. "He would pray before he ate. Like this." He pretended to hold a bowl in his hands, and he lowered his head. I was tempted to hide my head behind my arms and groan, but I decided to be a man about it. It wasn't as embarrassing, from him, as it might have been. He said, moving himself very deeply, "Gentle Zeus, Father of all mankind, forgive us all our stupidity and hate. Tease us to kindness and forgiveness of our enemies and, hardest of all, ourselves. Teach us to live with contradiction, and lead us, by your cunning ways, away from the dark pits of meaninglessness and despair. As we feed our restless, willful bodies, teach us to learn to love them, and all their kind."

The huge man sat like a boulder, still bent. His blind eyes were weeping, remembering his leader.

The bald-headed man at his side said gleefully, "He never forgave them Spartans, *that's* for sure."

The blind man's throat kept working, furious and grieved, and he couldn't answer. I moved away.

When the people were settling for sleep that night, I saw the thin blond girl who fought with the men. She was leaning on the wall in the darkest part of the room, alone, apparently at home neither with the men nor with the women. I sat against the wall opposite and watched her. It was amazing that she could stand in one position, not a muscle flickering, for so long. I thought of crossing to her, but I could think of no reason. And I was afraid of her, to tell the truth, though she couldn't be over seventeen. I thought of the breasts I'd seen when they were bathing her, after our rescue, and my mind's going back to it annoyed me. She had a beautiful face—only hard; harder than stone. Why had the woman who was bathing me turned my face away? To warn me?

I kept going over and over it, now wondering why they all kept clear of her, now wondering what I could say to excuse my breaking her isolation. Was it the girl who killed our jailer? I could come to no conclusion, and I didn't cross to her. I was interrupted. The old woman, Iona, appeared at the doorway to her chamber and stood squinting through the room until she saw me. She came over.

"Demodokos."

I nodded.

She peered at me, witchlike in the dimness. "Or should I say Peeker?" She smiled, and it was startling. A glimpse of Agathon's old friend through the horrible mask.

"That's what *he* calls me," I said.

"I know." She went on peering at me. At last she said, "Come." An order. She turned away.

We went into her chamber and she closed the double-planked door. It was a crypt. Torch rests without torches in them. Pegged to the wall, a rusty iron trident. In the center of the room stood a giant coffin, with candles on it and rolls of parchment. She used it for a desk. I moved closer.

"Menelaos's coffin?" I asked.

"Who knows?"

There was a stool beside the coffin. She motioned me to it. She herself never sat, apparently. She would have to stand to work at the high, makeshift desk, and anyway, she had some kind of demonic energy that gave her no chance to sit. She went around behind the coffin and leaned her elbows on it and again looked at me with her icy, drilling eyes. "We're sending you away," she said.

I said nothing, waiting.

"It's not because you're a nuisance," she said, and again she freed from its chains, for an instant, the younger, softer smile. She said, "Agathon's dead."

I started.

"Sit still. He died this afternoon."

I cast about the room for some sign of him, and at last, though it wasn't part of her plan, she said, "All right, this way."

I followed her to the dingy, pillared corner, once an altar niche, now a trash pile—torn canvas, old clothes, broken implements, worn-out sandals. She lifted a corner of the canvas, and Agathon's dead face stared up at me. I bent down to close the eyes, but she touched my shoulder.

"Plague," she said. She dropped the canvas.

"Then all of us—" I began. I felt nothing, yet, at his death. Only physical repulsion at the staring face.

"Not necessarily," she said, and gave a strange smile. "We talked, before he died. He says we're to die in blood. It's all very clear to him. The Spartans are pulling the army back home from the north, he says. Who knows if Seers really see?"

"You should believe him," I said.

Again the strange smile. "I do." Then: "In any case, the plague's reached Sparta. One way or the other . . ."

She showed no feeling—no fear, no anger, nothing. She touched my arm, gently for a half-cracked old witch, and guided me back to the stool. For a while she said nothing. Grieving? I wondered. When would *I* be-

gin to grieve? She said, "We have something of his—
and yours." She handed me one of the parchment rolls
from the coffin. It was the things we'd written in prison.
I looked up, waiting.

"I've read it," she said. "Take it to his wife."

From hatred? I wondered. Was she sending the scroll
to Tuka because it would hurt? Still no sign of feeling.
Her face was dead.

She said, "Have you any idea, Demodokos, how
much of all this is pure fiction?" I must have looked
flustered, because she said at once, "No matter, don't
think about it. One could do worse than become a cari-
cature in a senseless, complicated lie."

"But it's all so *earnest*," I said. "He wrote as if he
were driven."

"Am *I* the liar, then?" she asked, and smiled.

I thought about it and felt a flash of anger. "I guess
he really loved nobody but himself."

"Nonsense. He loved us all—and *wanted* us all. Even
you, Peeker. Otherwise he wouldn't have been driven to
make us up."

She turned away and bent her head a little. Then,
with no emotion in her gravelly voice, she said, "Take
it. Tuka will want it." And: "Go. Go to bed. When
we're ready to slip you out we'll wake you." Her right
hand moved to the coffin; not for support, I had a
feeling, though the fingers trembled. "Thank you for all
you've done," she said. "Good night."

I left with the scroll and closed the door behind me.
After I'd lain down I began to cry, purposely and crossly, conscious of my consciousness of crying.

A few hours before dawn we left. The blond girl
was not one of the four who guided me down to the
water and gave me to the boatman.

33   Agathon *(Last Entry)*:

Sunlight, someone's bed. I do not recognize the room.

Someone told me, or perhaps I dreamed, a strange tale. Lightning struck Lykourgos's crypt and split it end to end. Perhaps I saw it. The image, at any rate, is very clear. I am looking across a valley at a hill, a group of half-dead trees, a crypt, with lesser crypts below it, and above the door on this main crypt the name LYKOURGOS. It's night, but the moonlight makes it almost like day. There's a weird wind, not fierce but oddly charged, as though it were not wind at all but something alive and sentient, Time itself, perhaps. The crypt, placed exactly at the crest of the hill, is separated from everything around it by a low fence but also by something more, a severe, defiant dignity that the trees, the blowing grass, the lower crypts cannot come near. It commands the hill like a fort. But above it huge dark clouds are forming, piling up like mountains rising out of the sea to obliterate the sky, and the earth goes dark in sympathy until the trees, the grass, the fences, the hill, the sky are all one thing converging on the crypt. A sudden flash—a terrible three-pronged lightning fork —that turns the landscape white; then darkness and a shudder and a deafening crack as if not the crypt but the world itself were splitting. When my eyes adjust, the crypt lies still in the rain like the moonlit rib cage of a horse destroyed by fire.

Whoever told me the story of the lightning believed

267

that the gods had shown favor to Lykourgos. Favor?
Blasting him to bits? Yet perhaps it's so.

Whoever told me cooled my forehead with her palm
afterward. —Hers, yes. I remember that. I wanted to
reach up and catch the hand, bring the stranger down
to me, but all my body was inert. I could only reach
up with thought, hungrily, laboring to identify the kind
dark shadow above me. I strained to speak, but my
mouth was as stiff as the door of a cell. Was it Tuka?
Can that be possible? Yet it was, I think. It was my
wife. The room grew darker. The stranger-wife bent
closer, as if to whisper something in my ear, but I
could hear nothing any more, couldn't even feel the
hand if it was still on my forehead. I strained every
muscle of mind to seize and enclose her, own her. A
searing anguish went through me; I lost consciousness.
Hours later—there was sunlight in the room—I awakened, or else I dreamed I awakened, in a room filled
with flowers.

Dying. I understand my panic. No worse than that
of a child poised on a diving board. Hike your skirts
up, Agathon, love! Point your fingers!

Whoo*ee* am I scared!

I must think of some last, solemn, sententious word.

Cocklebur.

Ox.

34 Peeker:

And so, after three days on the river and at sea, traveling by night and fog, I arrived safe, with the gods' help, in Athens. I was sick on the ship, and I believed I had the plague. But no fever developed, and now five days have passed since the death of Agathon, and I'm still without a fever; in fact, thriving. I begin to believe I have mysteriously escaped.

A beautiful city—noisy with merchants' splendid carts, booming with mingled languages, theologies, political persuasions, and bright as a pinwheel with canopies, tents, great piles of produce, baskets, trinkets, the swirl of dancing girls and jugglers. . . . But never mind that.

I had a hell of a time getting someone to tell me where Agathon's wife might be found. No wonder, of course. I was dressed in rags, my face still gray from my sickness on the boat, and I spoke with a foreigner's cockled tongue and a strange store of words. But I was successful, finally. I found an old peddler, an escaped Helot with one arm, and after I'd followed him through the streets half the day while he hawked his wares, he saw fit to lead me to her house—that is, palace. The former home of Philombrotos, a shrine now. She keeps a few large rooms in back, helped by her two old servants. She has no slaves. Here too, at the steps of the palace, they tried to turn me away, and, when they failed at that, ignored me. At last I got one of her two servants to listen, not that I knew who the servant was at the time. "I have a message for Agathon's wife," I said. "—From Agathon." The old woman-servant glanced at me, full of suspicion. She had a face like a broken hoof. I pulled the parchments from their protecting rag and showed her. I guess she must have thought I was crazy. A long message to be bringing from Agathon! She went away without a word, and I didn't expect her back. However, she came. "This way," she said. I followed her.

We went what seemed miles down enormous sunlit hallways, chamber growing out of chamber—guards everywhere, government officials, janitors polishing the marble floors and the great, painted chairs where once Philombrotos and Solon and Pysistratos sat. There were busts of Philombrotos everywhere, dignified as all-wise Apollo, and there were documents he'd signed, implements he'd used, bas-reliefs of his life. Here in his own house he dwarfed even Solon and the great Pysistratos. We came at last to a closed door. The old woman lifted the iron hook from the wall, opened the door, and bowed, sending me in, then following. The door swung shut behind us like the door of a tomb. "Wait here," she said.

I waited an hour. A huge room beautifully furnished and, as far as I could see, never used. There was no dust, no decay. Only an aseptic lifelessness: motionless planes of light thrown over the gleaming floor from the alcove to the west where another small statue of Philombrotos stood, motionless carpets, chairs and tables draped in white, and over in the darkest corner of the room—I started as if at a ghost when I saw it—her harp: motionless, silent. I went to it, touched the wood. The gold and walnut shone as if with knowledge. It should be draped in protective cloths, I thought, like the tables and chairs. Did she sometimes still play it, all alone in the covered, abandoned room? I touched a string, just a brush of my fingertip, and the way the sound filled the room made me duck in alarm.

And then at last there were footsteps, far away, then nearer. They paused, outside the small door to the left of the harp, and after what seemed a long time, the door opened toward me. She remained in the heavy shadows of the doorway, examining my rags. At last she said, "I'm Tuka."

"I'm Demodokos," I said.

I thought about her voice. It was shy Soft. She seemed somewhat younger than the others—Agathon, Iona.

"I don't think I know you. Should I?"

"No," I said. "I've been Agathon's disciple these past three years."

A pause, then: "How is he?"

"He died three days ago."

In the shadows I saw her white arm move, pressing her hand to her chest. Then she said simply, "I see." And, after a moment, as if for my sake, "I'm sorry."

Another long silence. It came to me at last that she had no intention of coming into the room, into the light, where I could see her. She was right. I looked awful, and I was prying. I said, "I brought you this," and held out the scroll.

She hesitated, then extended her hand to accept it. Her fingers showed no sign of distaste for the foul rag that covered it. "Are the others lost?" she asked.

I had to snatch a moment before I connected. I said, "It's not part of the book he had. That was destroyed. This is something he wrote in prison. —Along with, I'm afraid, some shit of mine." As soon as the word was half out I wanted to grab the back of my neck and punch myself. I hurried on: "I would have separated my part out—I should have, I guess—but I thought . . ." What *did* I think?

"Don't apologize. Thank you." She half turned, about to leave. "Have you eaten?"

"I'm fine," I said. "Don't think about it!"

"No. Wait here, if you don't mind. I'll send Persaia."

She withdrew, leaving the door open, and I waited. In a few minutes the old serving-woman returned, more suspicious and hostile than ever. She nodded and ushered me through the small door and down another long hall—this one bare, uncarpeted, unfurnished except for a bust of Philombrotos and a statue of the goddess of cities, Pallas Athena. We came to a large white room that overlooked the garden and, beyond that, the vineyard. I could see the little slope, the stone tables and benches, where Tuka, half a century ago, had hurt the child on the wagon. It was a smaller and much more gradual slope than I'd expected. Beyond the vineyard, where the hill fell away, the sky was so blue it looked dyed. The old man, her second servant, looked up toward me from the hedge. He looked angry.

"She wants you to stay here," the serving-woman said, and before I could stop her she left. Stay for food? I wondered. Stay for the night? I could only wait and see. I looked out, hunting for familiar signs, but except for the slope of lawn, the tables, and the vineyard, nothing was where it should be. Klinias's hut—it should be beyond where the gardener pruned the hedge—had apparently been torn down long ago, and I could see no sign of the roundhouse or the well that Agathon had talked about. I sat down. The room was bare except for a couch with heavy, musty-smelling pillows, two carved chairs, once very fine but now in disrepair, and a table with a pitcher and a bowl. It was weird. Philombrotos must have been rich as Kroesos. What had she done with all the money?

After a while the woman reappeared with food—fresh fruit and wine and some finely spiced kind of meat I couldn't identify—and again before I could question her, she was gone. Seeing them against the fruit I realized how dirty my hands were. I ate. The servant-woman appeared when I finished as if she'd been watching all the time from some chink in the wall. I said quickly, for fear she might escape again, "Thank you very much It was excellent. But now I'd better be leaving."

She shook her head, alarmed. "You mustn't do that!" And again she was gone. It was beginning to get amusing. Or it would have been except for this: I kept having the feeling that that tricky old bastard Agathon had set the whole thing up. He couldn't have, I knew; but the feeling stuck with me. I suppose the feeling will be with me all my life, from time to time. I could see him hobbling from view to view. "Wonderful! Charming! Bless me!" Then, playing the other part: "We're *so* pleased you like it!" He was as real as ever, in my mind: volatile as a small sunlit whirlwind. His rags flew out as he inspected the walls, found dust on a chair back, pretended to be horribly embarrassed. My eyes filled with tears. How could he possibly be dead?

I waited on and on. It was ridiculous. He would have loved it. Finally the servant-woman appeared again. She did not like me, did not believe I belonged in Philombrotos's house. She stood stiffly at the door. "She wants to know do you want a bath," she said.

"I could use one," I said meekly.

She took it decently, considering. "This way, then."

Again I followed her. I was tempted to mimic her walk, *clump clump,* but I was nice. We went down some stairs and along a hall and came to a beautiful tiled room with high, small windows, and on the back wall faucets in the form of golden lions' heads. I'd never seen such a room before. She lit the lamps, grudgingly, I thought—it wasn't really all that dark—and turned the faucets on above the . . . pool, like. Regular water came out of one, and steam came out of the other. She went away and closed the door and I undressed. While I was bathing she sneaked in and stole my clothes. Hours later, feeling guilty, I suppose, she brought in some new ones.

"She wants you upstairs," she said, and left with a jerk.

So I hunted around in the cellar for a couple of hours and finally found my way upstairs. Agathon's wife was waiting in the room with the harp, and she wasn't alone. The covers had been taken from the chairs, and the room was warm with lamplight. The sky to the west was deep red, the sun glowing like a coal on the rim of the sea. The three of them were all dressed to the nines. So was I, come to think of it. In Athens they do things right.

The tall, middle-aged man who looked like Agathon gone sane came over to greet me. "So you're Demodokos," he said. It sounded like a put-down, though very genteel.

"Sometimes," I said. "Sometimes Peeker." I grinned, to be polite.

He looked at me harder. "You remind me of him," he said, and smiled, a little stiffly. Suddenly, for no reason, I liked him. He looked like a man who did things. Business, politics, expensive funerals, something.

"You remind me of him too," I said. "You're Kleon —his son?"

He nodded. "And this is Diana, my little sister."

I bowed. She was pretty. Blond hair, a dimple, a double chin. Unmarried. Insofar as possible, I made a point of not imagining her soft, fat tits.

"How do you *do?*" she said, and, as if in panic, made a smile.

I do horrible, I wanted to say, wringing my hands and wincing. *I beg from door to door, I kill people to steal their sandals, I rob oats from stalls for horses.* "Fine," I said. "I'm very pleased to meet you." She extended her hand, palm down, as she'd no doubt seen her mother do, and I did not drop to the floor and kiss it, merely touched it, lightly, politely, with my fingertips. I loved her passionately. I thought she was the funniest lady I'd ever seen.

Kleon said, "You and Mother have already met, I think?"

I turned to her, bowing. I'd been watching her from the moment I first came through the door—I would have said so if I could have thought of a way to write it and still cover all this other stuff I was walking through. She was seated, with her eyes on me from the first instant, neither kind nor unkind, neither suspicious nor trusting: watchful, like someone at a play. The statue of her father watched me from just above her left shoulder. Though she must be seventy, I knew, her hair was black as night except for one white streak. It stood out like lightning. And it was real, you could see; not art. Below the white, at her temple, she had a scar. By rights, whatever made the scar should have killed her. The scroll was in her lap, lying on her black wool cover.

"Sit down, Demodokos," she said.

Kleon pushed a chair toward me. When I seated myself, they too sat down, Kleon and Diana.

A silence. All of us were nervous except the old woman.

"Mother tells us Father passed away," Diana said.

I smiled—I'd lived too long with the critical old bastard—then covered my mouth quickly and shot a glance at Agathon's wife. She'd caught it.

"You loved him, didn't you," she said. Coolly, flatly. Merely an observation. "So did we."

"I'm sure you did," I said politely.

It was Agathon's wife's turn to smile. Holy Zeus but she was fast. No wonder she scared him.

Diana leaned forward with her dimpled hands folded. Kleon sat like his mother, just waiting and watching, but he wasn't as self-possessed. Diana said, "Could you tell us how . . . it was?"

"In prison," I said, then started over: "He was taken sick while in prison. . . . There was a plague of some kind in the seaport towns. We didn't think it could reach

Sparta but—" I glanced again at the old woman. She was hard to talk in front of. If she took a notion to mimic me she could nail me to the wall.

"Plague!" Diana whispered. Her eyes welled with tears.

"Come, come, Diana," Kleon said. He moved his hand as if to reach out to her, then realized he was too far away. It was Agathon's kind of scene. Kleon folded his hands, embarrassed.

With a quick, sharp grin, the old woman said, "Kleon's a lawyer."

"Kleon's what keeps this family together," Diana said fiercely, then looked startled, apologetic, then looked stubborn. I loved her. I would conquer elephants in her name.

There was another silence. The old woman simply waited; time was nothing to her. It was as if she had come to believe she would never die.

Diana wanted details. She was pitiful, sweet. I told her all I could, but cleaned it up. How the sickness mysteriously began (I didn't mention the rats), how it progressed, how the Helots rescued us from prison, and how, finally, he died. He died peacefully in his sleep, I said, and I said I was with him all the time. I didn't look at the old woman as I talked. Even if she hadn't read the scroll to the end, she would know how it was, I thought. If she wanted to contradict me, that was her business. If she opened the scroll up, I'd swear it was all lies.

The story took a long time to tell. I told it like a poet, and Diana kept using her hanky. It was dark outside when I finished. Diana sat now with her hands over her face, weeping and wiping her eyes with the hanky's edge. Kleon's eyes were a little funny, but he hadn't let us see him cry. He'd gone out for wine for all of us while I was telling the saddest part.

Kleon said huskily, clearing his throat, "He was a strange man."

I nodded. The old woman was watching me. So was the statue.

He cleared his throat again. "I remember when I was a little boy he used to carry me on his shoulders. He never said a cross word to me. Never once!"

I sipped my wine to keep from the old woman's eyes.

"He was an important diplomat for Lykourgos, you know. And Holy Apollo what a horseman that man was!" He laughed and shook his head, then shaded his eyes for an instant, afraid of breaking. "He'd gallop over the snow, hunting rabbits—Great Zeus, he'd be going a hundred miles an hour—and the rabbit would go under a six-foot hedge and he'd go over it as if the hedge wasn't there, and he'd lose the rabbit and he'd yell, 'Whoa, rabbit! God *damn* you, rabbit!'—mixing up the rabbit and the horse, you know—" He laughed again, loudly, and this time, having brought Agathon to life, he did break, and covered his face and made peeping noises. I could have told him it would happen. So could his mother. Or the statue.

"Poor, dear Kleon!" Diana whooped, and leaped from her chair and went to him and threw her arms around him. He sobbed on her bosom.

"He loved us," Kleon sobbed. "At least I think he did. You could never tell with Father."

The old woman watched me.

"I've read the scroll," she said. She sipped her wine.

"I thought you might have," I said.

She looked away from me at last, over at her children. She got up, not effortlessly, exactly, but gracefully all the same. I wondered if she could still play the harp. She crossed to them and touched the nape of Diana's neck gently, then touched her son's balding head. She looked back at me. "Come," she said.

We went down the hall and down the long stairs and outside to where the slope was, and at the foot of it, the stone benches and tables. The old serving-man peeked out the door and looked furious, then disappeared and returned a minute later with a torch. He carried it past us and set it in one of the torch rests beyond the tables, behind a thin statue whose features were in darkness. The servant never glanced at his mistress (much less at me), though she watched him like a critic.

When he was gone she said, "It's true, you know, that I loved him."

"I know."

"And Diana loved him too, though she's stupid, poor thing."

I nodded. "There are worse faults. I like her."

She said nothing for a long time. I watched the torch. At last she said gently, as if afraid of hurting me, "You're aware, of course, that Agathon too was stupid."

I said nothing for a while. It was a difficult moment. Then I said, "Yes, *finally*."

She smiled. Not old. You'd have sworn she was eternal. "However, I happened to love him."

"Then why did you leave him?" I asked as innocently as possible. A stupid question, she might say. But I'd risk it.

She answered easily. "Because sooner or later he'd have killed me, you know. —In one of those rages that Kleon can't remember." She smiled. "Poor Agathon hardly remembered them himself, to judge by the scroll."

I could see the scar very clearly, a shiny place in the torchlight.

"But if you loved him, as you say—"

"Think," she said. "If he killed me, and couldn't kill himself . . . with his history, you know—after riding his brother down that night, and later the awful thing with Konon . . . He *did* love me, Demodokos."

I nodded. Harp music floated down from the house.

"We were all crazy enough as it was," she said,

and laughed. Then she frowned, sudden as a spring-time change of sky, musing. "And of course I was young," she said. For the first time she evaded my eyes, stared at the death-white hands crossed over her knees. I wanted to touch them. I looked away. She said, "I needed to know he loved me—needed to know he could forgive me for being . . . unlike him." She frowned, fine creases descending to the sharp square chin as white as winter. "A woman . . ." She paused. She tipped her head up, looked at the stars, and smiled as if with amused compassion for all her kind. "A wom-an needs proofs of a sort no man can possibly under-stand. Sometimes even violence will do." Her eyes be-came tiny chinks and her hands tightened in her lap. "I gave up my death for his sake, Demodokos."

I nodded.

She mused, then she gave her head a barely per-ceptible jerk, as if driving away the first faint mumble of a dream. She smiled, slightly scornful, like a beautiful young girl. "That's stupid. I made it up."

I shrugged. "But interesting."

She smiled again and touched my hand. Her tremble went through me. "Ah, Demodokos, Demodokos! You do me good!" Darkness was pulling her outward like old light.

killing yourself, second by second
self knowledge comes down to
recognizing actions as the result
of impulses and nothing more

About the Author

Born in Batavia, New York, John Gardner attended Alexander Central and Batavia High School. "I grew up on a farm and wrote poems, novels, and plays on the typewriter in my grandmother's law office and under the tractor in the back lot when I was supposed to be plowing.

"Went to DePauw University, where I thought I was a chemist; left after two years and went to Washington University, in St. Louis where I thought I was a great poet and was going to die tragically young. Went to the State University of Iowa where I worked hard and wrote worse than in my childhood. Became, by accident a medievalist," writes Mr. Gardner.

He has taught creative writing and medieval literature at Oberlin College, Chico State College, Chico, California, and at San Francisco State. Since 1964 he has taught Old and Middle English at Southern Illinois University.

Mr. Gardner has written several articles, textbook, and four novels. He lives on a farm with his wife and two children in Illinois.